Once, Two Islan

DAWN GARISCH

Once, Two Islands

MYRMIDON

Myrmidon Books Ltd
Rotterdam House
116 Quayside
Newcastle upon Tyne
NE1 3DY

www.myrmidonbooks.com
Published by Myrmidon 2008

A catalogue record for this book is available from the British Library.

ISBN 978-1-905802-16-6 Export Trade Paperback
ISBN 978-1-905802-17-3 Hardback

Set in 11/14 pt Goudy by Falcon Oast Graphic Arts Limited,
East Hoathly, East Sussex

Printed and bound in the UK by CPI Mackays, Chatham ME5 8TD

1 3 5 7 9 10 8 6 4 2

For Jonathan

Be not afeard; the isle is full of noises.
William Shakespeare
The Tempest, Act III, scene II

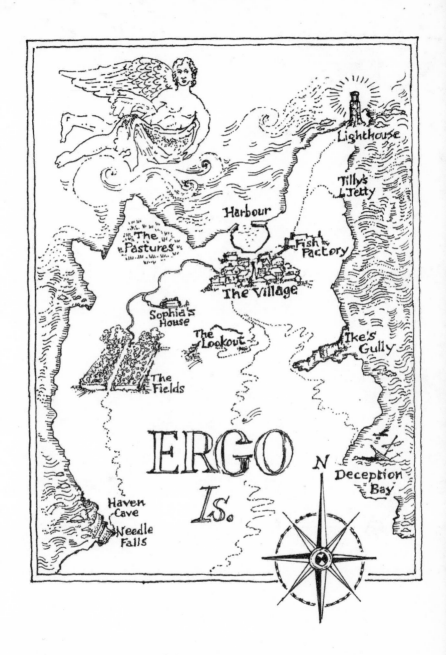

Lighthouse

Tilly's Jetty

Harbour

The Pastures

Fish Factory

The Village

Sophia's House

The Lookout

Ike's Gully

The Fields

ERGO

Is.

N

Deception Bay

Haven Cave

Needle Falls

Part One

Chapter One

There is an island situated in one of the three vast oceans of the world, an island which is actually a peak of a huge mountain, lying on the ocean floor like a sleeping dragon with only two scales of its humped back poking through the surface of the sea. Two, because near the island is another, smaller one, further east, which has all the qualities of the larger yet is different, like an echo. A man and his wife, some of the islanders call them, although their appointed names are Ergo Island (the larger) and Impossible Island (the smaller). They were formed long ago, before the beginning of time, by the power of the dragon, bursting out of the ocean with fire and ash and steam, affecting a quarter of the planet, causing tsunamis and black skies. But now they are merely two islands, the only comma and full stop for miles and miles in the blank blue page of the sea. To look at them, you would never guess the power of the dragon below, for they seem inconsequential, out of the way of the main shipping lines, in the way of the gales that roll in from Antarctica. Although the islands are made mostly of black volcanic rock, Ergo has an apron of settled sediment which is fertile, and on which people and their animals have come to live with the seabirds and seals and penguins.

Amongst them was a young girl, born on the island one winter's day while the spindrift wind sang strange songs around the cliffs. Her body had thus far been immersed in the music of her mother, the shush of the sea of her, the thrum of the blood drum of her, the tinkle and resonance of her belly embrace. She'd grown from a full stop to a comma, from a tadpole to a frog to a fish, the plates of her face slowly colliding to form her features. She'd put on flesh and hair and pushed out frontal lobes, preparing to leave the sea behind, to drag herself out of her mother's belly onto dry land.

The handsome doctor, Orion Prosper, washed his hands, snapped on a pair of latex gloves, and examined his wife again. Prostrate beneath his gaze, the brown mound of her belly tightening, Angelique gripped the bedpost as a wave of pain rolled through her.

"Not too long now," her husband informed her. "Remember, when the time comes, close your mouth and push!"

Angelique's thoughts strayed to her cow last season, lying and lowing, a black struggling sack emerging from under her tail.

"You must push into your bottom!" Sister Veronica concurred. She was childless, but trained in one of the best hospitals on the mainland. "Don't forget to push as though you are going to the toilet!"

Angelique remembered the beached whale last summer, dying under the weight of its enormous body, its sonar gone wrong.

Frieda, who'd had her own babies, held her young sister's

hand. "Soon you'll be seeing your child," she consoled her.

At that moment, all Angelique could see was the Virgin Mary hanging on the white hospital wall, left there by one of Veronica's predecessors, her face full of good sadness, her only son lost, lost, and all for a good cause. Another wave washed through her, flushing all thought from the pink coral of her brain as she clung to the side of the bed, and to an ancient body knowledge of how to give birth.

It seemed to Frieda that this birth was taking too long. Something in the flow of things had been arrested; the passage would not open, despite the doctor's modern chemicals flowing into Angelique's arm, up her vein, through her heart and down to her womb. She knew from her own son's birth what was required. Of course, Sophia should be there, but that was impossible, impossible.

Frieda wiped her sister's brow with a cloth and tried to keep her mouth closed. She liked the doctor enough. A confident man, a man who had brought all manner of good to the island. Why, he had saved her own daughter's life when her appendix blew. No home remedy from Sophia could subdue that beast, only the knife would do, and so her Liesa carried the mark of the surgeon upon her belly: a neat straight scar where her body had sewn itself closed around the doctor's stitches, a reminder forever that life can change in a moment. There were some things a woman knew better than a man, though, some things that the spirit world knew better than the human one, and some things better left to those who do not have to wrestle through the confounding drapes of love and ardour; the doctor was, after all, the patient's husband. Frieda watched the doctor's brow pinch and wished there was a way she could open him too: he was closed, as closed as the unfathomable language of his journals.

Her chance came an hour later, when the doctor and

Veronica were called away to attend to Elijah Mobara, who had fallen badly on the rocks at the Point, and to little Phoebe, Graça Bagonata's newborn, who had the croup. Frieda sat by her sister's bed, torn by the roar of warring loyalties inside her.

"Please!" gasped her sister as another spasm gripped her, lifting a face brimful of fear.

Frieda could sit and watch no longer. She went to the window and flung it wide open. The cupboard doors, too, she opened, and the taps till they gushed. She undid the ties that bound the curtains, her own shoelaces, and the ties of the hospital gown around her sister's neck and back. It was up to the ancestors now, she thought; she had done what she could.

When Veronica returned a quarter of an hour later, she found winter right inside the room, a gale blowing in the patient's hair, rain slanting in through the window. Like a whirlwind herself she stormed about, shutting out and cutting off water and wind, tying and closing, releasing from her mouth a torrent of horror directed at Frieda – "You people are a danger to yourselves, imagine exposing a woman in labour to the elements!" – while Angelique, gripped by the end-stage madness of her yawning womb, felt how her body had become an instrument, how the oboe of her body had opened, how her mouth moaned a long and perfect O sounding out of the foundation of her and somehow flowing in two directions, out through her open throat and through her dilated cervix simultaneously, a sound to move the heavens. There was no stopping her now.

The baby released her grip, pushed aside her mother's swollen lips and slid out into her life. The doctor, her father, arrived in time to cut the cord, too late to be told of Frieda's duplicity.

The doctor allowed himself a quick smoke and a whisky

before delivering the afterbirth. He had been afraid it might come to a Caesarean section. He was a good surgeon, clean, efficient, working by the book, taking no undue risks, but he did not relish the thought of putting his hand into the very centre of his wife's body. He was not a religious man, but somehow that would be going too far.

Of course, some would have said he took risks, delivering his own child so far from the help of obstetricians. They had considered going to the mainland for the birth, but it was a week by ship, and ships only visited the island four times a year, bringing provisions and luxuries. What if his wife had gone into labour on the high seas? Besides, if he was not prepared to deliver his own child on the island, what would the islanders think – that he was not a good enough doctor for theirs?

He went over to where Frieda was washing the baby, dousing the child in coos and smiles and warm water, and looked his daughter over, this sprung and fragile scrap that had something to do with his loins, with the nightly pleasure he took in his wife. Everything was present and correct, but he had to admit a moment of disappointment. He would have preferred a son; a daughter was too vulnerable to predatory men. He was a man who did not like to worry, and he could feel worry tighten in him already.

"Well done, my darling," he said, kissing his wife on the forehead. She smiled at him, happy he was pleased with her, happy the ordeal was over, that her wayward body had brought their daughter safely to the shore of the world.

*

Underneath, the dragon that underlies life shifted, almost imperceptibly, it's true, yet just enough to open up a rent in the fabric of things – a rent large enough for a woman to fall through. Two days after the birth, Angelique sickened, and despite the doctor's best efforts, she turned to worse, burning up in the middle of her white hospital bed like a forest fire, her chest crackling with the heat, her eyes bright with sparklers, her dry breath a desert wind.

Two days after that, she died.

Outside the storm continued, unconcerned. Squalls of rain beat against the windowpanes, against the fluffed and oily backs of the millions of skua, petrels and albatrosses nested in a myriad mosaic on Impossible Island, also against the bridge of a Chinese fishing vessel lurching about in the sea to the northeast.

Work at the crayfish and fish factory came to a halt; no one could put to sea in this weather. The workers took the time to wash down the tanks and tables and floors. The fishermen mended nets indoors and felt for the weather changes that started in their bones; they tapped their barometers in a gesture as natural and familiar as breathing. A few villagers sheathed themselves in their all-weather gear and waded out through the gale to tend the turnip, pumpkin and potato fields, but most kept indoors, waiting for the impersonal rage of the storm to dash itself to pieces. In homesteads and in the tavern, they waited in the still glow of hearth warmth that dotted the village: islands of comfort surrounded by the mayhem of weather. They mustered around their paraffin stoves and wood fires, preparing food, drinking tea and home-brew, and talked about this and that, and especially about the goings-on at the hospital: would she live, would she die? Whose fault was it? And why? The theories circulated, eddying from cottage to cottage, sucking in a fresh tributary here, spitting out dead wood there. Some said it was bound to happen after what he did to Sophia – didn't he realise who he was dealing with? A woman who brought in the living, healed the sick and ushered out the dead. Others said maybe, but that doesn't make it right. Another said to stop this superstitious nonsense, this dead-old-wives' tale. Here the conversation fractured: that was an unfortunate thing to say, it's a wife we're talking about here, she wasn't even old, and who knows how ill-considered words carry fate on the wind, to where it is sniffed out by the hungry old dog that waits for us all? They didn't know yet that she was already gone, sucked out of the tempest of her body, held loose and light in the eye of the storm.

In her stone cottage near the fields, Sophia spread pumpkin seeds out on a tray before the fire to dry. She could feel the shift coming, the one foretold in thrown bones. The birth of this child was a portent of the turn of the tide, a change of phrase that would alter the rhythm of things. There was a tightening in her, too, for the bones had had an awkward lie, and she knew no one on the island would escape the change unchanged.

The doctor sat a moment at his wife's bedside, tracing with his eyes her last exhaled breath, feeling the great insulated door of the freezer of his chest swing closed. What had happened, what had gone wrong? He had been the top obstetric student in his final year, he had won a prize for his fifth-year essay on "The Use and Abuse of Antibiotics: Keeping the Upper Hand in the War between Man and Microbes". His CV ran to several pages and he'd had as many options for his career path as there were fingers on both hands. He hadn't had to come and toil in this godforsaken windswept corner of the world, he could be advancing to professorship in a top academic hospital, he could be flying all over the world to conferences, delivering scientific papers on vaccinations for malaria, AIDS, prosthetic heart valves or proton-pump inhibitors. He had come here for a short adventure and had stayed for love, love of this woman now gone, now snatched away, this burnt cinder of his love still warm on the bed in front of him.

Sister Veronica closed Angelique's eyes, washed her hands, and left the room quickly to break the news to Frieda, asleep next door. She so badly wanted to rest her hands on the poor doctor's shoulders, to lift from them the weight that bore down so heavily. She wanted to take him into her arms and comfort him, to let him weep into her breast, to stroke his dark cropped hair. It isn't your fault, she wanted to tell him. She could've told him about Frieda's native stupidity, about how his wife had been exposed to wind and rain, she could have pointed fingers, and she did consider this. But she knew the fault lay with her alone and she would never be able to tell him why, never. She had trained at the best hospital on the mainland, there was nothing wrong with her technique or her hygiene or her knowledge, oh no. It was her thought that had spirited the young, unsuitable wife away. She would make it up to him, she would.

Orion could not look at his dead wife. His eyes instead traversed the hills and vales of the counterpane, travellers in search of rest, his very centre buffeted by the wretched commotion out of doors. Whoever would choose to live in a place like this? Angelique, that's who. She had persuaded him to stay and marry by falling pregnant, all against his desire, it now seemed, all against his best intentions to be successful, to travel, to shine, to be a name remembered. *Ghastly*, that sudden word leaping to his aid, a word he could not remember ever having used before: ghastly, the sudden horror of his name remembered in this fashion, associated with death and error, with loss and disgrace.

His gaze had climbed the wall in a separate act. While his brain was firing rounds of blame, ammunition going off uncontrolled in the horror chambers of his mind, his eyes had climbed the white hospital wall as though detached, coming to rest upon the Virgin Mary, whose eyes stared accusingly back down at him. The sight shocked him into action, a bolt of recognition shooting through his terror and confusion, threading his thought and will and body together onto one long string. He stood up, took the image off the wall, threw it into the bin and left the room. He instructed John Peters, the porter and general cleaner who, weak with shock, was leaning on his broom outside the tearoom, staring at a crack in the cement floor, to turn the mortuary fridge on. On no account, he added, was John to let Sophia in, with her superstitious ways and her supercilious smile. He could not bear to think of her hands on his wife's body; he would not stand to let her look down on the evidence of his failure. Nelson Peters, John's cousin, could arrange the funeral. He would have no other.

John nodded, not finding any word to fit his lips, and shuffled away to do his bidding.

The doctor went home and shut himself in his bedroom.

Chapter Two

Two islands, covered by mosses, fungi and ferns, by grasses and shrubs and stunted trees all set at the angle of the prevailing wind, and cultivated with potatoes, carrots, turnips and pumpkin, also a grove of apple trees. Two islands populated by three hundred and sixty-seven inhabitants, all of them living on Ergo (the population stable with the birth of one, death of another), the majority of the employable adults working at the crayfish and fish factory owned by Jerome Peters. Only seven surnames (not including those belonging to Doctor Prosper or Minister Kohler, who were still considered mainlanders): Peters, Bagonata, Bardelli, Schoones, Pelani, Mobara and Tamara. Four fisherman's cottages on Impossible Island, eighty-three buildings on Ergo, including cottages, the schoolhouse, the mayor's office, the community hall, the shop, the church, the tavern, the lighthouse, the dairy and the co-op. All of them – except the hospital, the boat sheds, the police station and the factory – built of hewn volcanic rock and salvaged pieces of shipwreck and topped by toupees of thatch made from island grasses. Eighteen fishing boats kept in Ergo's harbour, twelve kilometres of gravel track in the village and a half-kilometre track to the fields. One hundred and eighty head of sheep, three donkeys for the carts, numerous fowl (chickens, ducks, geese and peacocks), forty-two dogs and an unknown number of cats and cattle, some feral. Seventy-five graves set close together like a rosary round the church – the departed need their space, but not at the expense of the living. Only three graves left, up to two deaths a year.

And now another, unexpected. Officer Dorado Bardelli heard the news that morning from Liesa Pelani, who came over to the office. Dorado received the words released from Liesa's lips as though they were any other; it was only once she had closed the door on the departing messenger that she felt the dragging pain. She leaned against her desk, shocked, letting tears well and fill her eyes. She had been at school with Angelique; they had played house-house together, and nurse-nurse, and skipping games. Angelique had always been the patient, dying of some terrible illness, and Dorado would take her temperature with a stick under her tongue and listen with her ear to her flat chest to hear the bumping of her heart and the tide of her breath. She would boil up leaves for medicine and Angelique would refuse to take it, saying she didn't know what was in it; and so Dorado would decree that Angelique was dead, and she would play along, holding her breath and getting floppy. Dorado would run and call the doctor, Roland Kohler, who would come and save Angelique in the nick of time. Then she and Roland would get married and Angelique would cry and feel left out. But Roland had grown up and had left for the mainland and Dorado had fallen in love with Clarence, the mayor, a man already taken. Angelique was the one who had married a doctor; there should have been some insurance in that, but now they said she was dead. Dorado needed to see Angelique dead before she believed it. Perhaps she was just pretending.

She knew Clarence would arrive soon, in his all-weather gear and his agitation. She went to the mirror fastened to the wall over the hand basin and dabbed at her eyes. She must be strong for him, she must steady her hair, which was all over the place again. She would tie it back, braid it, force it into submission, except that it helped to obscure her ugly face. Things would only go from bad to worse now she was getting older. Why had the pretty one been taken away? She screwed her features into a knot, then stretched them wide open over the bones of her face. Clarence had confided his private theory to Dorado: that facial exercises done daily kept the skin flexible and firm and prevented the sagging of flesh, the dewlaps and the jowls from developing. It was ridiculous, wept Dorado, her face going gargoyle as she dragged her hairbrush through the dark thicket on her head. She mopped at her eyes again, wondering whether his wife knew, or whether his little vanity was their secret.

She heard Clarence's car drive up. She pulled her jacket down sharply over her behind, put on her best face and opened the door to him. He gusted in, dripping, hardly noticing her, already saying something, his arms punctuating his meaning with forceful gestures. She wanted to quieten him, to take him in her arms to reassure them both. But there were eyes all around – the office window looked clear out onto the road – so she busied herself, making him a strong cup of tea. Later, perhaps that evening when the fuss had died down, she could take him to her.

"It's an act of God," he declared. "I've called a council meeting at eleven. It's our duty, Dorado, to rescue the doctor from gossip and superstition. Orion Prosper has cured us all of something or other over the years!" He brought himself up in front of the mirror, and looked into it critically. "Jerome can make a sensible announcement in the factory cafeteria, and Minister Kohler can set the villagers' minds straight on Sunday." He turned and looked at Dorado for her response. She agreed encouragingly. Her tears had abandoned her. She was up for anything.

"We must go round to the doctor's house," Clarence decided. "Express condolences, a public display of solidarity." He looked at his hands, at the soft pulp of them. "It's so difficult, death. Awkward." He frisked his pockets, found his cigarettes and lit up. "You'll come with me?"

Dorado got ready, pulling on her all-weather gear, pleased to see Clarence relax a little. He touched her cheek softly. "You always know what to say, after the obvious."

Dorado and the mayor went out, pushing through the storm to the police vehicle parked beside the flagpole, on which the chivvying wind was playing the strings allegro: ting-ting. The officer paused a moment to wrestle with the loops in her thick gloves, lowering the flag to half-mast; there it wrenched about, threatening to tear away into the sky.

Chapter Three

Aunt Frieda held the small bundle of her niece in her arms, eased the bottle's teat into the baby's mouth and rocked her slowly to the rhythm of her grief. It came back to her like yesterday how she had done this very thing for Angelique, the last-born, the latecomer to the family, the angel. Frieda, the eldest, had had to look after Angelique as her own while their mother worked at the crayfish factory. The baby sucked hungrily, stopped and squirmed, torn between hunger and discomfort, sucked again, then broke her face into a grimace of complaint. Frieda stood, put the bottle down. She had been up all night like this, the night that she should have been keeping a vigil for her departed sister to smooth her passage into the afterlife. She'd lit a candle and had whispered the prayers of supplication to the ancestors while busy with the baby. It was the best she could do.

Frieda put the baby on her shoulder to wind her, the wails flailing against her ear, the tight gourd of the infant's belly straining against the colic. She'd seen this before. She knew what the problem was, what she had to do. Poor child, she had enough to cry about – her mother disappeared into heaven, her father into his bedroom. Her own tears ran down her face. She knew what she had to do, but she was afraid. Surely her dear sister would understand. And the doctor needn't know, it could be hidden from him.

She jigged around the room, patting the infant on her tiny back, trying to wind and soothe her. "Hush, now, hush." No mother, no father, grandmother and grandfather gone too, the doctor's parents and sister estranged and her other aunt away to the mainland, unable to get to the island to attend the funeral. What a story, what a beginning to a life! Aunt Frieda cooed and clucked over the poor young squalling thing while she changed her nappy, and told her stories of the island and how they came to live there, to distract them both from their great loss.

"Once upon a time, a sailing ship lost its way in a storm, blown away into the southern ocean while trying to go north. Oh yes, things don't always turn out the way you plan them, you'll get used to that fact." The baby whimpered and sobbed, pulling her little frog legs up, looking into Frieda's face with her deep, dark eyes. "That ship was a slave ship, stealing black people away from their homes and selling them across the ocean – those that survived, that is, for many died of dehydration and chest complaints and heartbreak, all crammed down in the hold like animals, though nowadays you'd go to jail for treating an animal so bad." She cleaned and dried and oiled the baby's bottom as she'd done for her own children, both grown up now, and shook her head. "Us humans, we've got a lot to answer for, we have." She put the baby's cap on – for she knew, like her mother's mother before her, that a baby loses most body heat through the head, where all the thoughts, lessons and memories are stored, and there was a cold rain outside. It thrummed hard on the roof of the doctor's house, reminding him in his bedroom at the end of the passage of his endless grief.

"This ship was due back home in the north, and after discharging her cargo, she set sail. The storm brought her south, and wrecked her on this isle, along with twenty survivors. They were both crew and slaves, for a few of the slaves, mostly favoured women, were being taken back to the old world. Already one was pregnant, for you know, slaves were forced to do whatever their masters told them. Oh, we have a lot to answer for! But good things can happen out of bad, look at me! Without all that I would never have been born, and neither would you!" And she laughed her gap-toothed laugh through her tears, and jigged and soothed her niece, and found some comfort there for herself.

The doctor was seated at his desk reading *The Annals of Modern Orthopaedics*, trying to concentrate on the diagnosis and treatment of osteitis, trying to block out the buffeting of the baby's cries and his own turbulent mind, when he heard a car pull up. That could only be a council member, or the police. He sprang to the window, peered out through the deluge, and saw the blurred figures of the mayor and Officer Bardelli hurrying towards his front door. Seized with rage, he found himself with his pistol in his hand, pacing. After all he had done for this dump, the dogs now turn on him! He had done nothing, nobody could pin a thing on him. He heard Frieda let them in; ear to the door, he tried to decipher words, but the damn weather drowned everything. How long must he suffer this assault from the skies? He had a wife to bury in the cold, wet ground before anyone started talking about autopsies. He locked the bedroom door, noticing with irritation how his hand was shaking. Pacing, pacing, his body restless, his mind caged in his head, in this room, this island, this life, imprisoned by the stories people told about him, by what people thought of him. Bastards, the lot of them, wanting a funeral to gawp and gossip and make a scene.

Frieda at the door, knocking, always at the door knocking, why wouldn't anyone leave him alone?

"I'm busy."

"But Mayor Peters . . ."

"Not now!"

Frieda retraced her steps to the sitting room where the two waited, hats in hands. "He doesn't come out except for the bathroom," she apologised. "Eats in there too, what little he does."

The mayor shook his head. "Terrible thing. Just wanted to pay my respects, you know. And to tell him there's nothing . . . to worry about." He looked at Dorado for help.

Officer Dorado Bardelli nodded. "Tell the doctor the police van is available for the funeral Saturday. I'll drive her myself."

She stared at the baby Frieda carried at her shoulder, amazed by how much noise could come out of such a tiny body. Every day she had a different feeling about babies; today she was glad not to have any and reminded herself to be more careful about taking her pill. Besides, the mayor had two of his own, both grown now; he wouldn't consider more, not in his position. She glanced at him, hoping her hair was lying straight and right, but he was looking somewhere else, always looking somewhere else.

"What's wrong?" Clarence asked, chucking the baby on the cheek with a bent forefinger.

"The colic," said Frieda. That was all they needed to know. It was what the doctor had diagnosed, getting John Peters to bring antispasmodics over from the hospital dispensary. "She'll grow out of it," is what the doctor had said. Then he'd left it up to Frieda, burying his head under pillows when it got too much.

Mayor Peters glanced at Officer Dorado again; he wanted to escape, but she wished there was something more they could do. Dorado had never heard a baby cry for its mother like this: a shuddering wailing tearing at her ears. "Well, we'd better get going," the mayor decided, making for the door, pulling Dorado in his wake.

They were not the only visitors. People came in dribs and drabs throughout the next few days, bringing presents for the baby: crocheted blankets and caps and knitted jerseys, milk formula, teddies for the bed and ducks for the bath. For the doctor they brought home-brew and condolences. Whatever they might say to each other in the confines of their cottages, they knew the right thing to do. They knew that, come an emergency, a slip on a rock or a gall bladder gone bad, your life could suddenly fall into the doctor's hands. Who knows, if he already held a grudge against you, his hands might be too full to catch you.

But whoever came to the house, the doctor would not come out of his bedroom. The presents piled high on the table in the sitting room, presents wrapped in patterned paper blurring and sagging with the tear and pluck and wet of weather, hand-made and shop-bought gifts resting and sogging, but still the doctor would not come out. Not even when Nelson Peters arrived to take instruction concerning the funeral arrangements. Not until the day Frieda answered a knock at the door and there stood Sister Veronica, braced against the gale, wearing her body like a corset.

"It is time," she said to Frieda as she whisked briskly past her, past the wailing baby and down the passage (how did she know which was the doctor's bedroom door?). She knocked. "Doctor," she announced firmly to the wooden barrier, "Mr Arthur Bardelli has cut his finger to the bone with his fishing knife, and that Peters child, Sasha, has a bronchospasm I cannot break. And Katerina Schoones cannot stop vomiting, her sugar is off the scale. I have done all I can, but we need you, sir. I am sorry to disturb you in this difficult time, but I fear . . ." What she wanted to say was that she feared death might come again, but that could not be said, not with his wife still above ground.

Still no answer, but she knew what would rouse him. "People might start to turn elsewhere, sir, and you know what will come of that." Already there was a queue outside Sophia's door in the mornings, already people's heads were being turned.

The door opened and Doctor Orion Prosper emerged, pale and unshaven, his eyes underlined with pain. Veronica's heart leapt to see him. I'll save him, she thought. I will make my body a raft for him to lie on, I will bear him away to tropical shores where the wind never blows, and the water is clear and still, and the sun will thaw his heart so he can love again.

The doctor shrugged his coat on, knocked back some pills. "Let's go," he said to Veronica, and went out of the door as though it was his idea.

Chapter Four

A storm can set in for days around Ergo Island, but it is also possible for the weather to change six times in twenty-four hours. Later that morning, the clouds above the isle broke open above Frieda as she looked outside. The waterlogged sky divided – just like the Red Sea, she thought. It was an omen. The doctor had come home for lunch as though nothing had ever happened, sitting at the table eating pumpkin soup and telling Frieda that the chest had opened, the finger was sewn and intact, and that the sugar levels had dropped. She nodded encouragingly, glad to see his appetite, glad to hear him whistling in the bathroom, glad to see him take a peek at his sleeping daughter.

"She looks like me as a baby," he said, getting out his photo album to illustrate the point. Baby Orion stared with unfocused eyes out of the page, dressed in white, his floppy newborn body held up like a trophy by his proud father. His mother looked on anxiously, her hands ready to catch him if he fell. There was some difficulty between the doctor and his family on the mainland, perhaps because he had married a young pregnant island girl. There had been someone else marked for him, rumour had it, someone appropriate to his station in life. Whatever it was, in the three years he'd been here, the family had never come out to visit. Frieda tried to pick up any sign of hunger or fear in the doctor's face as he stood looking at the photograph of his parents, who were gazing up at his tiny potential, hopes for his future life blooming in their faces; but he snapped the album closed and turned to his daughter. His hand hovered above her, as though afraid to touch her, in case this gift too might disappear. "She'll go far," he decided, before pulling on his coat and striding back to the hospital.

Frieda had been waiting for this, waiting and watching, for she knew what she had to do. She sent word to her daughter, Liesa, via one of the children playing in the street. They were the messengers of the island, the telephone network, the communication system; the children were often the first to know what was going on or who had gone where. Occasionally the system broke down: a child was distracted by a kitten while running a message, or some of the words were forgotten or misremembered, and what started out as "We have run out of milk" arrived as "The cow has got out again" – but then, what telephone system doesn't have faults?

Liesa came soon enough from the co-op where she carded and spun island wool, and nodded as her mother gave her instruction. She was a young woman of few words, a bowl of a woman who could be trusted to store what needed to be stored and not allow little leaks to develop, running out here and there into other people's ears. But Frieda was careful not to tell her daughter too much; only that she needed to go out for a short while, that she was going shopping, and would not be long. All of which was true. Frieda was not the kind of woman to tell a lie.

She kissed the baby, who was screeching again, and made her way carefully along the slush and slurry of the gravel road, skirting puddles glinting in diluted sunlight. The children were out, every one fattened up with clothing against the cutting wind. She smiled with pleasure to see them running to the harbour or to the shop, dogs at their heels, or just running from sheer release of the tension that builds up in children's legs when they are forced to sit inside day after day because of weather or school or some such thing. Raef Peters, Gilbert Tamara, Al Bardelli, Harry Pelani, Kali Mobara, Rayla Schoones, Sasha Peters, Yero Tamara ... children she had known since they were born, who yelled greetings as they passed: "Hi, Aunty!"; children who played in the nooks and crannies of the island as her own had done, collecting eggs, rounding up stray cows, building rafts and houses out of drift-wood that came in with the storms. Wood that had once been rooted in places too far away to imagine, that brought with it, in its weather-beaten grain, ideas of other places, of worlds that existed beyond the horizon. Often she would see these children staring out to sea, holding some object that had washed ashore, setting sail across the globe of their brains to visit places they had only seen in the few books from the school library, or heard about from occasional travellers. Television had not yet come to the island; that would only happen once satellites were employed to flood remote places with images of what people should desire and aspire for, of what their island lives lacked.

Frieda was headed for the potato fields. A side path led up to the edge of the volcanic cliff, where a little cottage stood away from the others in a small thicket of trees. She didn't want anyone to see where she was going; people would jump to conclusions, probably the correct ones. Word always got round. A few other women were hurrying to the fields, making the most of the dry spell to deal with the grubs that could spoil an entire potato harvest and bring the community to the brink of ruin and starvation. She greeted them and walked with them: Martha Schoones, Rumer Peters, Octavia Pelani, Elaine Peters, Layla Bardelli, Graça Bagonata. At the same time, she wanted to fall behind as though she had forgotten something; but they were naturally full of questions about the father and the funeral, and about the tiny crying one. The women shook their heads and clucked, and Graça suggested peppermint water, which had helped for her own little Phoebe, and Elaine recommended Telement drops, and Martha asked if she could help, take a turn with the baby, and Rumer gave a look which said the thing that none of them could say, and before they knew it they were at the fields.

Frieda helped for a while, then said she had to get back to the baby and hurried off with their good wishes. Through the gate, then quickly right, up the track when she thought no one would notice. No stopping now; she had to hurry to get among the stunted trees and in front of the small stone cottage.

It stood slightly skew on its base, white smoke snaking out of the chimney to fade against the grey sky. Over the front door hung a sculpture made out of a length of driftwood that Elijah Mobara had carved for his cousin Sophia, with a hand at either end that seemed grown out of the grain: one open, receptive, the other closed into a fist. Frieda had always liked it, for it showed the balance of things, how God both gives and takes away. But today her heart felt fisted over Angelique, and she had a sudden urge to break the sculpture, or to burn it. Another watched her as she wiped at her eyes: beside the door stood a large figurehead washed ashore from some wreck, the carved figure of a woman with partially furled wings. She would have been an angel, except the sculptor had given her a beak instead of a mouth; a birdwoman she was, holding to her naked breasts something crusted in dried barnacles. Frieda rapped on the door, not wanting to stand on the step any longer; there was something about the figurehead's eyes that saw straight through her. The lace curtain lifted a moment, the door opened and Astrid Tamara, her distant relative, stood in front of her in a purple coat, her green eyes wild, her toothy mouth smiling widely, her red hair shocked about her head.

"Afternoon, Astrid."

"Hi, Aunty." The large young woman glanced over her shoulder, shifted her weight on her slippered feet, her every movement unsettled, unsettling.

"I've come to . . ."

"She says bring the baby."

"Bring . . .! I couldn't! She knows . . ."

"Tonight."

"But . . ."

Astrid laughed and closed the door.

Too proud she was, thought Frieda, too powerful for her years, too mad and wild. Astrid had set fire to her father's boat when she still lived with him a year back, burning their very livelihood, running naked down the road in winter, shrieking that her father was the Antichrist. The doctor had put an end to that with his needle and six men holding her down – six men! Then she'd spent nine months sitting quietly in the corner of her father's cottage, or shuffling round, her mouth hanging open, her brain chained to safety by bottles of pills.

There was talk of sending her to an institution on the mainland, but her father had a stroke and did not have the wherewithal to sign for it, and the mother wouldn't have it.

Instead she had brought her to Sophia, who took her in and vouched for her, and said she was special. Special! laughed some of the menfolk drily down at the tavern. Sure she's special! Suppose we're all devils and it's our boats next! They approached the council to try to force her off the island, but this could not be done without her mother's consent.

And so the tide began to turn against Sophia – because of that, and also because of the distrust people had of a woman living alone when she could have had a husband (for there were many she had turned away, including the mayor himself, some said), and also because of the disagreements between her and the doctor. Now people rarely consulted Sophia, for fear of her or of what the doctor and the mayor or others might think, or for fear of Astrid, sitting on the roof, laughing at the women walking to the fields. They carried charms and made the sign to ward off evil and hurried on, and wished for Sophia, midwife, healer and undertaker, to live somewhere else. It was affecting the crops.

Frieda walked back to the doctor's house, leaning into the freshening wind. Sophia never made things easy. Annoyance twitched in her. Now what was she to do. But she knew, she knew. She had to take the baby.

Still, that night, after the doctor had finished his dinner of fish and potatoes and had gone back to the hospital to assist Danny Schoones through his withdrawal from alcohol, Frieda sat in the sitting room at the fire, and felt her stomach knot at the thought of it. Tired she was, so tired; she had hardly slept since she took over the care of the baby six days back, poor little thing; and there she started up again, the endless crying, the yelping for help, the mewling of a lost kitten. She picked up the baby, jigged her, felt their helplessness, alone in the night.

"I don't know what to do," she said out loud to herself, to

the child, to God. And outside, as if in reply, the wind dropped. The whining, winding howl outside quietened, and along with it the child; then a hush like waiting, like listening: what next, what next?

How could she take her out into the cold dark, and only ten days old? Sophia knew better, it was against the old ways. But then, so much was happening that defied how things should be, and here in her arms, a scrap baby wailing again with such desperation crumpled into her face. But if she went and the doctor came back before her? Would he notice they were gone, or assume they were asleep? Cross each bridge as you come to it. Do the next right thing, the rest will sort itself out.

Frieda wrapped her niece up and strapped her against her bosom, pulled on her cumbersome all-weather gear – the waterproof and padded jacket with hood, the stiff, resistant trousers – and stepped outside. At the Point, to the east, the lighthouse blinked, holding its light up into a sky full of stars. They were like a million eyes pinned to her secret errand. It was late, all was quiet except for the music from the tavern at the end of the road and the generator going at the police station. Most people went to bed early, tired after the buffeted round of their island lives – except the readers, whose windows glowed as they read into the night: old favourites from the small library housed in Martha Schoones's study or from the school library, books that were coming apart at the spine.

Frieda turned away from the houses, skirting the main section of the village, and made her way to Sophia's cottage. It was done. There would be consequences, but that was the way of life.

Chapter Five

"So this is the doctor's daughter." Sophia gathered the baby up and cradled her along the length of her forearms, the tiny capped head cupped in her palms. The infant was shrieking, her little legs pulling up to her belly, her face exhausted and crumpled and dry, her tears used up.

"Also my sister's daughter!" Frieda replied, surprised by her flare of irritation. Light from the fire blazed as Astrid fed and stoked it, light lapped at patches of shadow on the rough stone walls and at Sophia's soft face, her brow puckered as she peered at the child. It was absurd, thought Frieda, that Sophia refused the convenience of electric light in this day and age.

Sophia lifted her face and looked at Frieda long and hard, turning something over in her mind, as if to say – what? What was in that look? What was there left to say after the tragedy, after the facts of the matter? Here was a baby who needed help. Surely Sophia wouldn't hold the father against her?

"She's our daughter," muttered Astrid, feeding dry grasses into the crackling fire.

Frieda looked at her sharply. Astrid was unpredictable; she felt uneasy in her presence. What did she mean?

"It's time you did your own crying, Astrid," said Sophia. "Leave this babe, she carries enough."

Astrid only laughed at this, a high, loud laugh that shocked the child to silence for a moment, then merged with the cadence of her renewed cries.

"Light the herbs," instructed Sophia.

Astrid reached up and took a bound plait of dried leafy twigs down from a bunch hanging from a rafter and immersed the end in the flame. As soon as the plait took, she removed it and extinguished it. The glowing cinders unravelled a grey and pungent smoke onto the air.

Sophia took the plait and leaned over the baby. She blew the smoke gently onto her forehead, her chest, her belly. Startled, the baby's cries choked off into coughing. Frieda restrained her impulse to leap forward and take the child away. The use of herb smoke cleansed the spirit and invited the ancestors in, yet it surely was no good for newborn lungs! It was wrong to have come. Yet she could not bear the thought of going home to more nights of wailing.

"Angelique is here," Sophia said quietly, putting the baby down on the sofa next to her and lifting the baby's clothing to reveal her belly.

Frieda tried to sense her sister's presence in the air around her but failed. Why was it that some were chosen and others not, that some had this gift of seeing and healing? Frieda had known Sophia her whole life – and yet she barely knew her. She remembered her as a wilful and overindulged child, the only progeny of elderly parents who regarded her as a miracle given by the ancestors – yet this supposed miracle had picked on Frieda for being short and fat. Then, as a prepubescent girl, Sophia had become very ill, dreaming dreams that belonged to the deepest hour of the night, growing thin and wasted. Aunt Kora, the local herbalist and midwife, came to explain to the parents that Sophia had been called, and that Kora had been waiting for this sign of a successor. Kora said that if Sophia did not come into apprenticeship, she would become crippled or die. Becoming a healer was the only possible choice for Sophia: this was her destiny. The parents did not want their only child to become a healer, a difficult and exacting life bound by strict ritual, observance and service. It was also a marked life: a potential target of awe and fear in the community. So they consulted the doctor at the hospital. Despite his medication, Sophia worsened to the point of death. The doctor explained that she needed to be hospitalised on the mainland, that specialists could help her; but the next ship was only due to arrive a month hence, and that might be too late. Frieda remembered hearing this news as a child with deep satisfaction. But Sophia hadn't died. Instead she had convinced her parents to let her go to Aunt Kora, dreaming every night of an elephant that carried her away. By the time the ship arrived, she refused to go to the mainland for treatment, despite the doctor's insistence that the sickness would no doubt return, that she was only in remission.

Frieda recalled the day Sophia did not come back to school, and her feeling of relief and envy. The chosen child no longer played with the other children and was seen only occasionally, at a distance, by herself or with Aunt Kora, her beautiful braids shaved off, her face washed with white, a stranger, a spirit, unreal. She spent her days walking the island, gathering indigenous plants, immersed in ritual, preparing for life as a healer.

Then, some years later, when Angelique was born, Sophia arrived at Frieda's mother's house as Aunt Kora's midwife apprentice. Frieda remembered how she quietly did what she was told, carrying in the basins of water, wrapping the afterbirth to prepare for ritual burial, ignoring Frieda in her own home. Frieda had barely been able to look at her, knowing she was chosen and Frieda was not – even though she knew Sophia got up at four in the morning in winter to gather certain plants, and washed in cold water only, and was not allowed to eat fish.

Yet here she was, asking her old enemy for help, against the doctor's beliefs and wishes.

Sophia leaned over and put her open mouth onto the baby's abdomen, drawing her cheeks in with a gentle sucking, so that when she raised her head, she left a reddened oval mark on the baby's belly. She leaned forward and spat a hissing globule into the fire, then took some oil from a bottle warmed at the hearth, and rubbed it into the baby's belly, her hand moving in slow circles.

The baby's sobbing breath, catching on itself, slowed as Sophia began to sing a string of song.

"Stranger to this world you come,
sent by those who know your fate,
love has given, love has taken,
may all storms in you abate."

Sophia blew gently into the baby's blinking eyes and open mouth, down onto her chest still lurching with occasional sobs, down to her belly, to her legs which had relaxed.

"Child of poverty, child of plenty,
may your small boat find its bay.
Daughter of shipwreck, child of moonlight,
let your life show you the way."

Sophia took a length of knotted blue yarn from a basket beside her. Frieda stiffened; not this, not this! "The doctor will not stand for that!" she objected.

Sophia ignored her, tying the yarn around the baby's belly, blessing it with a few of the old words. "You will find a way to keep it from him. We refuse the way of the ancestors at our peril, Frieda, you know it."

Frieda shook her head, dismayed, as Sophia pulled the baby's garments back over her belly. She should have known: the yarn was the old way to keep the child safe, tied to the guidance of the ancestors. But the doctor never bathed or changed his daughter, so perhaps . . .

"What is she called?" Sophia asked.

"She hasn't . . . been named yet." Frieda saw disapproval flash through Sophia's face. "The father's been . . . in mourning, not capable . . ." Surely this healer could have compassion for a grieving man?

Sophia waved any idea of the father away. "You know our way."

Frieda felt exasperated. Times had changed, why did Sophia insist on making things difficult? "Our way is not the way of the father," she stumbled.

Astrid, sucking at a strand of her red hair, mumbled wickedly: "The father must have his way, the father must have his way . . ."

Sophia inhaled audibly, impatiently, not bothering to respond. She opened a packet of powder and placed a pinch on the baby's tongue, then picked her up into the crook of her arm and lifted her own jersey. She stroked the baby's cheek with the tip of her ample nipple, crooning to her. The child's tiny head turned towards the offer, wobbling hungrily, her mouth open, eager and instinctive, then latching and sucking, sucking and sucking, sucking and sucking, then pulling away with the wail of failure.

What was she doing? "Is that . . . is it for the comfort?" asked Frieda, astonished. Sophia shook her head.

Frieda understood. "I didn't mean for you to . . ."

"What did you expect?" Angry, there was an anger in Sophia. "You could do this too, if you put a mind to it and took ergonot root."

"Me? My lastborn eighteen, and me almost in the change?" Frieda shook her head. "I don't think so."

Astrid rocked, laughing, shaking her fiery head. "I don't think so," she repeated, "I don't think so!"

Sophia handed the child back to Frieda. "The milk will come, if she sucks every day." She looked at Frieda. "You'll bring her every day."

Impossible. Impossible! Surely . . . there must be another way.

"Astrid will help. If she sucks also, the milk will come."

Astrid stood abruptly, struck by the thought. "I am not a baby."

"No. You are not a baby." Sophia gestured: come, come and sit beside me, you are not a baby. Astrid tensed with indecision, her eyes looking at Sophia longingly, then away with feigned indifference.

"Together we can help this child, who is a baby."

Astrid glanced at the baby whimpering in Frieda's arms, then gave in and came over and nestled against Sophia, desirous, afraid; then she lifted Sophia's jersey. She looked at Sophia's pendulous breasts lying like a feast on the table of her chest, then her eyes darted back to Sophia's face.

"Suckle me," instructed Sophia. Astrid bent her brazen head to Sophia's breast, her lips open, her tongue finding the dark nipple, and closing her lips around the halo of the areola, she sucked, pulling it deeply into her mouth. Frieda watched, embarrassed, amazed, as Sophia put her arm around the shoulders of the suckling woman to support her. It looked like love, like lovers, what did it look like? She glanced at the windows; the curtains were not drawn; what if someone saw, what would they think?

In her own arms, the baby had fallen asleep.

Sophia indicated that Frieda should take the rest of the packet of powder with her. "Add a pinch into each feed. And bring her back. Tomorrow." In her arms, Astrid had started crying, suckling and crying. Unconcerned, Sophia stroked the side of Astrid's face and watched as Frieda wrapped the baby up and strapped her to her chest.

Frieda pulled on her jacket, put the remedy into her pocket. "Thank you," she said. "How much . . ."

"An egg-laying hen," answered Sophia, who never took money as payment, "and a bag of flour. And leave food out every day. You know it, Frieda. This island is full of the ways of the mainland, the ancestors are starving."

Frieda nodded, torn. She turned to go.

"Gulai," said Sophia.

"What?"

"The ancestors say her name is Gulai."

Chapter Six

"Gulai!" The doctor banged his coffee cup down and glared at Frieda.

"It was her mother's wish." Not a lie, Frieda never told lies, and the ancestors had spoken.

"What kind of a name is Gulai?" The doctor stuck a finger behind his collar and tugged at it as though it was strangling him.

"It is a good Ongala name. It means born in the rainy season."

"It sounds like a man digging in mud! Besides, she isn't African!"

"She's part African. So am I. So was her mother."

"Hardly." The doctor picked at his moustache irritably. "She never mentioned that name to me! Gail was the name we agreed to. It was Gail, you have made a mistake. It's just a few of the letters swapped round. Look at her, she's not a Gulai!"

*

So the baby had two names: Gail for the father, meaning father's joy, and Gulai for the mother, meaning born in the rainy season. It was Gulai who sucked at Sophia's breast every day until the milk came, and continued suckling for two months thereafter. Her crying stopped and the doctor told all who would hear how Gail had responded to the miracle of modern medicine, and they nodded their heads in agreement, knowing full well that his daughter drank witch's milk every day, for it was no longer a secret. Often enough, Sophia would come to the doctor's house to feed the child while the doctor was at work, and everyone could see how the baby grew fat and happy, full of ancestral magic and miracles.

There came a day that Frieda cut the cord around the baby's belly and hid it away in an envelope, for she argued within herself that the child was now healthy and out of danger. The ancestors would understand, it was surely prudent to take only the risks that were strictly necessary. It's true she lived with the worry that Sophia might discover the yarn's absence; but there was no pleasing everyone, and Frieda knew it was a miracle that she had got away with what she had.

Yet there were those who shook their heads in the privacy of their own homes, or even in the tavern when the doctor was not there; no good could come of this situation in the long run, no good at all. No one ventured to inform the doctor about Sophia and Gulai – for who wants to be the bearer of unwelcome news, and while the weather is fair and mild, why rock the boat? Things will emerge in their own good time.

Why was it that the doctor was the last to know? Well, his mind was on many things, busy he was, keeping certain feelings at bay; and being the only doctor for several thousand miles around he was, fortunately, a busy man. After the funeral – a sad, windswept affair with Minister Alfred Kohler's blessings tossed this way and that over the open grave so that the mourners heard only snatches – Orion filled up his spare time reorganising the hospital's filing system. This was not his job, but he was a methodical man who understood the way things should work.

He was fortunate in that Sister Veronica was available to help him in her spare time. Often enough he came home late and a little drunk, having stopped off at Veronica's for a bite to eat and stayed on longer than he had intended. It was a great solace to him that his assistant pointed no fingers; on the contrary, she relieved him of all blame, to the extent of suggesting, while she rubbed his shoulders, that he apply for a prominent post on the mainland. She never added, *before it's too late*, but he knew that was what she meant: too long in the backwaters, and you would not be taken seriously by the mainstreamers. He knew this should be his next move, yet he could not act on it. Something stopped him, something tightened in him, preventing him from reaching out to open the envelopes containing monthly academic journals that arrived in batches by ship three or four times a year, with adverts for positions displayed in the back. He had lost his nerve, that thread that strings body and will together, and instead he was filled with a fear that he would be found out. Found out? What would be found out? That he was a fraud, if truth be told. That the error of his wife's demise was not just a momentary slip, but a sign of something that underpinned his whole career; that he was not good enough for anything but a backwater where people did not know better, where his mistakes could be buried without an inquest.

Nevertheless, he was pleased that Veronica thought him good enough for the mainland, thought they were both too good for the island. He also liked the way her hands slid under his shirt, and the smell of her, a good, well-scrubbed smell. Before long he lay himself down on the comfort and support of her; he allowed himself to be consoled in the rocking cradle of her, her hands on his back absolving him in long strokes, telling him he was lovable, that he was not floundering, shipwrecked on some godforsaken shore, but up and sailing on the good seas; that satisfaction and prosperity and, yes, even ecstasy, were still visible on the horizon, still within his reach.

Chapter Seven

Some say it was the fact that Frank Bardelli saw Astrid down at the boat sheds that night that started the avalanche of events. Some say it was not a fact at all, and to call that a fact left out others, like the fact that the fishermen hated Astrid, and the fact that Astrid was not the only person with red hair on the island. Some say it could have been prevented, but then there are those who say it was meant to be; who are we to argue with fate?

It was true that Astrid liked to wander at night, and that she liked to light and stoke the fire in Sophia's grate. Frieda knew that from the times she'd visited late, when people were in bed except for the drinkers at the tavern. It was true, too, that Astrid still had an edge about her: strange turns of bodily expression and phrase, and behaviour that made you feel as though you had lost the path and wandered into an unrecognisable landscape. But she was no longer excitable and violent, and she no longer took her clothes off in public places. She had calmed herself in the year she had been living with Sophia. Some said the doctor's medicine had reset her connections, some that Sophia's remedies had cured her. Whatever the case, Frieda did not think Astrid's behaviour so strange that she would commit arson again. Yet the alarm was raised one blustering night; the villagers rushed out, pulling on their jackets, to see great orange tongues of flame roaring out of the windows of one of the boat sheds, licking at the cold night air, and to hear the exploding of petrol cans, and the sigh of the roof as it collapsed. People ran with hosepipes, buckets, sand, anything, for this was their livelihood: the fish and the crayfish, best in the world, frozen and exported four times a year to the fancy restaurants in Japan, England and America. Without their boats, they might as well pack up and go . . . where? There was nowhere to go, this was their home, this was their foothold upon the planet, the reason for their existence, the place their ancestors had built from nothing.

Jojo Schoones's boat was destroyed, Frank Bardelli's badly damaged. One boat shed was a smouldering shell with the remnants of hoists sticking through like charred bones. Light was cracking the eastern horizon open when the men marched through the village and along the track to the fields, turning up the path to Sophia's cottage and demanding that Astrid come out.

Sophia emerged, said Astrid was in bed; what did they want?

You know, they shouted. Come out.

There is no reason, no charge, no cause, said Sophia. Leave my property. Now.

Why weren't you there, fighting the fire!

What fire? asked Sophia, concerned.

Ask the ancestors! someone shouted. Didn't they warn you?

Ask Astrid! yelled another. Astrid knows!

The mayor arrived, and Officer Bardelli.

54

Arrest Astrid, the men said. Enough is enough! She will burn all our boats, she will kill us all! She is crazy, a man-hater.

She is not crazy, she has been hurt, said Sophia.

Hurt! raged the men. Hurt! Look how she hurts us! We'll show her hurt!

It's unnatural what the two of you do! blurted one.

Tell these men to get off my property, said Sophia quietly to Officer Dorado Bardelli. Officer Bardelli looked at the mayor.

We will have to take Astrid to the office for questioning, said the mayor. Just a few questions from the council. And an examination. By the doctor.

Jojo Schoones was the one who saw her run out of the back door and away up the mountain, and they were off, thirty-four men after one woman, mad they all were, mad with rage and history and blame and revenge.

Astrid knew the mountain well after years of trying to escape, she knew her way even in the dark; but the sun was already prising open the lid of cloud, the sun was shining on her red crown of hair, red like fire against the black laval rock, as she ran for what felt like her life.

They could have waited for her; they could have gone home to drink coffee and clean up, they could have waited until Astrid came down the mountain of her own accord, cold and tired and hungry. By then the tempest of tempers would have died down, by then they might have discovered that Danny Schoones had drunkenly fallen asleep in the boat shed with a burning cigarette falling from his fingers. The detail of that evening was gone – it was one of many nights in his life that he would never recall; but he was told, on finding himself in hospital being treated by Sister Veronica for burns to his face and hands, that he was a hero for being injured while fighting the fire. He was pleased to have been of service, sorry he hadn't been in time to save the boats.

They didn't wait, they were after her like hounds baying for blood. They say Astrid slipped and fell at Ike's Gully, that Jojo Schoones and Nelson Peters tried to save her, poor mad girl, that the two men tried to prevent her from jumping, but they were too late.

Chapter Eight

"This is monstrous!" paced the mayor. "Right before the elections!"

Nelson stared at his boots, which were peeling a rim of drying mud onto the mayoral office carpet. Dorado closed the blinds and wished that Clarence would keep his voice down. She had never seen Clarence's younger son like this – struck weak by a vision, run through with shock.

"I'll get Mannie to come with me, and the doctor," she said, feeling ill at the thought of collecting blood and bone, at the thought of the spirit of mad, wild Astrid forever gone. "You go home and get some rest, Nelson."

"Stupid, stupid girl!" Clarence pulled hard at his lower lip, reining himself in. "Look, my boy, you did the right thing, coming to me before the rumours get going. What's happened has happened. The autopsy will set things straight. I'll have a word with Orion."

Clarence tugged open the blinds with such force they jumped and jangled. "Only one grave left," he worried, glaring at Elijah Mobara trundling past with his barrow.

"We'll look into opening up ground for the new cemetery," consoled Dorado. "I'll add that to tomorrow's agenda."

"You better," Clarence warned, "Or the dead'll be buried at sea."

Across the road, a tall woman in black appeared, striding towards the hospital, her greying hair swept back into a knot, several children pulled into her wake. He swung on Dorado. "It's that Sophia," he railed, "causing trouble again, obstructing the peace! If she hadn't defied the doctor's instruction, none of this would've happened! That girl needed professional help."

"She should've gone to the mainland," agreed Dorado, trying to placate.

"Sophia is an obstruction! A remnant of the old days. Remember that business with old Rozi Bagonata? This damn woman dealing in boiled herbs and charms had a nerve, brazenly telling the doctor it was Rozi's time to die!"

Nelson expelled a sudden, disparaging chestful of air, relieved the focus was not on him, eager it should remain so. "The doctor put her right. Sophia hasn't midwived a baby at home or anywhere else in years."

Clarence's brow smouldered round the problem. "With Astrid, she's gone too far."

"You heard, she was going with that girl," Nelson stoked.

"Imagine!" Something flared in Clarence's face that terrified Dorado. "That a middle-aged woman would seduce an unstable girl! There was a time she could've had pretty much any man on the island."

"Perhaps that was her problem all the time," offered Nelson. "You know. Lesbian."

The conflagration leaping in Clarence's features made a small explosion in the back of his throat. His hand moved underneath his cardigan and fiddled with his navel. There was a way of salvaging the situation. He took a deep breath. "Now there's a death on her hands," he noted quietly. "Dorado, you'll be with me on this in the council meeting. She has to go."

Orion looked at the young woman lying on the mortuary table, at her face stark beneath her matted red hair, slivers of glass-green eyes showing beneath the drape of her pale eyelids. Her jersey was tinged with blood from the laceration in her scalp and her right foot lay at an unnatural angle. He put his gloved palms on her iliac crests, pushed down with the weight of his body and felt the give. Pelvic fracture. She had fallen from a height onto rocks. Accidental death caused by bleeding into a pelvic fracture and/or head injury. No need to look further.

He pulled off the gloves. Nothing more required here except to get Nelson in to do the necessary. It bothered him, this crazy mixed-up island where the butcher doubled as undertaker. Wouldn't be allowed in a civilised place. But Nelson was the mayor's son and Jerome's brother, and thereby related to two of the most influential men on the island; there was nothing to be done about it.

He filled in the death certificate. It made him angry. This girl should have been in one of the institutions on the mainland. She could have done well. With recent advances in psychiatric medication, bipolar disorder was not the problem it used to be. This was a tragedy. But what could one do? To commit her required parental consent, and the mother would have none of it. He wondered how she felt now, having chosen to put her psychotic daughter in the care of a charlatan. That choice should not have been there in the first place. That's why, in civilised countries, there were peer-review councils, medical boards, licences to practise. Guardians of the basic standards were essential. People needed to be protected against fraudsters taking advantage of a primitive propensity for magical thinking. Rule and science prevented anarchy and quackery, they allowed people to sleep peacefully in their beds.

He looked again at the body. Death looked so extraordinary, so unnatural. One moment the body animated, responsive, electrical circuits firing and in order; next, this bag of flesh and bone. He could never get used to it. It was a failure, a giving up. He felt a sudden anger towards Angelique. She had given up on him, she had reneged on her responsibility to bring up their child, to be a partner to him into his old age.

He knocked a cigarette out of the packet and lit it. He wanted a drink. There was one more smoke-inhalation patient waiting for him in the casualty department, but he had time enough to go there via his office, where there was a bottle of whisky and one of breath freshener in a locked desk drawer. He washed his hands, noting again the puckers in the skin of both palms, then rubbed them roughly as was his daily habit, hoping this could stop their progression. Then he closed up the mortuary and strode down the corridor.

With some ambivalence he saw two women related by marriage, Rumer and Cyn Peters, waiting for him outside his office. "Good morning, ladies," he said, noticing how Cyn, the older one, pivoted, holding her body towards him, her contours softening. He must tread carefully, for she was a good-looking woman, troubled frequently by mysterious gynaecological complaints, whose husband the mayor's attention had wandered elsewhere. Rumer, on the other hand, irritated him by stubbornly refusing to notice he was a man at all. "Get John to draw your folders and I'll see you in the casualty. I'm on my way down there now."

"Oh no, Dr Prosper, there's nothing wrong with us," said Cyn, flushing. "There's just something . . ." She glanced at her daughter-in-law.

"There's something you need to know," Rumer said firmly.

Chapter Nine

Frieda was putting out food for the ancestors: some potato soup. She hadn't been able to help fight the fire because of her small charge, but she also hadn't been able to sleep until she'd heard via the children's network that the fire was out and no one badly injured. Exhausted, she had gone to bed, but Gulai had woken early, and shouted and laughed and sang from her cot until Frieda gave up and got up. She'd fed the little mite her breakfast, then set about making the doctor's lunch, knowing he would come home from the hospital tired and hungry. And now, in the garden, she stood a while quietly, thinking of her father, lost at sea; mindful of her mother, silenced by a stroke; her paternal grandfather, diabetic, infected; her paternal grandmother, who went to sleep and never woke up; her maternal grandmother, lost to a cancer that flowered in her breast; her maternal grandfather, yellow with liver failure; her own husband killed in an accident on an oil rig, and one of her sisters taken suddenly one afternoon with headache. And Angelique, Angelique. She said a prayer to them all, made supplication on behalf of the living, gave thanks that the alarm had been raised timeously, that only one boat had been destroyed and no lives, for health and food and shelter, for her niece's recovery, and for her place in the weave of things.

She had not yet heard about the crowd that had congregated in the early hours at Sophia's cottage; she did not yet know about Astrid's death.

She poured a little soup out onto the ground in the customary manner, to give thanks to the ancestors and to the earth from whence all life comes.

"What the hell are you doing?!" The doctor, bearing down.

Frieda stepped back, startled out of prayer. "Giving thanks . . ."

"Thanks!" Behind him stood Sister Veronica, her mouth pulled tight.

"It is our custom . . ."

"It is your custom to throw food away, to lie and steal!" Orion's rage erupted red and raw from deep inside the well of him. He had been hoodwinked – why, the whole village knew about the betrayal! They had all been laughing behind his back these months. "I will not be made a fool!"

"But . . ."

"I know what you've been up to with that . . . that charlatan! Your problem, you know what your problem is? You like undermining authority! That's the last of it. Pack your bags right now. You're a bad influence, you stay away from now on!"

That is how Frieda moved out and Veronica moved in; how the motherless child of many mothers lost two more, gained another.

On the other side of the village, another woman was forcibly brought home and told to pack and leave. They say she fought like a wild animal, refusing to go until she had seen Astrid's body in the mortuary and had prepared her charge herself for the spirit crossing. A needle quietened her. Thereafter, the doctor accompanied the mayor and Officer Bardelli across the channel to Impossible Island in the police launch with Sophia, drowsy and shackled. They released her there to live in a fisherman's hut with the basics for survival.

A notice was posted at the police station by the council that thenceforth Impossible Island was to be used for exile purposes for miscreants and outcasts. No landing would be permitted save for the regular guano- and penguin-egg-gathering expeditions; fishermen were only permitted to land if forced by inclement weather. No one except the authorities were to have contact with the exile. Anyone found breaching these rules and orders would be fined a month's wages.

There were those who read the notice, made the sign to ward off evil and nodded their heads, satisfied that the witch had been exorcised. For who but a witch could produce milk when she was near the change of life and had never had a baby of her own? Who but a witch would harbour and encourage an arsonist? And when she gave birth to a son eight months later, they made the sign again. Must be the devil's child, they concluded. It was unnatural to bear a child at her age, and with no man in sight!

There were also those who shook their heads, appalled, but they did not dare to question. After all, look what happened to those who did.

Chapter Ten

Nights are very long if sleep refuses you; you lie wide-open-eyed inside earth's shadow with nothing to distract you from intractable ghosts.

Since that terrible night of Astrid Tamara's death, since preparing her broken body for the funeral, Nelson had been shaken awake in the early hours by violent dreams of blood and falling. He lay and lay for hours beside his wife's deep, deserted body, suffocating under the dark blanket of night as it pressed down on his chest, wanting yet afraid of sleep – and thus waking to that nether world of relentless torment. Wandering through the house like a spectre himself, he'd enter their two-year-old son Raef's room and sit at the foot of his bed, listening a while to the tide of his breath, wishing there was a way to keep him from harm forever. The world was suddenly full of danger, with no way of keeping it all at bay. Worry wormed away at him, the days and nights dragged themselves slowly through his exhausted body. He was always in a twilight zone of partial sleep, terrified that his attention would slip one day, and with it his hand beneath his butcher's blade.

"What's happening to you?" asked Condolessa, his wife, at dinner. "You never hear what I say."

What? Nelson had no recollection. It occurred to him that sleep's measured absence perhaps restored the daytime capacity for presence of mind. He pushed his chair back and left for the tavern, where he found his brother Jerome, his cousin Jojo and the others, joking as in the days before falling women.

" . . . there were times he didn't know which end to hang over the gunwale!" laughed Jojo Schoones.

"He's talking 'bout David," explained Arthur Bardelli, chortling. "Poor boy ain't cut out to be a fisherman, that's for sure!"

"He's on a drip at the hospital." Jerome waved his younger brother into a seat next to him.

"He'd be better off here, trying to fix his reputation!" said Samuel Pelani. "The boy can hold his brew better than he can weather the sea!"

Frank shook his head with exaggerated shame. "What to do with a landlubber."

"Makes you wonder where he got his genes," said Jojo. "Thought he was born from fisherfolk."

Frank joined in the laughter, although his was a little strained; it was his mother's virtue Jojo was questioning.

"Something eating you?" Samuel Pelani handed a glass of home-brew to Nelson.

Nelson stared back out of red, burning eyes. "I'm fine," he said.

"That Tamara girl's death still getting to you?" asked Arthur Bardelli. "Must have been quite a mess you had to sort out."

"You did a good job," Samuel Pelani reassured him.

"What you could see at the funeral looked like her."

"You'd think Nelson was used to the sight of blood," jibed Jojo, his eyes across the table cold as fish. "Deals with it every day."

Nelson felt rage river through him, but he kept his mouth shut.

"Get over it, man," proclaimed Frank Bardelli. "It's for the best in the end. Terrible life, wired to madness."

"Poetic justice," pronounced Arthur, with an eye on Samuel, who was related to Astrid by marriage. "She was a proud girl."

"So was the witch," agreed Frank.

"What's David going to do then?" Nelson turned to Jerome abruptly, shifting the focus back. He had come here to escape the millstone of his memory, not to dwell on these matters. He was horrified that both Samuel and Arthur had seen something in his face.

"He'll apprentice himself to old Absalom. Electrician's a respectable job. No good catching fish if there's no way to preserve them."

Nelson downed the shot, made excuses and left them to their stories. Deep inside the belly of night, he found himself sobbing outside the church, the cold biting at his ankles. He was going mad, the world a blur of sludge dragging at him, nausea rooting his belly.

"You're looking terrible," Graça Bagonata informed him the next day. Phoebe, her one-year-old girl child, was on one arm, a puzzled sheep on a leash attached to the other. "You need a break."

Nobody had ever said that to him before. Nelson grunted, ashamed, unshaven, and told her she could fetch the cuts the following day. He took her sheep through to the back. Gripping the bleating animal fast between his knees, he pulled her head back and cut her throat with a quick slice of his sharpest knife, and felt how her struggling life bled out into the bowl, how her body went limp and sagged down onto the floor.

Tired, so tired he was, splitting the still-warm skin, but he was terrified at the thought of time alone with his own madness. He had almost forgotten himself at the tavern, almost said something to Jojo that could never be unsaid. That's what exhaustion did, as effectively as alcohol: it loosened the tongue and muddled the judgement. He would cause problems where there were none – except those inside his own head. He could not go on like this.

He gutted, beheaded and hung the animal and washed it down. Then he cleaned up, changed and went up the road. At the junction, he hesitated. Which way? Ahead of him stood the church, with Minister Kohler's house propped next to it. He suspected the minister was better at preaching than listening; besides, there were certain things he could not say in the cold, clear light of day.

To the right squatted the hospital. Above him, a petrel slewed into the wind; a dropping spattered white onto his jacketed shoulder. He cursed, brushed it off with his handkerchief, and turned towards the hospital.

That evening he shook a diamond-shaped pill out of its container. Hard to believe that this small compacted tablet contained the essence of what had eluded him for so long. Extraordinary that swallowing this tiny dose was sufficient to put an end to his suffering. He downed it with a tot of island brew for good measure, and lay down wide-eyed as an expectant bride. Before long the room tilted, a warm haze oozed in; Nelson felt his body twitch puppet-like before he slid effortlessly down into the muffled velvet depths.

Chapter Eleven

The end of each year heralded highlights of island life: this was the time of the sheep shearing and the potato harvest, the Hunt and the Summer Solstice Masked Ball, Christmas and then New Year – busy times for both the doctor and Minister Kohler. As December approached, the minister's sermons would become longer and longer. His congregation fidgeted under his stern gaze as he wheezed out his warnings of the peril that lay in wait for the soul indulging in activities traceable to pagan rituals and heathen practices.

"Desire and restraint," he announced, "quarrel over our every waking moment, they fight over the weakest part of what makes us human! Consider, ladies and gentlemen, the situation in the Garden of Eden." He loved the pauses in his sermons: the abyss of quiet like a cliff edge that launched his words towards God for His blessing, then allowed the meaning to parachute down onto the field of upturned faces. "Eve and Adam and the serpent all succumbed to desire in the full knowledge of their sin!" He watched for a sign of the impact of his words, praying for assistance in this thankless task. "Consider too: Christ in the Garden of Gethsemane! He desired to live! He feared death! He appealed to God: 'Take this cup away from me!' Yet he was the Son of God, and despite his fear, despite his desire, he practised restraint and submission, saying: 'Thy will, not mine.'" He leaned right over the pulpit for emphasis as he said this, looking down on his pitiful flock in the corrugated landscape of the pews. Often, of late, he had considered going back to the mainland. He felt weakened by the daily labour of his mission, an eternal pushing of a boulder uphill. Yet this was his restraint: God had lashed him to this cross, this place.

Minister Kohler rocked back on his heels, gripping the edge of the pulpit, and contemplated the beams that held the thatch roof of the church in place. "And so, as we near the time when we celebrate the anniversary of the coming of Christ to the earth, let us be mindful of the choices we make. Choices to obey God's mighty will – or to follow our own corrupt one." He never went as far as to name the Hunt and the Masked Ball; everyone knew what he was referring to, and for the following month few in the village could look him in the eye. Nothing was going to dissuade the majority from these observances – surely God knew that they were only a bit of revelry, which never got so out of hand that a prayer or two wouldn't rectify matters? Only Fabio Bagonata, who lived in perpetual dread of the end of the world, would shout "Amen!" with enthusiasm at the end of the minister's service, and avoided the temptations of the Hunt and the Ball each year by going fishing.

The build-up started with the sheep shearing and the potato harvest. The potatoes were said to be the best in the world, and the portion that was earmarked for export had to be bagged, and the wool carded and spun in time for the departure of the December ship. This same vessel brought to the island post and gifts and books and supplies, as well as occasional locals returning from the mainland, and island teenagers returning from boarding school for the summer holidays, full of stories to savour of life away from an island existence.

Officer Dorado Bardelli was the first to know the expected time of arrival of a ship, as she was in contact with the captain by radio. Sometimes a ship would arrive during the night, and the children would wake early and run down to the harbour, where the bay beyond accommodated the large and imposing ship, too big by far to fit into the small fishing harbour. The best was when it arrived in the day and the weather was good. Mrs Mobara would let the children out of school to climb up the black volcanic slopes of the mountain to the lookout point, trying to be the first to see the speck on the horizon that would slowly grow into a huge ship carrying dreams from far away.

As soon as someone had spotted the vessel, the children would run down to the harbour, hearts racing, to see how the bow thrusters brought the ship to a halt out in the bay, and how the huge anchors fore and aft were released with a splash into the water. They crowded onto the end of the breakwater, barely heeding their mothers' shouts to them to be careful. The barge, run by Frank Bardelli, would set out for the ship, coming alongside to receive the cargo hauled from the holds by the ship's crane and swung out over the barge in nets and containers. Then the barge would ferry the precious items into the harbour, where the process would be repeated with the cranes onshore.

In her office, Officer Dorado Bardelli, who doubled up as the customs official, would oversee the issuing of the goods the islanders had ordered. Some things could be opened straight away and savoured, others had to wait for the Summer Solstice Ball or Christmas or birthdays, when they would provide a further surge of pleasure. Fabio Bagonata always received one of the largest parcels: all his spare earnings went on tinned goods, which he stacked in his increasingly cramped cottage in preparation for the end of the world.

By night, half the islanders would be drunk, getting into fights and throwing up their imported wine and food over their new shoes. The year after Sophia was sent into exile, Mr Bacon – as the villagers called Giorgio Bagonata, the shop-keeper, the fourth person on the island rich enough to order a vehicle – mistook two poles for a road, rendering the car undrivable and plunging half the island homes into darkness. It took two days for David Peters to get over his hangover sufficiently to get the electrical circuits sorted out, and three weeks for Mr Bacon's broken nose, rearranged by the steering wheel and then pushed back into place by the bemused doctor, to heal, but it took two months until the next ship brought a new radiator, bonnet and fender to fix his vehicle. In the meantime, it stood forlornly at the back of his shop – a reminder to the whole community never to overdo it, reflected the doctor.

The night after the ship came in, yet other islanders plunged into the intoxicating worlds of books, music, art. Liesa Pelani, who had discovered a love of painting, would open new boxes of water?colours and enamels, Mannie Mobara would caress his new guitar like a lover, Martha Schoones would fall into the arms of the latest prize-winning novel and Elijah Mobara, who spent his spare hours combing the island for driftwood, would set to work with a new set of chisels.

The next day was the day of the Hunt. Years ago, someone had made the mistake of importing to the island a breed of cattle that had a tendency to be excitable; a number had got loose, disappearing into parts of the island that were barely accessible, breeding and going wild. Catching them was near impossible, and if the islanders went out and shot a few, it was difficult to get the large carcasses down the steep mountain paths and back to the village. But the December ship also happened to be a research vessel with a helicopter on board, and the mayor had an informal arrangement with the captain: in exchange for one carcass, some world-class crayfish and five crates of island-brewed spirits, the captain would assist the islanders by airlifting the cattle carcasses down to the village for the Summer Solstice Ball.

First the cattle had to be shot; but the day after the ship came in, there were few able to aim straight. The women would mutter prayers and shake their heads as the men lurched off, fish and crayfish nets forgotten, in search of larger prey. One year, Ricardo Bagonata got shot in the leg when Frank Bardelli mistook him for a heifer; another year, a wild bull gored Lucien Peters while he was trying to remember how to release the safety catch on his rifle. Both injured parties had to be airlifted to the hospital.

Once the cattle carcasses had descended from the heavens and been deposited in the square in front of the community hall, everybody fell in. While some helped Nelson Peters prepare for the feast, butchering and soaking the beef in huge tubs of marinade, others laboured to load the frozen fish, crayfish and potatoes destined for the world markets onto the ship, which sailed the following day. Because the time of the arrival of the ship and therefore the day of the Hunt was uncertain, the islanders always held the Summer Solstice Ball three days after the ship's arrival, whether it was the true solstice or not. Great fires were made in the square, both for atmosphere and for cooking. It was understood that if anyone was in the jail cell, they would be let out for the occasion, and any hospital patients were wrapped up and wheeled out under the night sky, some even on oxygen. The cleaning tables from the fish factory were carried out and laden with bowls of salads, and breads, and nuts and fruits brought from the mainland. Jojo Schoones's hi-fi was cranked up until the volume of the music competed successfully with the noise of the generator, and young and old joined in to celebrate after two months of hard work: eating, dancing, singing, flirting.

There was only one rule. Everyone, from great-grandparents to great-grandchildren, was required to wear a mask. Some spent the whole year making their masks spectacular, not only in an attempt to win a prize, but also because they needed to believe they could spend one night each year incognito on this island where everyone knew practically everything about everyone else – even though you could easily hear it was Cyn Peters's high staccato laugh, or spot at a glance Elijah Mobara's loping gait or Mr Bacon's potbelly. Masks allowed for some abandon. As a result, an unusually high proportion of the islanders had their birthdays nine months later, in September – another busy month for the doctor – and the fathers of September babies would look closely at their offspring, trying to discern familiar features.

Dorado Bardelli glued the last few strands of dried seaweed onto her papier-mâché mask. She was pleased by how she had managed to crimp and plaster the forehead and cheeks the previous night into a fierce, rugged face with heavy brows. The seaweed created a ragged beard, adding to the effect. But she was annoyed with herself for having left it so late: there was a danger of the glue not drying adequately by the evening. She placed the mask next to the crown, then started on the trident, fixing a parabola of wire to one end of a broom handle to create the fork, then padding it by winding strips of sea-green cloth around it. Clarence knew what she would be wearing; they would find each other in the throng that night, and he would surreptitiously cup her buttock in his hand and press himself against her. Later they would find a way to be alone; they would wash up together in a delicious, cocooned island moment. For a while she could pretend it was just the two of them, marooned in each others' arms, falling into paradise.

She glanced at the clock. She was almost late for work: signing out the goods for export, calculating the export duty and harbour tax, and stamping the crew's passports. She was meeting with Clarence at two to discuss the adequacy of the fire extinguishers in the co-op; their attention to business would be punctuated by their hands brushing occasionally in anticipation. Her days were organised around these moments, these brief encounters that made her thrill with a painful pleasure.

By two-thirty he had not arrived. This was unusual. Dorado sent Absalom Pelani's youngest son, Harry, to look for him; he came panting back to say that the mayor had last been seen in his boat early that morning, heading off in the direction of Impossible. Something tightened in Dorado's chest; what on earth was he doing? Some time ago, Clarence had taken to going fishing: something he had come to late in life, a solitary pleasure he insisted on despite Dorado's concerns for his safety. But today was one of the busiest days of the year, what with the ship in and the preparations for the Ball; the mayor should be available to be consulted about any attendant problems. Dorado went outside and felt how the wind was picking up and swinging round from the south, scrubbing the surface of the sea into a corrugated washboard, feeding her own turbulence. She locked up the police station and went to check herself. Clarence's boat was not in the boat shed. She went to Jerome Peters, Clarence's elder son, for help. The factory was closing early. The ship had been loaded in record time, and men and women were hurrying home to wash and change for the festivities ahead. Jerome checked with his mother; it transpired she was unaware that her husband had gone off in his boat.

Dorado prepared the police launch for the search with a double dread. In living memory, there had been three occasions when men had gone missing at sea – but none had been found. Also, why had he not told her of his plans?

Jerome and his brother Nelson came with her. The launch ploughed through the ruck and chop, heading for Dead Man's Cove on Impossible, where the fish were so plentiful they almost jumped into the boat. By the time they reached the cove, the sky was heavy with grey constellations of cloud, and visibility was becoming poor. There was no sign of Clarence's boat, so they put in at the landing beach and went to interrogate Sophia, her young son crawling at her feet. Three hours later, when they could not get Sophia to admit she had seen Clarence or knew his whereabouts, they were forced to sleep over in the fishermen's cottages.

Nelson lay in the darkness listening to his brother's breathing, his body tight and cold, his father lost, perhaps forever. This woman Sophia had something to do with it, he knew; he remembered his father's scratched face on his return after he had escorted her into exile.

Jerome thought this idea far-fetched. "He should never have gone out alone," he said, raising his voice above the wind's whine.

"The sea was calm enough most of the day," Nelson pointed out, wanting his wife's warm arms around him, angry with his brother for not seeing the obvious.

"You also don't know the sea, Nelson. It's not only storms can wreck you."

Nelson did not sleep much that night, not having brought his tablets with him, and with his father's ghost already sitting on his chest, whispering disparaging comments in his ear. The past could not be changed; certain memories stood solid and immutable, set in stone amidst the flux and wash of vague recollections. Certain events called him back, back, pulling his attention away from sleep, from life itself, refusing to let him go despite his best efforts to put them behind him and not look back. He was Lot's wife turned to salt, mesmerised, punished, pointless.

Had he pushed his father? He gasped at this notion, this mad idea sprung from the dark, ambushing his brain. Had he been a good enough son? His father leaving, always leaving, since he could remember. He had not managed to make him stay, even for his mother's sake; he could not bring her relief by staying with her himself, then or now. He had to make it up to her somehow.

The trapped fish of his thoughts revolved without respite in the dark bowl of his skull.

For Dorado, too, there was no chance of rest. The walls of the cottage were false shelter; she needed to feel the rip of the wind on her taut skin, she needed the tumult of weather to wrench the horror and grief from her mouth. Most of the night she was out on the cliff, her body wired and waiting, trying to pick up any trace of hope in the salt air; then plunging into despair like drowning, wanting to throw herself off the earth and down to Neptune's feet, joining her Clarence in one last act of immersion. But perhaps, perhaps he wasn't drowned. After all, he'd recently come to an agreement with Minister Kohler about the last gravesite at the church, claiming it for himself so as not to lie one day in the stony, cold cemetery near the sheep pastures. Clarence would've hated the thought of his flesh soaking off his bones in the freezing deep, his remains dancing to the tug of shark bites with the cold eyes of fish watching. It just wasn't possible. She had to know the truth, she had to stay alive until she'd found out what had happened.

Those moments when the wind tore the mist to woolly shreds, allowing glimpses of Ergo, she could see the lights of the village, where the Ball was in full swing. Or was it? She had radioed back to Mannie, who was doing duty at the station in her absence, reporting that they were safe but marooned by weather. The villagers would all know by now about the disappearance of their mayor. How could he do this, on the day of their celebration of life?

The following day, the weather had abated sufficiently for the three to continue their search. They found nothing: no boat, no body, nothing. When they arrived back on Ergo with the news, there were those who were dazed; there were those who made the sign to ward off evil, silently vowing not to voyage near Impossible again. Minister Kohler was tempted to say something about God's timing at the memorial service held four days later around the absent mayor's gravesite, but found that God had stopped his tongue; instead, to his surprise and embarrassment, he wept.

Chapter Twelve

Cyn Peters encouraged both her sons to stand in the council elections, in their father's shoes as it were. "Keep the weak and deceitful out," she instructed Nelson, her face dark with storms. He knew whom she meant: Dorado, the police officer and his father's erstwhile mistress, had, together with Jerome, made herself available for re-election to the three-seat council.

While clearing his father's personal effects from the mayoral desk, Nelson had sat himself down for a moment in the swivel chair, and found himself at the helm of the island. He felt what it must have been like for his father to sit there, steering this tiny ship through troubled times, making decisions to determine her course; even the small ones of a few degrees setting a completely new direction, which would ultimately take the community far from the original destination. There were times, Nelson reflected, with a sudden fist in his middle, that his father might have consulted him as well as Jerome on important matters; running government was not that different from running a business, and although his butchery was not as high profile as Jerome's factory, it was a going concern.

From his position, he could see through the window all the way down to the harbour, where the morning's harvest of fish was being off-loaded from the boats into bins, ready to be hauled to his brother's factory. He decided right then: he would stand for mayor. There was work to be done and he would do it. The vision he had for the future of the island was in danger, he felt it in his bones. In a few years, his home would become unviable, submerged under the dross and tinsel of the new millennium or drowning under a deluge of mad old ways. If they were to survive, he had to find a middle path, a way that worked for everyone, one that ensured that the best survived and flourished. Ergo Island was in danger of becoming a retirement village as the youth started leaving for the mainland. Even Raef, his own son, would be tempted unless there was a secure and exciting future on Ergo.

And besides, a mayoral job would be a new challenge, it would occupy his mind and make a good man of him.

The doctor's pills had closed the gate firmly on nocturnal apparitions. Nelson was back in the middle of his life, back as the lead voice in the male choir, welcomed back into the centre of his wife's body. But always, always, he carried a phial of tranquillisers on him in case a rush of terror ambushed him. It was a miracle, really, how a pill could restore equilibrium, reason, even sanity when the world suddenly turned unstable and began to jag in angles.

A few weeks later, he was able to marvel still further that a mere tablet, produced by the history and weight and miracle of modern medicine, could be a decisive factor in an election outcome. He, the son of the missing mayor, was now mayor himself, and his brother voted in as a councillor. For most of the villagers, there was something comforting in that; balance was restored and life could continue its lift and slide.

Cyn was not satisfied. She heard the news as she was moving in with Jerome and Rumer – she was too lonely in her cold house up the road. "Bitch," she muttered to Rumer, unable to celebrate her sons' triumphs, for Officer Dorado had maintained her council position. "That bitch just won't let go."

Chapter Thirteen

Winter came around again, flying across the world to fill the spaces autumn had prepared; winter tilted the light to slant from the north and tossed capes of roiling cloud over Ergo and Impossible, dusting snow on their tips. The seas boiled cold; their salt-tipped waves scurried after seamless corridors of roaring air.

It was Gulai's second birthday. She stood inside a circle of well-wishers in front of a cake baked by Katerina Schoones, with two candles standing astride the iced top, and watched amazed as the candle wicks leapt alight when her father held a match flare to them.

Orion Prosper watched, and saw the flames dance in her dark-pool eyes, so like her mother's. This was his child, his alone since Angelique had turned away. He watched her face break open with delight as she looked around at those that sang the birthday song to her: the Peters brothers and their wives and children, Graça Bagonata and her daughter, also Veronica, and Lena, their mouths pouring song onto her.

Gulai raised her tiny hands and poised them to clap and clap again, to demonstrate her perfect pleasure.

He saw, he watched and saw, as though a curtain had flung open, that his daughter was the most precious thing he had. He would guard her from a world that would ensnare and beguile her. He promised himself he would not fail her.

The doctor was not a man prone to sentiment, and he was alarmed by an unexpected pricking of his eyes, a minor tremor of his lip. Abruptly, he fixed his mind on the task at hand, concealing his traitorous face behind his camera.

Part Two

Chapter One

"What?" Mr Bacon leaned over the counter, the overstuffed pillow of his tummy bulging onto the countertop, and glared down at Gulai.

Mr Bacon had a shop filled with all kinds of fabulous things brought by the ships from the mainland. He sold everything from combs to coffins, serving spoons to toothpicks, screws to floor polish. Gulai loved to walk through the rows and rows of tins and boxes and bottles and tubes and toys, and marvel at the abundance that could be found over the sea. Mostly she didn't buy anything. Sometimes she came on an errand, to buy toothpaste or flour, but today she held up her hand and uncurled her fingers so that Mr Bacon could see her treasure: a sinker she'd found on the stony beach near the harbour.

"A toffee, please, Mr Bacon."

He frowned at her, took the sinker, turned it over in his palm. "Where'd you steal this from, eh?"

Her face went hot and red with feelings she did not yet have names for. She turned and ran for the door.

"Hey! Come back! Where you going so fast?"

Something in his voice made her stop. She didn't understand grown-ups, these giants who were so powerful, so
unpredictable, so hard to please.

"Come here, you silly."

Reluctantly she dragged herself back to the counter, her
feet ready to run again.

"Where'd you get this?"

"The sea stole it, Mr Bacon, from a trawler that passed in
the night, and gave it to me so you could have it and I could
get a toffee."

He smiled at her then. He weighed it carefully in his hand,
pretending to weigh the offer in his head. "P'raps it's worth
two," he said, and Gulai laughed and was rewarded with three
whole toffees for her efforts.

The doctor didn't believe in toffees. "They rot your teeth,"
he'd say, "and cause diabetes." He didn't have to know.
Neither did Veronica.

Gulai ran all the way down the track that led to the fields,
heading for the abandoned cottage in the thicket. Children
were told they shouldn't go there, that a witch had lived there
once upon a time, the same witch that now lived on
Impossible Island with her deformed son. Some said her
cottage was haunted by a red-headed ghost that screamed and
cried all night; you could hear her on the wind. Gulai had
listened to these stories with a clutch of her heart, and had
joined in games with the other children – sneaking up to the
cottage as close as they dared, then running away screaming
with horror and delight when they heard a door creak or a
rustle in the undergrowth. But soon she realised that she was
different from the others; that the closer she crept, the more
at home she felt, the more the tight stony place inside her
relaxed. She was drawn, too, by the wooden woman with

wings who stood by the door, the paint peeling off her in strips and bits like a skin disease, the grainy wood of her stained and even rotting in places. Her mouth was covered by something, perhaps a mask, rendering her speechless in Gulai's mind, and in her arms she held something encrusted in barnacles: a tiny baby perhaps? She held the baby close to her exposed breasts, but she looked straight ahead with eyes that seemed to see right to the horizon, right into tomorrow. Gulai pretended to be scared along with the others; she even made up stories about how she had heard a terrible wailing from the chimney, and seen a light in the cottage in the early evening. She realised that keeping the others at bay meant she could come to the cottage on her own and be undisturbed.

One day, venturing alone to the cottage, she was dismayed to find the wooden woman was gone, perhaps flown away. Some windowpanes had been broken, the front door forced, and the interior ransacked. No ghost had done this. She immediately set about putting things as right as she could, sweeping the dust and cobwebs out with a fistful of reeds, smuggling in boxes for a table and chairs, washing what was left of the windowpanes. Slowly she turned the cottage into a place all her own, with a mat on the stone floor and a bed made up in the corner for her doll. She wished she could do more – maybe fitting cardboard into the frames where the panes were broken, to keep the wind outside; but she knew she mustn't be found out.

Sometimes she would lie on the old lumpy mattress in the bedroom, curled up under her coat with her arm as a pillow, listening to the sounds around her. There were songs in the wind about the cottage, a singing that soothed her and made her sing too, softly.

Often enough, Veronica would scold her when she returned home – saying nobody could find her, where had she been, she

knew she was not to wander off. And Gulai would say she'd
been down at the harbour behind the wall. Her father the
doctor, from behind his medical journal, would mumble about
her being a dreamer; some day she would have to grow up and
become responsible.

That day, with three toffees in her pocket to savour long
and alone, Gulai paused on the track to the potato field as she
always did, pretending to tie her shoelace, glancing about to
check that no one would notice where she was going; then she
ran up the path towards the cottage. She stopped, for there
were voices. Slipping behind the bushes, she crept closer.
They belonged to the members of the council: Mayor Nelson
Peters's voice, and councillor Jerome Peters's and Officer
Bardelli's. She realised with a catch in her belly that they were
talking about Sophia:

" . . . time she came back here, that son needs schooling . . ."

" . . . depends, if she'll agree to . . ."

" . . . have to be careful . . ."

" . . . need some fixing up . . ."

Gulai ran away, afraid of being caught, turbulent and
brimful with this new idea: that the witch and her son were
coming back to Ergo Island, to this cottage. It felt strange,
exciting, like the beginning of a new chapter in her life.

Chapter Two

Gulai sat at the breakfast table with a book pinned under each arm, trying to cut her French toast. It was Veronica's way of teaching her not to fly. "A nine-year-old should know how to keep her elbows to herself," she reprimanded. "You take up too much space."

Gulai chewed miserably, looking at the floral design that swept round and round the border of the plate, as it had since before she could remember. Her arms and shoulders ached.

Veronica set a cup of coffee down in front of the doctor. "I don't know what we'll do with her when we get to the mainland."

"Umm," said the doctor, whose elbows weren't anywhere near his sides.

Gulai knew they weren't really going to the mainland; it was just Veronica's dream, which she dragged around with her like a ball and chain. Veronica didn't love the island; she wasn't attached to it by an invisible thread like Gulai and her father were, a thread that went all the way from the centre of their hearts to the graveyard. Gulai knew it was her fault her mother had died. Every day she tried to make it up to her father. If her mother hadn't died, they wouldn't have to put up with Veronica.

"Now look! Tomato sauce down your front!" Veronica grabbed a dishcloth and scraped away at Gulai's jersey.

Gulai looked at the doctor from under her lashes. Now and then a flutter would start up inside her, a worry that Veronica might get her way. He wasn't responding. Gulai hoped that Veronica would give up on both of them and leave all by herself.

"Eat up now, you'll be late again." Veronica cleared the dishes away crossly, a small tornado swirling around the island of the breakfast table. The doctor sipped his coffee as though deeply involved in a sacred ritual. Gulai wondered where he went to inside his greying head. Sometimes it seemed he had already left, gone off without either of them to a place where no one else was welcome, as though his eyes could look in two directions at the same time: out onto their common world and also inside, into a secret place. Gulai wondered whether he was happier there, whether it was a place like the witch's cottage, where he could be alone and undisturbed. She wished she could show him her secret – then maybe he would let her into his. But she knew she couldn't. She knew her father disapproved of the witch.

"Gail," warned the doctor, and by that she knew she had been humming again; though for the life of her she didn't realise when she did it, so how was she to stop?

After breakfast, the doctor drove Gulai to school. There were only four children who were driven to school: the mayor's son Raef, Jerome Peters's children Sasha and Leon, and herself. Everyone else walked in all weathers, unless the storms raged so wildly that even the adults could not get to work. Gulai remained sitting in the car when her father stopped.

"Go along now, my princess," said the doctor. "Be good." He patted her knee, going off again into his head.

Gulai knew that being good meant getting out of the car without a fuss, walking neatly into the school grounds, not minding or telling when Hans Schoones tripped her up on purpose to try and see her panties, agreeing when Mrs Mobara, the teacher, told her she was a stubborn girl, sitting still and coming first in everything. She wanted to be good; she wanted to tell her father she was sorry she had failed him. Instead she said, "My tummy's sore." Sometimes that worked, and her father took her to the hospital with him, and tucked her into one of the big white beds, and told Sister Lena that she had a V.I.P. today – a Very Important Patient. Sister Lena would smile and bring hot chocolate to make her better, and she would read and her father would pop in and tell her she was the most beautiful patient in all the world. Then Veronica would come into the ward and find out and Gulai would have to get up and go to school. Other days, like today, it didn't work, and the doctor said she would be all right, to hurry up now, he was late.

Gulai's tummy was sore right into the second lesson, until she remembered that the witch was coming back. Then she got lost in thoughts about how to say hallo to a witch and how to stop her father from knowing, and before she knew it she was in trouble for not listening.

At break she wondered whether to tell her best friend, Phoebe Bagonata, about the witch – but then she would have to tell her about her cottage, and then Phoebe would want to know why Gulai had never told her about it before, and she might get cross and hurt, and Gulai wasn't sure about telling her that part of the secret anyway. But when the witch came back she would lose the cottage; besides, the secret worried at her tongue.

So after school she took Phoebe down to the church. She passed the grave reserved for the ex-mayor, Clarence Peters, who had mysteriously disappeared, should his remains ever wash ashore. Gulai glanced at the empty grave with the ornate headstone: *No man is an island, for God is with him.* She wondered at this – whether God was like the sea surrounding an island, or like a dolphin swimming alongside you, or more like a boat that connected an island to the mainland. Her mother's grave nearby had a white stone angel planted in it; the angel held a scroll inscribed with the dates of Angelique's birth and death – her death only four days after Gulai's birth.

"Okay, what?" Phoebe was already at her grandmother's grave, her right hand pressed to the tombstone.

"Swear."

"I swear on my grandmother's grave, I won't tell anyone – 'specially not Hans Schoones!"

Gulai laughed. She went close to Phoebe and lowered her voice.

"The witch is coming back. Her son is coming to school."

"Really!?"

There, it was out, her secret golden coin, spent into someone else's ear. The two of them fell on it, this treasure, looking at it from all sides: what would this mean to their island lives? Gulai ended up taking Phoebe to show her the other secret, half of her sad that she was losing her solitude, and half glad to have someone to share this with. Although it was broad daylight, Phoebe gripped Gulai's hand. "You come here all by yourself?"

Gulai nodded. How to explain: the fear was only in the game.

They fell into playing out scenarios: Phoebe as the witch,

Gulai the witch's son, or Hans, being turned by the flash of a finger into a pig – snort, snort! The girls laughed at this with tears in their eyes, although Gulai wanted a turn at being the witch.

"What if she doesn't like us?" worried Gulai. She wanted this witch on her side, this woman people were so afraid of they put her on another island, the woman who could make the mayor disappear.

Phoebe shrugged. "Then she'll turn us into pigs," she said, and snorted her way through to the bedroom, where she sat and bounced on the mattress. "You slept here?!" she asked. Gulai nodded. Phoebe looked at her with narrow eyes. "You know she's a lesbian."

Gulai was ashamed to admit she didn't know what a lesbian was.

"They say she did it with a ghost too."

"What?"

"You know. Sex."

This information embarrassed and confused Gulai further. She knew that sex made babies, and had something to do with the shameful place between her legs, something to do with the noises like the sounds of suffering that came from her father's bedroom at night.

"Maybe she'll want to do it with us too," said Phoebe, flinging herself back on the bed, squealing with horror.

Gulai squealed too, so as not to be left out, but inwardly she was truly horrified. Her beautiful secret was being spoilt by these ideas she didn't understand. A brick solidified in her belly. "Let's go," she said.

As they ran back home, Gulai felt fear creep in, fear that could spoil everything.

Chapter Three

"Tell me a story," pleaded Gulai as the doctor tucked her into bed. Veronica was out playing bridge, a game the doctor considered slow and pointless. Unless there was a call from the hospital, she had her father all to herself for the evening.

"I don't know any stories," the doctor would always reply.

"Yes, you do! Tell me the one about the Viceroy of Uganda!" It was true her father didn't know any traditional stories about fairies or dragons – those she had to read for herself in her own small collection of books, or the few battered ones in the school library – but he would sometimes allow himself to be pressurised into telling her stories out of his head about the mainland, stories so strange they could be out of Grimm's anyway.

"Oh, you'll never believe that," he teased solemnly. "That's a story too good to be true."

"Please, Daddy!" She loved to hear the same stories over and over: the horror and thrill of them, the way they were a thread that bound her father to her, the same story living in both their heads at the same time.

"All right, but you mustn't tell anyone else or they'll think I'm a liar."

The doctor settled himself down next to her on top of the blankets, her room full of his rough male smell, her body squashed against the wall to make room for the bulk of him. She didn't mind: these were the best times, when the doctor lay back and contemplated the rafters, his handsome face inches from her own, allowing her to study at length the mystery of her father. She watched closely to see where a chink might open so she might fall into his grace.

"Well, once upon a time there was a man who was sent out from England to rule Uganda."

"Where's Uganda?" Gulai had a vague idea of the rest of the world from the globe in the classroom. She suspected it was probably not all that accurate; although she'd searched for evidence of her existence, there was no sign of Ergo Island on it. Mrs Mobara made excuses for the company who'd made the globe, saying the island was too small for the printing process to stamp it on, but Gulai wasn't convinced.

"Uganda is in central Africa, you know that." The doctor frowned at her, then resumed. "In those days it was difficult for people to communicate because it was before telephones and radio, before cars and roads and aeroplanes. It took forever to get anywhere. The British government got news that the war in North Africa was spreading south, and they hadn't heard from the Viceroy for ages. They thought he was in trouble. So they hired an explorer and paid for an expedition to go to Uganda to save him. During that terrible journey through the jungle, half the expedition died, killed by marauding tribes and head hunters and mosquitoes."

"Mosquitoes!"

"Well, yes, certain mosquitoes carry parasites called malaria, and if they bite you they can kill you, just like that!" The doctor snapped his fingers like a gun going off. He stared at Gulai for her to be quiet and listen and not pretend she didn't know. "They got to Uganda to find the Viceroy living comfortably with ten local wives and forty-four children."

"Ten wives!" Gulai was sure that at the last telling there had only been eight; even so, she could hardly imagine such a thing. Why would anyone want more than one wife?

"When the expedition told the Viceroy they had come to save him, he refused to leave. So they were forced to kidnap him to complete their mission and take him home."

Gulai had an image of a man in silk garments, sitting on a red sofa surrounded by beautiful women – then being dragged, protesting, away from his life. She wondered what his wives and children had thought of this, whether they had tried to hold on to his ankles. "And then?"

"He died falling from a window trying to escape his rescuers," said the doctor, leaning over to kiss her forehead. "Time for bed."

Gulai couldn't be left alone in the dark with head hunters and mosquitoes and the sad madness of falling men. "Please, Daddy, tell me another one, the one about the girl and the cows!" She hated this story, but her father loved to tell it and she wanted him longer.

The doctor settled back on the pillow. "Once upon a time in Africa, long, long ago, there was a young girl who told her tribe she had a dream from their god. She told them that if they sacrificed all the cattle in the village, the ancestors would drive the white settlers into the sea and their tribe would be prosperous. The girl was so insistent the old people believed she was a prophet. So they killed all the cattle."

"What happened then?" The horror of error and death bumped inside Gulai's chest.

"Well, obviously, the fields were full of rotting carcasses and there was nothing for the tribe to eat and they starved to death." The doctor pushed himself off the bed. "Africa's such a crazy mixed-up place."

Gulai couldn't bear for him to go. "Tell me about the witch, Daddy!" she begged. It was out, the thing that kept ferreting round in her mind.

For the first time, the doctor looked at her, straight at her, as though trying to see into her. "What witch?" he asked, an edge in his voice.

Gulai wished she could suck her words right back into her chest; she hadn't given them permission, they'd just leapt out when she wasn't thinking. Frozen, she stared at her father.

"What witch do you mean?" he asked again, sitting down on her bed, his attention fully on her.

"Hansel and Gretel's witch," she said, forcing her voice.

The doctor looked at her one long moment, then stood up again. "You know I don't know those silly stories," he said, hitching up his trousers.

She knew he knew she'd lied.

"There's no such thing as witches or prophets, only silly muddled girls who believe in things that aren't there." He leaned over and ran his fingers through her hair. "In the old days, the church used to round up women who meddled with herbs and superstition and burn them at the stake because they were afraid of their influence – yet the church was as muddled as they were. Nowadays we know better. We can just ignore all that nonsense."

The doctor switched Gulai's bedside light off. "Good night,

my princess," he said, and closed the door behind him.

Outside, the wind wound its growl around the house. Gulai switched the bedside light back on again. Even with all her blankets covering her, she felt cold. Even though she told herself that none of the stories were true, the room skulked full of burnt shadow.

Chapter Four

Waiting for Sophia and her son was agony. The thought of her coming back threw open a catch releasing flocks of other thoughts. Phoebe and Gulai continued playing out scenarios, trying to imagine the witch's life, trying to tease out her story. Phoebe banished Gulai to a rock near the Point, but she complained about the bird droppings, so they asked Officer Bardelli if they could rather use the jail cell adjacent to her office. It hadn't been used in living memory, except for when there were brawls in the tavern and someone had to cool off, and the time a woman ran mad in the village, taking off her clothes and burning things – imagine that! Gulai and Phoebe argued about who would be the prisoner, for the cell was horrible, with only one high, barred window to frame a shred of sky, and a bed and a chair and a potty under the bed – enough to turn anyone mad. The door had a small sliding hatch to let the jailor check up on prisoners and give them food and water; otherwise you were left alone.

Gulai took first turn as prisoner, and only lasted a few

minutes before bursting into tears and banging on the door, pleading to be let out. Officer Bardelli dried Gulai's eyes and gave them both a cup of tea. Sitting there in her big important office, she told them about the old days.

"I was best friends with your mother when we were girls," she told Gulai, "just like you and Phoebe."

"What was she like?" asked Phoebe.

Officer Bardelli sat back, remembering, looking through the film clips stored in her head. Images that Gulai could never have: pictures of Angelique alive and well and laughing. "She was like a bird," said Officer Bardelli. "I bet she's flying free right now, looking down on all of us."

Gulai had always imagined her mother trapped in the cold dark earth. But she wasn't sure this version was reliable, even though it came from a police officer.

"And the witch?" Phoebe glanced wickedly at Gulai. The "W" word was out. "What's she like?"

Officer Bardelli raised an eyebrow. "You mean Aunt Sophia? Call her by her proper name, she's not a witch."

Gulai wasn't sure she could trust this information either. "Then why was she sent to Impossible?" She knew the story – that Sophia had tried to teach a young girl to fly, and she had fallen on her head and died – but she wanted to hear it from her mother's friend.

Officer Bardelli tapped the desk with her pen. "You children are too full of questions. I have work to do."

"They say she's coming back."

"Maybe," said Officer Bardelli, getting all quiet and looking at other pictures in her head. "Maybe."

Sophia did not return that summer, nor the next, nor the next. Rumour had it she refused to come back, despite the fact that her son was long of school-going age. Gulai would go and stand on the harbour wall on a clear day, with the gulls careening and keening through the salt air around her, and look out across the channel towards Impossible Island, rising out of the ocean like a sail set for far away. She wanted to know more about Sophia: why she had left, why she refused to return, whether being ignored was better than burning. Did the witch need saving? Did she want to be saved? Gulai had looked up "lesbian" in her father's dictionary; it turned out to be a woman who was sexually attracted to other women. Gulai didn't understand. She knew it took a man and a woman to make a baby; the witch had a son, how could she be a lesbian?

A white albatross swooped close by, its long black-tipped wings arcing smoothly and effortlessly through the grey light. A glance from its black eye skimmed over Gulai before the bird tipped and slid above the crumpled sea, heading for Impossible. Could that be her mother? Did Angelique know the witch?

"You sing beautifully, like your mother." Gulai swung round, embarrassed to see her cousin Liesa, standing at the steps. She hadn't realised she'd been singing as she stood there. "Hallo, Gulai," Liesa said. There were only a few on the island who called her Gulai; the doctor had forbidden it.

"Hallo, Liesa." She didn't know Liesa well, nor the rest of her family. Her father had never forgiven Aunt Frieda for not caring for her properly after her mother's death. He had banned the family from the house, and confiscated any presents that arrived for Gulai on her birthday.

"My mother wants to see you."

How did Liesa know? Aunt Frieda couldn't speak much, silenced by a stroke that had stiffened her leg and hooked her arm up to her chest like a chicken wing. Still, Gulai knew, there were ways other than words to let people know what you were thinking.

Gulai shook her head. "I can't."

"It's important. She has something for you from Aunt Sophia."

This put a new angle on things. Gulai felt the tug of a double intrigue, but she was afraid. She looked away, out over the sea.

"My mother loved you as her own. And Sophia grew you up on her own milk."

Gulai was shocked. Her father had warned her that her mother's family was not to be trusted, and here they were: monstrous lies. But Liesa's face was not closed, like the fist of a lie, meant to hurt; instead her manner held something like a gift out to Gulai.

She turned apprehensively, and followed Liesa to her cottage near the church, worried that word would get to her father if a child came skipping past and saw. Aunt Frieda was sitting in the garden in a patch of sunlight, the wind playing with a strand of her hair. Gulai, now twelve, stood awkwardly and wondered what it was like not to be able to talk and walk properly.

"Over," said Frieda, looking at Gulai with tears in her eyes. "Over." It was one of the few words left intact after the stroke had burnt the library of her brain and the proper connections to one side of her body.

"My mother says she loves you," offered Liesa.

Aunt Frieda nodded emphatically, holding her good hand out to Gulai. Gulai didn't want to take it, but she didn't want to hurt this old woman either; she was, after all, her mother's sister. Aunt Frieda's bony hand gripped Gulai's with urgency.

"Over!" she said, appealing to Gulai. Confused, uncomfortable, Gulai looked at Liesa.

"She wants to give you something," said Liesa.

With her good hand, Aunt Frieda pulled an old creased

envelope from her pocket and handed it to Gulai. "Fine," she said, with something like relief.

"Open it," translated Liesa.

It was slightly bulky, containing something other than paper. Gulai tore the envelope open and pulled out a short length of twisted and severed homespun blue yarn, with a knot where it had been tied into a loop. Gulai knew what she was looking at. Some of the village children wore them round their bellies, but it was uncommon, considered old-fashioned and superstitious.

"Over," explained Frieda, pointing to Gulai.

"She says it's yours," said Liesa. Then, remembering: "It was yours as a baby. Sophia gave it to you to keep you safe." She lifted her jersey to show she wore one too.

"Why . . . ?" Why are you giving this to me now, who cut it off me, why, why have you got it, Aunty, why is it blue, why . . . ? Gulai wanted to ask these and many things, but instead she ran away down the road, clutching the yarn, her heart hammering in her chest, the thought pounding in her brain: the yarn that was supposed to keep her safe had been severed. She ran back to the harbour wall and hid behind the rocks. Across the channel, Impossible Island was still sailing away, swirled in the mist of the coming rain. Gulai searched the sky, but the birds had gone; the air was strangely, suddenly, devoid of life.

Her safety ruptured, her life divided. She took the yarn out, wrapped it tightly around her hand, felt the ache start up in her belly.

It's only a piece of wool, for God's sake. Her father's voice. In the old days people were burnt for the stupid way you're thinking.

Something was wrong, but she didn't know what it was. A sob rose from within her, a huge bubble of grief rising, breaking the surface of her with a sound like lament for the life she might have had with other mothers. A song without words broke open in her, a song she sang towards Impossible, now being erased by encroaching cloud.

The mist rushed towards her on the back of the gusting wind, swallowing up first Impossible Island, then the sea; the world was vanishing in front of her. As the grey hit the stony beach, Gulai felt rain sting her face like ants biting. Water trickled down her face and into her collar. She would get into trouble for getting wet, but she didn't care. She could hardly see more than the few rocks around her; she was a boat alone and lost in grey, attached to one end of a rope that had been cut from certain moorings. She thought of her mother alone in her grave, rain trickling down through the earth, falling like tears on her cold face.

The next morning, Aunt Frieda was found dead in her bed.

Chapter Five

There was no way round it, the doctor realised, looking at the X-ray. Frank Bardelli required a general. Despite Frank's attempts to dislodge the fishbone, eating half a loaf of bread and then making himself vomit by sticking his finger as far as he could down his throat, it would not budge. On the X-ray, Orion could see the shadow of it wedged in the oesophagus, a crescent like the thin clipping of a giant toenail, but he could not see it using an ordinary torch. So Frank sat unhappy and drooling for the six hours required for his stomach to empty before he could be wheeled into theatre.

It was one of the great advances of science, thought the doctor, as he closed the gas mask over Frank's mouth and nose. In his hands lay the power to induce a near-death state in another human being, in order to perform a procedure that outsmarted death. Before the days of anaesthetics, that deeply embedded fishbone could have killed Frank, causing sepsis and gangrene, a horrible end.

After a few breaths of gas, Frank's body relaxed on the table.

Orion touched his eyelids, checking for reflex movement, ensuring he was deeply under before introducing the laryngoscope. Levering Frank's tongue and jaw forward with the instrument while tilting his head backwards with his other hand, he brought the larynx into view. Orion loved the symmetry of the body, the secret of it. Here, revealed to his eye, was the delicate portal to the lungs, held open by a substance as simple and complex as cartilage, and draped with the membranes of the vocal cords. It was inspiring, really, how the tissues of the body had evolved, how random change could hit upon the perfect combination to precipitate development.

Behind the larynx lay the oesophagus. Orion gently opened the slack tube with the forceps, and the offending fishbone came into view. He removed it with satisfaction and placed it in a sample jar. Frank would want to take it to the tavern to show to the boys, show it off, laugh about it: this fish that nearly got its revenge.

He repositioned the mask and turned up the oxygen to flush the artificial sleep from Frank's brain. In a moment, his patient would be awake, a good future ahead of him. There were no scopes at the hospital, a problem should a fishbone be lodged further down. Still, he would have made a plan; that was what was required of him, so far from any assistance. There was something both terrifying and gratifying in that. The villagers both loved and respected him, feeding his ear with their concerns and their praise, and his hand with gifts of gratitude for pain relieved and death thwarted. They had forgiven him that terrible day, so why should he not forgive himself?

Later, in the tearoom, he caught himself pressing his hand down on the table, trying to stretch his palm and fingers completely flat. It irritated him, his own superstition –

pretending that he himself was not headed for the operating table. Not that this was a life-and-death issue, and his scarring was not yet pronounced, but Dupytron's contracture unattended could cripple you. He brought his hands together, turning them palm up like an open book, as though trying to read what lay imprinted there. In the folds and ructions of his skin he saw tectonic plates colliding, a welling up and sliding under, a subterranean story pulling his hands closed. These hands were the tools of his life, tools he used to diagnose and treat, to eat and wash, to wipe his arsehole and to make love; hands he used to help the living and to close the eyelids of the dead.

It was a secret, and must remain so. The islanders must not know of his weakness, his deformity. He would stop the booze. That would help. Perhaps by stopping drinking he could even reverse the contracture. Terrible stuff, alcohol; it fooled you into thinking that all was well.

He made his way to the clinic. Dorado Bardelli was the first patient, sitting with her back straight, her liberal bottom perched on a chair. A reasonably good-looking woman, going prematurely grey. Not taken another lover since Clarence went playing high jinks on the open seas, as far as he knew, and he knew pretty much everything. He wondered why; what a woman her age did about sex.

Orion closed the consulting-room door and sat down at his desk. "What can I do for you, Officer?" He saw the flinch and smiled inwardly. So easy to get a rise out of this kind of woman. Just a slight inflection on the title "Officer" was enough.

Dorado folded her arms over her chest. "I . . . have a lump."

She was behaving as though he'd never seen breasts before. He was used to it. Incredible how shy people were about their bodies. He talked her down, told her to strip to the waist, did a thorough examination, and sent her on her way with the reassurance it was only glandular.

Next was Rayla Schoones, who had arrived back unexpectedly on the May ship – and into the arms of Harry Pelani. She sat down, her mouth fluttering with anxious half-smiles. Rayla was the first baby he'd delivered when he came to the island, a difficult birth, one which had nearly gone wrong because of that woman who pretended she was capable of medical practice with no formal training. It was thanks to him Rayla was alive and well, although she might have come out brighter if the labour hadn't taken so long.

He knew why she was there. "What is it, Rayla?" he asked, sitting down heavily at his desk.

Going a deep puce, she explained that she wanted contraception because she and Harry Pelani were to be married. Orion stopped himself from giving her a lecture on wasting her life; it was pointless, these people had no ambition. He asked the relevant medical questions and took her blood pressure. It was shocking to him: really, she was still a child, sixteen years old; but child marriages were not uncommon in this backwater. Rayla and Harry's parents could have refused permission, but the truth was they were happy at the prospect. Seventeen-year-old Harry had not gone to high school on the mainland, but had stayed to fish like his father, and was well on his way to the means to his own boat; with Rayla home without finishing her schooling, she too would not disappear into the world. Marriage was the net that saved the youth from troubles relating to sex, the mainland and being on your own; it gathered them back into the arms of the community and safeguarded the future. And approved marriages made bloodlines more secure.

What everyone wanted to know was whether Rayla was pregnant already or not. She'd been going with Harry for some time and, as Jojo pointed out at the tavern, her shape might disguise more than just her bones. The doctor was aware of this; also that her coming to him for contraception might well be an excuse to find out whether she was expecting, without the embarrassment of having to ask directly. To his practised eye, she could well be: there was a certain flush in her face, but that could be due to anxiety or happiness at the coming wedding. At least she had the sense to come at all. Everyone knew the story about Graça Bagonata, also a big woman, who had arrived at the hospital with what she thought were intestinal cramps heralding the onset of gastroenteritis – and within an hour had produced a baby. He didn't want complications, not any more than could be expected. But Rayla's urine tested negative, and she said she was sure of her period dates, so he issued her with a card and told her how to start taking the pill.

Gulai sat on the side of the bath, running her hands through the gush of warm water. She'd seen her blood that morning and knew: this was the end. Blood meant death. Now she'd have to wear these thick bandages between her legs as though she were wounded, and keep this terrible secret.

The water streamed comfortingly over her fingers; water that had travelled far to come to her bath, across oceans, high in dark clouds. Perhaps this same water had been in someone else's bath once, someone from the mainland – an important person staying in a hotel, maybe a famous singer preparing for a concert.

"That's enough!" shouted Veronica. It wasn't as though the island was short of water, but Veronica came from the mainland, she still had mainland ways. Gulai turned the taps off, got undressed and looked at herself in the mirror. Her image was clouded over, blurred to nothing, so she wiped the mirror and stared. Her nipples pouted from her chest, and a knot of hair announced her vagina, her vagina out of which blood came. Why would God organise it this way? Why the waste, why the hard-earned blood lost? A red spot fell to the floor; Gulai wiped it away, then perched on the side of the bath opposite the mirror and opened her legs to have a better look.

The sound of the doctor's voice entered the house, reminding Gulai that the bathroom door was unlocked. She stood to lock it and in that moment it opened, and there was her father: large, masculine, his dark eyes thatched over with frowning brows – eyes that had unexpectedly lifted their shutters and stared out at her, fixed on her vulnerability and filled with . . . what? Gulai shrank from that gaze. His look was terrible. Before Gulai could say or do anything, he was gone, closing the door behind him. Quickly she locked it, her heart racing.

Gulai slid into the bath, shaking and ashamed. Her father disapproved of her; her father, who had probably seen everyone on the island naked at some point, didn't like what he saw. She wished she were little again, sitting on his knee in her pyjamas, safe and warm.

The doctor didn't come home that night in time for supper. Veronica and Gulai sat and ate fishcakes and turnips in silence, the food falling like lumps into Gulai's belly. She went to bed early, waking when her bedroom door opened. It was dark, but she could just make her father out. She felt the weight of him settle on the foot of her bed, and smelt his sour smell: whisky and smoke. She sat up, glad of the darkness after their bathroom encounter.

· "Where were you?"

"Pelani's bachelor."

It was always like this: the men getting wrecked the night before a wedding, the groom looking ill during the ceremony as he wound his strand into the marriage plait. That was the one ancient ritual Minister Kohler permitted that wasn't out of his marriage book: one strand for the man, one for the woman and one for God.

"There's food for you," she offered, knowing that food was ballast for a drunk man.

He didn't respond, just sat, his face hidden from her. She wanted to throw her arms around him, reassure him that she hadn't really changed.

"You know, Gail . . ." He ran his fingers through his hair, elbows on his knees.

"What?"

He sat a long time without saying anything, until Gail thought he had fallen asleep sitting upright, his head in his hands. At last he looked at her out of dark sockets, this man she had known all her life, this stranger. "There are things you only find out too late."

What was he saying? Gulai tried to prevent his words slipping through the crevices of her brain.

"There are things you need to know, Gail, but nobody will be able to tell you, you're too damn young."

"I'm not that young!"

"I didn't want a girl, you know." He sighed, as though the effort of talking was costing him everything. "Girls are too much trouble."

His words hit Gulai like cold water; she felt herself go cold.

"Just don't you be stupid," he said, standing, nearly falling. He corrected himself and leaned unsteadily over her to tousle her hair. His fingers smelt thick with smoke. "Just don't you be bloody stupid. Like your damn mother."

He lurched out of the room without closing the door. When the argument started up in his bedroom, Gulai closed it herself. She lay awake for hours, the stupid wedge of cotton between her legs making her a stupid, stupid girl.

Chapter Six

Next day, the bleeding hadn't stopped. Gulai went round to Phoebe's, but she wasn't there. On her way to the shop to look for her, she saw Officer Bardelli and her new sidekick, Calvin Tamara's son Yero, coming out of the police station carrying boxes and bags to the police van, and went over to help. She would find a moment to ask her mother's old friend whether there was something wrong with her period. Gulai got into the van with them and drove down to the harbour to help load the parcels onto the police launch.

"Where are you going?" Gulai asked.

Officer Bardelli nodded in the direction of Impossible Island. "Taking Aunt Sophia some supplies," she said.

Gulai stared at Impossible, dark against a background of black cloud. "What supplies?" she asked. What would a witch and her son need?

"She grows her own vegetables, and of course there are plenty of eggs and fish. We take her other provisions, like flour and meat and toiletries. And schoolwork for Callum."

Her son. "What class is he in?"

"Same as you. He's the same age as you, maybe a little younger." Dorado thought, casting the net of her memory back. "Yes," she said slowly. "A bit younger."

"They say he's stupid."

"Mrs Mobara puts him up every year. Can't be that dumb."

Mrs Mobara had been sending the witch's son work all this time!

"Can I come?" she found herself asking.

Officer Bardelli shrugged. "Ask the doctor."

Gulai ran to the hospital to find her father. He was in the procedure room, trying to extract a tooth from John Peters's head. "Come, you bastard," he said, wiggling and yanking, with Sister Lena restraining John's head against the pillow. The effort involved looked enormous. A dentist only visited the island once a year, arriving on the ship with his tools and amalgams, his plates and braces. The remainder of the year, the doctor made do with oil of clove, antibiotics and extractions.

"Officer Bardelli says I can go with her on the police launch! Can I? Please!"

The doctor stopped, pliers in hand. He and John and Sister Lena turned and looked at Gulai. "Where is she going?" he asked.

"To the witch," slurred John helpfully through his bloody, numb lips. And that was the end of that.

As Gulai watched Officer Bardelli and Yero Tamara ride off in the launch, she realised she had forgotten to ask about her period.

She wandered home, adrift, insecure, aimless. Bored. Angry. Sitting on her bed, she remembered the piece of blue yarn Aunt Frieda had given her. It was still at the back of her bedside drawer, where she had hidden it. To think she had worn it as a baby, that the witch had given it to her, had actually touched this insignificant-looking thread.

Gulai went over to the co-op. Blue wool was what she wanted, blue as a dark sea, and she was prepared to spend her precious pocket money on it. She found Liesa; when her cousin heard what it was for, she didn't charge for it. Gulai ran back home wondering about secrets, the shame of her bleeding womb, the mystery of a piece of yarn. Carefully she cut a length and doubled it. She twirled and knotted it in the style of the short older piece, then tied the two together. Now it was long enough. She fastened it around her waist, loose enough so as not to feel it most of the time, but tight enough that if she pushed out her belly even a little, she would feel the bite of it, the reassurance of the noose that held her.

It was only a piece of wool, but it made her feel better. A lot better, for some strange reason.

She went outside to look for Phoebe.

Chapter Seven

The year Gulai turned thirteen, the year she got her thread back, was also the year she finished junior school. The February ship the following year would take her and her classmates – Phoebe, Levona, Theo and Darius – across the ocean to another life, pulling them out of the embrace of the island, discharging them into the world.

That December, Gulai was the first to see the ship making its way towards the island. She felt glad she wasn't like Levona Mobara, who wore thick glasses but couldn't see much anyway. "Where?" asked Levona, screwing up her eyes and peering out to the northeast. "Oh, there!" Gulai knew she was only pretending. As the ship rounded the promontory, she and the other children ran down the path to the harbour, Levona stumbling behind.

They tried to make out the figures on the deck as the ship slowed amidst a churn of bow thrusters and dropped anchor. Before Frank's barge was even halfway to the ship, someone on the lower deck gave a male yell and launched himself straggle-legged into the air, falling through the long plunge to the sea.

"It's Raef Peters!" exclaimed Phoebe, clutching Gulai's arm.

"Never," said Gulai. Raef of a year ago was short and quiet. There was no way he was the tall figure who'd yelled and leapt off the high side of a ship into cold water.

The figure was striking out for the harbour through the chop, his brown head sleek as a seal's. As he passed the barge, he raised a hand to greet Frank Bardelli, but refused a ride. True enough, it was Raef, rising dripping and shivering up the slipway, his smile bracketed by long dimples. The islanders crowded round him in welcome, his mother, Condolessa Peters, shrieking that he would catch his death, then shrieking even louder when he drenched her with a hug. Mayor Nelson Peters shook his son's hand and slapped him heartily on the back.

Gulai watched this creature emerge, magically transformed, as though the sea or the ship or the mainland had changed him. She studied Raef's face through the gaps in the crowd. People were jostling now as the barge came ashore with the other returning sons and daughters: Hans Schoones, Tomas Mobara, Di Peters, Leila Kohler, Gilbert Tamara, Al Bardelli and Sasha Peters. But it was Raef, Raef and his astonishing new face – leaner, more confident, turning to greet his other relatives and friends – that drew Gulai. She would meet him at the Ball, she decided. With her mask on, he would notice her.

For years, she had been collecting peacock tail feathers from the birds that paraded around Mr Bacon's shop, tyrannising the island dogs and cats if they came too close. Her blue mask covered her face except for her mouth; over her nose was a yellow beak and at the back of her head, where the mask fastened, she had glued and stapled the feathers into a delicate halo of luminous eyes. The night of the Ball, she pulled on blue jeans and a jersey, then carefully donned the mask and surveyed the effect in the mirror.

"Hallo, Raef," said the mouth under the beak, her lips black and strange with the lipstick she'd bought that day from Mr Bacon's newly imported summer range.

Raef was not going to be interested in a thirteen-year-old, she knew. Two years was nothing between older people like her father and Veronica. But two years at her age was like the distance between Ergo and Impossible.

The front door opened: her father and Veronica were back from the hospital.

Veronica's voice was taut, a wire at breaking point. "We could start over, forget all this . . ."

They were fighting more and more, Veronica getting thinner, with red eyes in the mornings.

"There's nothing to forget." Her father. "Drop it!"

"I didn't want this!" sobbed Veronica.

Good, thought Gulai. She hated Veronica. She wished she would die.

"It's always about what you want!" There was an angry, unstable edge to the doctor's voice which frightened even Gulai.

He needs a whisky, she thought, going through to get him one. Veronica and the doctor swivelled and stared.

"What the hell is that stuff on your face!" glowered the doctor. At first Gulai thought he was referring to her beautiful mask. "You look like you've got leprosy of the lips! Take it off right now, young lady, before I scrub it off myself!"

Veronica behind him, smiling tightly. Behind the two of them, mounted on the wall, the sculpture she had loved since she could remember: the sculpture Elijah once told her he had made for his cousin Sophia, that had hung over the front door of her cottage. A piece of knotted driftwood, with hands carved into each end: one open like yes, the other fisted into no. She realised for the first time that her father must have stolen it.

Gulai felt her body clench. Then, before she had time to think, a word welled and spilled from her peacock lips. "No!" she said, shaking her plumage, her feet rooted to the ground.

Veronica was upon her in an instant, her hand coming down on Gulai's arm, slapping a red mark into it. "Don't you ever, *ever* say 'No' to your father!" she breathed at her. "You will not go anywhere tonight unless you do what he says!"

Gulai turned and went to the bathroom, shame and rage blurring into a long smear of pain. She laid the mask aside and watched tears trickle down her cheeks in the mirror, past her quivering black lips. Yes. No. Yes. No. It was only lipstick, she reasoned with herself. It was nothing, really. She broke off a piece of cotton wool, wet it, and watched as she erased her beautiful mouth.

"Imagine what would happen to her on the mainland," she overheard her father as he poured himself a drink. "Even here she manages to get hold of that kind of rubbish."

That night, wandering through the crowd of clowns and ghosts, warriors and witches, animals and royalty, monsters and zombies, she saw someone she thought was Raef in a beaten tin mask, standing and laughing in a group. Hans Schoones was among them, instantly recognisable despite a large stamped envelope addressed to Hell over his head, eyes and mouth cut out and the words "Letter Bomb" on the back. A little later, she caught the tin man alone at the bar, opening a beer.

It was now or never.

"Remember me?" she said.

He peered at her through the punctured eyeholes, sipping his beer through a straw that disappeared into the small hole of his mouth. "The most beautiful bird in the world?" he offered.

She laughed, for inside the mask she could be anything, anybody; perhaps tonight she could fly. "Peacocks are supposed to be vain," she replied. "Who are you? The most beautiful tin in the world?"

He considered this. "I'm a cross between the Tin Man and a beer can. Hell, beer wasn't supposed to be drunk through a straw. I'm getting froth up my nose."

"What was the Tin Man looking for? In the Wizard of Oz?" Gulai wondered, to keep a connection going.

"All I want is a tin opener to make my mouth bigger."

"I've got one," she offered.

Next thing, they were up the road and outside her house. She was going through her front door with Raef Peters.

"You're Gail," he mused, noting the house. "What do you know, the doctor's daughter. Just the person to help me with a bit of surgery."

He hadn't recognised her before; she too had changed. Gulai handed a tin opener to him, aware of their hands brushing. He took his mask off, then pointed the opener at his face. "I've shown you mine, now show me yours."

A rush went through Gulai. She wanted to open herself to him, but she was afraid of what he would see. "That's breaking the rules," she objected.

"What rules?"

She tried to laugh it off, but her voice was strained.

"I thought you were different," he said, and bent over his task, widening the mask mouth into a jagged leer.

Gulai pulled hers off and stood before him, naked-faced,

exposed. She wished for black lipstick.

He stopped and stared. "You know what, you're okay," he said, and kissed her, a brief open-mouthed kiss.

It was the kiss of the very life she craved. She was safe in his embrace, held by the yarn and his arms about her shoulders.

Raef pulled back and laughed into her eyes; then he took his beer from the sink, donned the mask and tested the new aperture. "Perfect!" he exclaimed.

Back at the party, they ate and danced. Gulai had some swigs of Raef's beer and felt herself flying. Phoebe came up to her in a papier-mâché mask that looked like the globe, with Africa coming down over her nose, and threw her arms around her and told her she was beautiful, and Gulai didn't even mind when Hans Schoones kept making fart noises under his arm as he usually did just to annoy her, and that Raef was leaning just a little too heavily on her, and that he also danced with Sasha and Kate; she was happy and the night was beautiful, and in the new year she was going with Raef to the mainland.

Suddenly Raef was gone, without saying good night.

What had she done?

"He drank too much," said Phoebe. "His dad took him home."

Gulai walked away from the music and singing and dancing, down the track to the Point, to where the lighthouse stood tall above her, lit with a hurricane lamp to guide the sailors out at sea. She wanted to be alone with the taste of Raef in her mouth, to listen to the wash of the waves. Across the channel, Impossible Island was visible tonight in the clear moonlight. Gulai saw, or thought she saw, a flicker of light puncturing the dark island mound, like a star fallen into a swamp and in danger of being extinguished. She was seized with fear, and turned and ran, ran, skirting the village, ran along the moonlit track that led to the fields, turning at the juncture where the path led off to the witch's cottage. She hadn't been there for ages.

Gulai was perturbed to hear muffled sounds from the bedroom of this house, *her* house. Who had invaded? She listened at the window, heard the creak of the bed. There were people in there, a man and a woman, the man grunting and moaning in the way she'd heard in the night at home. Did all men sound like her father? Gulai felt sick. She ran back to the Ball to see if she could find him, to prove herself wrong, but he wasn't there.

At home she found Veronica, enraged and waiting. As Gulai came through the door, she swung on her. "Where the hell have you been!" Her fury spat livid, but through the anger, Gulai saw the rent of pain in her eyes, and she understood: it was not Gulai Veronica was angry with, it was the doctor.

He mustn't be found out.

"I was at the party. With my father."

"You're a bloody liar! That's all I get from you, lies!"

Gulai went into her room, slammed and locked the door. She was shaking and close to tears, but it was better that way. Let Veronica hate her, she could take it. She slid her hand under her jersey and felt her safety net. With this thread, she could take on anything.

Anything except not seeing Raef again.

Chapter Eight

A couple of days later, Phoebe arrived with the news that Raef and Gilbert and the others were renovating the old shack at Deception Bay, and they were invited if they brought something to contribute. Gulai took an old stool she thought her father would not miss, and Phoebe took half a tin of paint. The two girls set off. The path to the cliff above the bay wound slowly up through screed and brush. Phoebe was complaining about her old shoes pinching her, but she didn't want to buy a new pair from Mr Bacon when the variety of the mainland was only weeks away.

"I'm so sick of this place!" she said. "I can't wait to get out of this hole."

Gulai didn't have a dream of the mainland like Phoebe did, a dream of adventure and novelty, of freedom and choice. To Gulai, the island was not a hole but a touchstone, well worn, well known. She was afraid to leave, afraid of the storms that lay beyond the horizon, which looked like the edge of the world.

They had reached a vantage point above the cliff. On a clear day, you could see the fishing boats dotted about in the glinting sea like floating islands, and beyond them the sudden mound of Impossible, rising like a beacon out of the ocean. Below them, at a dizzying depth, was Ike's Gully. The surf there was a growling mouth of white teeth, eating at the very foundation they stood on, trying incessantly to topple their island back into the ocean.

Gulai couldn't look down: it felt too much like falling, like the story of Sarah Tamara's daughter who, they said, took her own life here. Looking down was like looking into the mouth of the beast, the beast that could never be satisfied, that could suck everything and everyone in. Not here, not this, not her.

"Come on!" Phoebe's voice from up the path, waking her from the trance of falling, pulling her back up the mountain to safety. The path now dipped down to Deception Bay, an inlet that looked like a natural harbour from the sea, but was in fact riddled with sharp submerged reefs that could tear a boat apart. The torpid shadows of two ships that had been opened in this manner lay on the bottom of the bay. On the rim of stony beach, she could make out a cluster of figures busy at some task, displacing the usual straggle of penguins.

Again a tug pulled at her, a tug towards Raef . . . all the parts of her captured together like shoals of fish in a fishermen's net, hauled together – towards what? A certain death? She felt like dying in Raef's arms, dying to be born again a different person. A person perfect for Raef, so he would love her, always want her; so they could get married and live happily ever after.

As the two girls descended through a small thicket of tree ferns, they disturbed two wild cows that bolted off to some scanty shade further up the slope. Gulai began to regret coming. With the sun riding high, there was nothing to hide behind. She would be seen for who she was. She was sweating, the loop around her waist chafing; she was putting on weight, she was fat and lazy and stupid and superstitious. These kids she had grown up with were changing, they all were – except she was going the wrong way. Which way was the right way? You could die trying, you could fall or get wrecked on rocks.

Raef wasn't there. He had gone back to the harbour in his uncle's rubber duck to fetch more supplies. Gilbert showed them the repairs they were making to the dilapidated structure.

"Who used to live here?" she asked.

Gilbert shrugged. "My dad said his father stayed here with a group of guys when they were our age," he said vaguely. "It hasn't been used much since then."

The shelter was rickety and leaky; building materials needed for repairs were scarce on the island. Gulai recognised a piece of fence scrounged from outside the boatshed sticking out from underneath the tarpaulin.

The rubber duck was coming round the headland. There was a second person in it, someone with long brown hair. Sasha Peters, Sasha who had just finished school and now worked at reception at the fish factory. A family business: she was Raef's cousin.

Gulai didn't like the way she called him Raffie, nor the way she hooked her arm through his – playfully, but with a certain . . . what? Flirtatiousness? But even Phoebe teased Raef; it was the way things were when you grew up close to people.

They went down to the rock pool and the boys jumped into the water in their shorts, their bodies leaner and more muscular than Gulai remembered from the previous summer, with scrapes of hair on their chests. "Come on in," shouted Raef, and Sasha stripped down to her panties and shirt and scrambled down into the water with a shriek of shock at the cold.

Phoebe was already wriggling out of her jeans. They had swum many times before with these boys; but their bodies were changing. Gulai was overcome with shyness. Her backside was too big, her breasts too small, and there was that stupid yarn tied around her waist; she would be found out, laughed at. Phoebe was in, enjoying herself, and Gulai was left on the rock, high and dry in self-exile. She wandered off, trying to escape humiliation, following the shoreline to where the rubber duck was pulled up out of the water. A cluster of penguins inspected her with curiosity. Gulai gestured angrily at them, sending them waddling in consternation into the sea. She wanted to take the bread knife she'd noticed sticking out of the picnic basket and plunge it into the boat. Stupid. What a stupid thing to think. A boat was the only way off this island, unless you were a penguin.

Raef had access to a boat.

Across the channel loomed Impossible Island, a fortress rising from the sea.

Gulai slid her hands beneath her shirt, took the yarn in her fists and pulled on it until it bit hard and sharp into her fingers, until it broke. Then she wound the length of blue into a coil and put it into a jeans pocket, and pulled off her shoes and jeans.

She would show Raef, she would show everyone that she was capable of breaking things. She could be anything he wanted her to be. She turned, sucking her stomach in slightly, and walked tall and determined back to the pool.

Chapter Nine

The ship that arrived early that February was a cruise ship, stopping off for two days at Ergo Island on its way from a port in the far north to one in the northeast. It brought tourists and supplies, taking away goods for the international market and the scholars bound for boarding school. The tourists, with their mainland accents and their fancy cameras, disembarked through Officer Bardelli's customs, then picked their way through the village on a guided tour led by Martha Schoones. They stopped off at the shop to buy cool drinks and postcards and T-shirts with "Ergo Island – been there, got the T-shirt" emblazoned on the front, or at the tavern to lunch on crayfish thermidor; they were impressed by the relatively modern conveniences at the hospital, and by the quaint notion of no television. And all the while, they looked at the villagers as though they were creatures in an exotic zoo. They photographed everything: from the seals at the harbour, the penguins at the Point and the boats coming in with the day's catch, to old Katerina Schoones sitting on her front veranda with two teeth and a leg missing, the dogs that all looked the same, the potato fields and the ghost house. Those who had the strength in their legs photographed the view of the village from the lookout, and took the path past Haven Cave to get shots of Needle Falls cascading off the edge of the cliffs straight into the sea. They bought pieces of carved driftwood from Elijah Mobara, home-brew from Samuel Pelani at the tavern, homespun, hand-knitted woollen socks and jerseys from Layla Bardelli at the co-op, painted penguin eggs from Liesa Tamara and models of the fishermen's boats from Harry Pelani. Frank Bardelli would chat up young single women, offering them a ride around the island in his barge at a special price, and Danny Schoones would try to chat up any woman at all in the tavern with his stories of volcanoes erupting and fish that got away – even though he was already married to Jolene, who had fallen for his bait several years previously and hadn't embarked on the ship when it sailed.

It was time for Raef and Phoebe and Tomas and Gilbert and Al and Hans and Di and Leila and Levona and Theo and Darius and Gulai to leave. Gulai walked to the lookout, surveying this place that was imprinted in her. Down in the village she could see a group of boys walking, Raef amongst them. On the ship, perhaps he would put his arms around her and reassure her that her father would still be alive when she returned, that the ship would stay afloat, and that she wouldn't get lost on the mainland.

When she got home, the doctor was sitting in his favourite chair, drink in hand. It was too early; he should still be at work.

"Sit down," he said. Gulai sat, afraid of the look on her father's face: angry and defeated and shaky. He looked across the room at the framed photo of her mother on the sideboard, a photo that fixed for Gulai who her mother was: a young bride, half turned away; a bride whose eyebrows arched over her dark eyes like a bird's wings sailing on the air, whose hair was pulled back from her sensitive face into a knot with a curled strand trailing, whose slender neck slanted down in slopes and valleys to her bared shoulders, whose shoulders sloped and disappeared into a blur of ruffled white. "You're looking more and more like your mother," observed the doctor, extinguishing his cigarette. "She was very beautiful."

Gulai came upon a sudden foothold of pleasure in her sea of anxiety. Her father had loved her mother; he was telling Gulai he loved her too. Yet something was coming: she felt it the way fishermen can feel storms before clouds smudge the horizon.

The doctor leaned forward, his tone shifting gear, becoming brisk, directed. "Veronica is going back," he said. "She has to . . . go to her mother."

Gulai knew Veronica's mother was dead. It didn't matter, because the thing Gulai had prayed for for years was coming true. She waited to feel joy, but didn't. It was the wrong timing. Instead, a question shot through her like a lead bolt: who would look after her father?

"I've decided you'll stay and do correspondence." He stood up, declaring the conversation over. "Unpack your bags and make some supper. She's already on board. You'll have to pull your weight round here."

For a moment the doctor's news fuelled the tiny fire inside her; rage erupted within her, a rage that could burn down the house.

"Understand?" The doctor, standing above her, demanding co-operation. He put the pressure of a palm on her forehead, combing his fingers through her fringe, his eyes for a moment open as water. The great wave of his need washed over her, dousing her. She understood. Her father required help; her mother needed her to look after her father. Her job was to make this difficult time better for him, to make amends for the problem she presented. And Raef? Raef didn't need her at all.

Gulai nodded, burnt out, inert, extinguished.

The doctor ruffled her hair, relaxing now there wasn't going to be a scene. "Good girl," he said. He picked up his stethoscope and went out of the door.

She hated Veronica, Veronica who had come and taken, and left without even so much as a goodbye.

Phoebe tried to persuade Gulai to board the next day as they loaded the barge. "I'll hide you in my cabin. You can be a stowaway, just think! You can't let your dad stop you!"

Gulai turned away, feeling dead, dead, watching Raef and Hans play the fool, pretending to throw Gilbert's luggage off the harbour wall. Raef's cousin Sasha was at his side, laughing. Raef had shrugged when Gulai'd told him, said she was lucky to be staying, boarding school was full of stupid rules. He'd held her face in his hands for a moment, and she'd nearly died, falling upwards into the blue lakes of his eyes; and then he'd kissed her, a short, sweet kiss goodbye. But now Frank Bardelli was telling the boys to behave and get into the barge, he was glad to be rid of their nonsense.

Gulai watched as the barge pushed off from the quayside. Maybe it was not too late. Maybe she could fling herself off the harbour wall and swim out to the ship before it left; maybe if she plunged into the water and swam out to the ship after him, mirroring his arrival, maybe that would impress him.

Phoebe was waving from the barge, as were Di and Tomas and Gilbert, but Raef was pretending to throw up over the side, fooling around with Hans. He didn't look back, not even after he climbed the rope ladder to the deck. The last Gulai saw of him was the blue of his jersey disappearing through a doorway into the ship. She stayed at the harbour long after everyone else had gone back to their lives, watching until the horizon closed over the ship like a lid.

Chapter Ten

The only other person left behind and doing correspondence was the witch's son. The books with the projects and assignments for the first term had arrived on the December ship, and Officer Bardelli had already delivered them to Impossible. The doctor paced the house as though cornered; he mumbled that Gulai would have to wait until the May ship brought her own set of books, she could catch up then. Finally, when Gulai pointed out the obvious, he declared he would have nothing to do with a charlatan. So Gulai went herself to Officer Bardelli and asked her to take a message to the witch, printed out carefully in her best writing, asking her whether she could borrow the course work to get it photostatted.

A box of books came back with the officer. Gulai looked through them, feeling in her hands the weight of texts full of knowledge that would somehow have to enter her head, feeling the texture of paper that had lain in the witch's son's hands. The margins of the first few chapters were annotated in a sensitive script. Callum had already started working from them. Officer Bardelli helped her photostat them at her office.

That night, when the doctor came home and found her bent over an assignment, he paged through the copied files, exclaiming he was glad Gulai had been brought up properly, not to write in books. Gulai had decided to suggest that she and Callum could work together, but she could see it would be pointless bringing the subject up.

She threw herself into housework every morning, so that her father might be pleased with her; she cooked his favourite meals and took him sandwiches at lunchtime. She did school-work in the afternoons, but was restless for something that drew her yet eluded her, like the slippery edge of a dream on waking. Something paced in her, caged and reckless, so she would escape to the mountain if the winds allowed, following paths in both sun and rain. On days when the weather lifted, she climbed to the edge of the extinct crater, which rose higher than the highest point of Impossible Island across the channel. Gulai would stare down at the lake that had formed in the volcanic basin, imagining the time when the volcano had burst through the ocean's surface, releasing the pressure of the earth's core. This island had once been a safety valve so the whole world didn't blow.

Gulai felt like exploding. Alone on the mountaintop, she would shout or sing loudly anything that came to mind: nonsense words, rhymes, notes; she would string sounds together until they fell like a rosary of comfort around her, weaving them into a melody that gathered her like a net and lifted her. Sounds left her lips like ripples; they looped round on themselves like a magic ring of stones, or like the rim of the crater she stood on; and somehow the music circling from this impulse soothed her, and made it possible to descend to the village and start her day over.

Every day arrived the same: mundane, boring, constricted. She would go mad counting the days until the May ship arrived with letters from Phoebe, and maybe from the others – even, she dared hope, from Raef. She wrote to Phoebe and Di and Gilbert, but she wrote to Raef the most. Another release valve: long flowing letters to him stacked up under her mattress where her father would not find them, containing news when there was some – like Mr Bacon's kidney stones, and how Elijah Mobara minded the shop while Mr Bacon was in hospital, and by mistake sold Katerina Schoones salt instead of bicarb, so her cakes turned out like salt bricks; and how Kylie Tamara got her finger bitten by a fish that was supposed to be dead, but it was just reflex, it happened sometimes. And how Mayor Nelson Peters was negotiating a telephone link with the mainland so the villagers would not be reliant on radio communication alone, and then she could phone Phoebe at school and talk to her, their voices flying miraculous and light to and fro through wires that ran under tons of water on the sea bed. Also how Layla Bardelli was walking down the road, pushing her new grandson in the pram, when she thought she saw a snake cross her path – never mind that there have never been snakes on Ergo, it was just an unconscious reaction to a piece of seaweed, the doctor said – and she got such a fright that she let the pram go, and it rolled away down to the harbour. If it wasn't for Frank jumping out to stop it, the baby would have had an early christening and maybe even have drowned.

Gulai didn't know whether she dared to send the letters with the May ship: the news was so boring compared with the mainland. Restless, she was restless, so she redoubled her housekeeping efforts and walked further and further each day, walking faster as the days shortened in order to be home before nightfall, getting fit and strong, trying to quieten this wayward spirit in her. She forced herself to do more schoolwork; the assignments for the first quarter had to sail with the May ship.

The ship arrived in the night; first thing, Gulai went down to the harbour. She had to wait patiently as the passengers disembarked and Officer Bardelli stamped them in, smiling politely as they exclaimed about the quaintness of the village; wait until Frank Bardelli had taken the mail bags from the barge and delivered them to the police office where Officer Yero Tamara dispensed the post. The villagers gathered round like children hungry for sweets when there are more children than sweets to go round. There could be no hiding who received and who did not. Gulai received one fat letter from Phoebe, written diary style, a short letter from Di and two postcards, one each from Leila and Gilbert. Nothing from Raef. But of course not; how could she have expected anything at all. His mother received four letters, and Gulai heard her exclaim over one of them: from Raef.

She went home and read and reread Phoebe's letter. It was full of the extraordinary. Everything was so big on the mainland, Phoebe enthused: the buildings, the trees, the roads, the shops; it was as though the gales that buffeted Ergo Island reduced everything to quarter size, but in the relatively good weather of the mainland, everything could flourish and grow. And the variety! Imagine, twenty kinds of toothpaste in the shops, twelve kinds of spaghetti, more than fifty kinds of car she'd counted thus far ... although Gulai couldn't see the point of that.

Phoebe loved the school. Imagine: a different teacher for each lesson, and fields the size of the whole potato farm for playing sports, and a swimming pool the size of the community hall! And the fruit! Such variety, and so fresh, she was never going to eat tinned fruit again. And the boys! Even more variety, and they tasted even better! And the books!

The library at the school was fifty times the size of the one on the island, and she was learning about computers, incredible machines that gave you access to any information you wanted, not like the old one at the factory that only did accounts and letters; on the mainland there were phones, and everything and everyone was connected to everything else.

Gulai counted her letters to Raef. Forty-two. She went outside, stacked them and lit them. She watched as her love flared into a rich blood-orange, as her words smudged into smoke, leaving black husks of ash scattering in the wind.

She went inside and started cooking supper.

Chapter Eleven

Gulai turned fourteen in the middle of a winter squall with snowfall swirling right into the village, but that did not stop her going to her mother's grave. It was her ritual, the thing she did often during the year and always on her birthday. But on this her fourteenth birthday she felt nothing: no happiness, no excitement for the year ahead. Life stretched out before her like a long monotonous road.

Someone was there already: Officer Bardelli, sitting on the bench, puffed up in her anorak and cap against the cold, breathing into her gloves. "Sorry, Officer," said Gulai, turning to go.

"Why sorry?" asked Officer Bardelli. "Come sit with me."

Gulai resented this intrusion, but she felt obliged. She sat down.

"Call me Aunt Dorado." Gulai couldn't get used to that. "Happy birthday. It's today, isn't it?"

Gulai looked away over the line of stunted trees to the fall of black cliffs to the sea. "I'll never have a happy birthday."

Dorado studied her face. "The day you were born was a happy birthday," she pointed out. Gulai looked at her doubtfully. "I went to see your mother in the hospital. She couldn't take her eyes off you. You were exactly what she wanted."

This was news to Gulai. "Then . . . why did she leave?"

Dorado shrugged, looked straight ahead, her gaze resting on the old mayor's tombstone marking an empty grave. "Sometimes we can't have the thing we want most in the world. But your mother was lucky. She had you for four whole days."

Dorado's eyes were sad, but Gulai felt anger lick in her chest. "Four days isn't very long!"

"It's better than nothing."

"If I wasn't born she'd still be alive!"

Dorado shook her head. "Don't imagine you are that powerful." She stood up and turned to Gulai, forcing a smile. "Sometimes we take things too personally," she said. "Have a good birthday, Gulai, and may life bring you gifts you haven't yet imagined." She bent forward and kissed her cheek, and Gulai did not know whether it was a drop of melted snow that fell from Dorado's face onto hers, or a tear.

The September ship brought something she was not expecting: Raef himself. Raef, the mayor's son, expelled from school. The details were in Phoebe's letter. He had been caught running a bar for the boarders out of a disused storeroom behind the cloakrooms. It was hilarious, a scandal, heroic.

As soon as Gulai saw him there was purpose and desire in her life again. Raef had more interest in her now, for she was a little older and very striking, with her mother's bird bones, dark eyebrows and lit smile, and he had cupped a hand around the back of her neck one evening behind the co-op and pulled her to him, into the vortex of him.

The doctor noticed that Raef had noticed his daughter, and he wasn't happy. "That boy is no good," he informed her. "You stay away from him."

But she knew she wouldn't; her every fibre was aligned to him. She would see him when her father was not around, the secrecy of their meeting half the pleasure of it. Raef was studying correspondence and working for his uncle, Jerome; evenings he was often at the tavern, a forbidden place for Gulai because of her age. Desperate, she would wander on the mountain paths and through her assignments, waiting for those moments they shared, when the world dissolved into a flush of pleasure. She felt her body respond like an instrument to Raef's touch, her heart and body so open and full of desire after what felt like a century of tight-corseted misery. Gulai was a stone that had miraculously transformed in the palm of another into something precious and lucky, something chosen and wanted; she was the secret pearl formed from a piece of irritating grit by this container of care. But in the background scampered anxiety: could she have this? Could she take what she wanted and survive?

Secrets are meant to be found out. It wasn't long before the doctor came home unexpectedly one afternoon and found Gulai on the sofa with Raef's mouth on hers, his hand inside her jersey. She surfaced from paradise to find her father towering and furious above her.

"Out!" he commanded.

Raef left without a word, leaving Gulai to her father's wrath.

"I don't want to see you near that boy again!" he thundered.

She stared up at him, dislocated, severed, her inner threads trailing. "I like him! You can't stop me!"

She wasn't expecting it. Out of nowhere, her father's hand came down; her father's hand – that had healed every member of the island community of something at some time, that had delivered almost every baby on the island for the past fifteen years, that had fought to save her mother's life, that had caressed and loved her mother – came down and slapped her face.

"You are *fourteen years old!*" raged the doctor. "You don't know what boys are like, you don't know *anything!*"

Gulai gasped, her hand at her stinging cheek, her eyes blurring tears. She wanted to run, run and keep on running, she wanted to steal a boat and sail across to the witch and never come back. That was impossible, but it wasn't long now before she would escape to the mainland. Her father had raised his hand to her. This could mean one of two things. Either her father was bad, or she was. She already knew the answer, from deep in her bones, from the day she was born. The world without her would have been a better place. Without her, her mother would have lived and her father would've been happy.

If she'd never been born, no one would've missed her.

Winter, with its unpredictable weather and gales that tore the surface of the sea into white strips over dark relentless water, was passing its hand round to the other side of the world. Gulai and Raef met certain afternoons in the shed behind Raef's father's house – Gulai knowing this could not make her any worse in her father's eyes, and why not look for comfort? Her breath catching as she felt his desire hot in her hand, the release of him pungent like the sap of an exotic plant. She wouldn't let him touch her there, she was too afraid of pregnancy, of being found out, of him not liking what he found. One time he'd walked away, saying it was time she grew up, loving someone was an all-or-nothing act, it involved taking some risks. She'd run home to her bedroom and spent an hour crying, fear caught and snagged in the prickly thicket in her belly.

One afternoon Raef was late again, and Gulai hung around the back of his house, afraid that his parents, Nelson or Condolessa Peters, would come back early from work and find her there and tell her father; afraid, often afraid. Through a window, she could see the figurehead taken from the witch's cottage, standing restored next to the fireplace. She went closer and peered in, for now she could see that the woman's mouth was a beak, and that she held a snake to her breasts. The figure looked incongruous inside, like a lion in a cage with its mane trimmed and nails clipped. The birdwoman stared out of her beautiful head at the Peters' lounge suite, at the china ornaments displayed on the other side of the room. Gulai had the sudden urge to fling the doors and windows open, to let the woman escape.

Raef arrived, pulling her into the shed and into his arms. She found herself telling him that she wanted him to take her to Impossible Island.

"Why?" Raef's face registered incomprehension, as though she had just asked him to eat paper. Gulai had hoped her idea would ignite him as it did her, that he would see it as an act of rebellion and daring – even ingenuity, on a par with the construction of the hut at Deception Bay or running a bar in a boarding school; that it would elevate her in his eyes. She'd hoped it would bind them together as co-conspirators, soul mates, that through this act they would understand each other better. Now her mind went blank. For as long as she could remember, she had wanted to meet the witch, but here was the question she'd never really answered, even for herself: why?

It had something to do with her life, with the milk she had suckled, with the birdwoman standing restored but somehow crippled in Mayor Peters's house. It didn't make sense; part of her knew that a work of art should be indoors and polished, not left out in the elements to deteriorate, slowly disintegrating back into the natural world. She felt ashamed, as though a secret treasure she'd kept close to her heart had been revealed as a piece of grit. What to say? Anything she could think of was laughable.

"Never mind," she said. "It was just something, you know, something to do. This place is so boring."

"It's the witch, isn't it? You want to consult her." He was laughing at her.

Gulai shrugged, attempting nonchalance. "Sometimes I wonder about her."

"Come here," said Raef, pulling her into the warm embrace of him, the smoke smell of him. "I'll kiss you better."

His mouth was on hers, his passion rising. Gulai felt a dread start up in her: dread of the pressure he put on her, dread of refusing him, dread of refusing her own desire that said, you can do what you want, you can have this, stop spoiling everything. She pushed his hand away, knowing that if he touched her, that wild beast within would rise up and take her.

"Tell you what," breathed Raef in her ear. "I'll take you to Impossible Island if you do it with me."

Chapter Twelve

They decided to go on the next clear day. Raef would take his
uncle's rubber duck out on the pretext of checking the nets.
Gulai would pretend to be going for a walk, and Raef would
pick her up just around the Point at Tilly's Jetty. From there it
would take about half an hour to get to Impossible.

Three days later, the wind died and the day broke open still
and light, the great yolk of the sun sliding into the pale sky.
After breakfast, Gulai wandered down past Raef's house. The
stone at the gate was overturned – the sign they'd agreed on.
She went home, got ready, left a note for her father, then
headed for the Point.

Raef was late. Gulai waited at the jetty, watching the
seaweed lift and drift in the cold sea, her irritation rising and
gusting with the wind. What had started out a perfect day was
shifting. She searched the sky. No clouds; it should still be
safe. The sea sucked and swelled and sighed at her feet, it
rolled slowly across the channel in large gestures suggesting
infinity, but nothing looked threatening.

Perhaps he had been held up. Or changed his mind. Gulai felt suddenly bitterly glad that she had made him wait. "Afterwards," she'd told him. "After Impossible." Two seals lifted their dog heads out of the water and stared at her. She wished she were a seal. Life would be so uncomplicated then, a life of fishing and swimming and mating and dying. What you had to do and how to do it was in front of you, a clear path, with no razor choices or dead ends.

An hour passed. Dark clouds began to boil out of the line of the horizon. It was too late. Gulai got up to go; as she did so, the rubber duck rounded the Point. She waited for Raef to reach the jetty and idle the engine.

"Hi," he grinned, reaching out for a post to steady the boat with one hand, his other held out to her. "Come aboard the Jolly Roger, my pretty maid, and prepare for a solid ravishing."

"It's too late."

"No, it's not." Raef looked at the horizon. "Those clouds are going the other way. The forecast is fine, wind only up to five knots."

Gulai hesitated. Impossible Island beckoned across the channel, so near, so far.

"Juliette, Juliette, wherefore art thou, Juliette?" Raef was smiling up at her again, one of his long-dimpled, irresistible smiles, as though she were a classical beauty on a balcony, not a schoolgirl on a jetty; as though he loved her. The question was being asked in the wrong direction by the wrong person, she knew that, but it spoke to her heart. Wherefore am I? She didn't know. All she knew was her island life; all she wanted was to get to Impossible, to put something restless in her to rest, to be lovable and therefore loved.

"I lovest thee, oh Juliette, now get your stubborn ambivalent posterior into my boat before I drinketh this can of poisoned potion!" Raef was enjoying himself, waving a beer at her. Gulai had to smile at him, her heart pulsing flushes of happiness. She climbed into the rubber duck, and they were off.

"We must hurry," she pointed out above the drone of the engine.

"We're at full throttle." Raef frowned. "It doesn't help to worry, you know. It just spoils what could be a good adventure."

Gulai nodded, pulling on her anorak. He knew the sea better than she did. Still, the waves were starting to crest, the sky was darkening. The boat was not making good headway against the roll and dip of the waves. She started to feel ill. Please God she wasn't going to be sick! She had a sip of Raef's beer to try to wash the feeling away, but it didn't help. Impossible Island rose and fell unstably in front of them; Ergo Island beckoned from behind, cosy and warm and welcoming, bathed in a last shaft of sunlight. Gulai gripped the seat, fighting fear and queasiness. Her belly, always her belly, let her down. A spot stung her face, then another. Rain. They were heading into a squall, and Impossible Island was vanishing slowly in a cold, white vapour. Raef's face was silent with worry, but he had not altered course.

"Turn back!" shrieked Gulai, tugging at his trousers, overwhelmed with terror and sickness. "For God's sake!"

Raef glowered at her and brought the boat around. The waves were now behind them, and they practically surfed down the face of each as they passed. "Hey, this is great!" Raef was in his stride again, enjoying the thrill, the challenge of managing the boat in this precarious sea. But for Gulai, this was the end. She put her head over the side of the rubber duck and emptied her breakfast into the water.

"Pity I didn't bring my gaff along," shouted Raef. "That's good bait!" The thought brought another wave of nausea. She

153

retched until there was nothing left, and still she retched. Wiping tears from her eyes, she saw that the mist was closing in fast, and Ergo, although not far ahead, was barely visible.

A wave broke over the boat. "Bail!" ordered Raef, handing her a bucket attached by a rope to the boat. Gulai didn't care about bailing, about living or dying, about anything, she felt so awful. She just wanted this nightmare to end.

"I said bail, goddammit!" Raef's tone of voice pulled her out of the queasy fog. "Fuck it! Hurry up!"

Gulai had never seen Raef like this – not in control. It made her even more afraid. Ahead she saw glimpses of the shelter at Deception Bay, painted orange, the only paint they'd been able to scrounge. Now it was a blessing, guiding them towards the shore as the mist swirled then lifted, lifted then closed. As Gulai scooped water from the bottom of the boat, she remembered the shipwrecks below, and the sailors who had embarked on the adventure of their lives only to die here, broken on the rack of Ergo.

With a scrape and a lurch, they were aground. Raef leapt out and helped Gulai through the tumbling surf, pulling both her and the rubber duck out of the water. Gulai sank to the ground, drenched and shivering, her hands closing around solid rock. Raef pulled the rubber duck up the beach and secured it with ropes and rocks against the rising gale.

"Come," he said, pulling her up. Hunched against the wild wind, he led her to the shelter and opened the door. "Welcome to my humble abode," he said, bolting the door behind them. They stood, dripping, their hair plastered down around their faces. "I can't believe the ordeals I have to go through to get you to come and visit me!" Raef smiled at her, welcoming, warm, then looked through his pockets. His cigarettes were wet. He swore, and rummaged through a box on the shelf, searching desperately for a dry one while Gulai looked around. There was a single mattress with a pile of blankets, a gas cooker, a few boxes and tins of food on a shelf. The wash of nausea receded into a hole of hunger. Hot food would help. She picked up a tin of baked beans and one of meatballs. She would get warm somehow, the storm would die down in half an hour, and she'd get home before anyone noticed. Raef had found a cigarette and lit it with relief; then he opened a bottle of brew and offered her some. She shook her head – cold, too cold for that. She lit the gas stove and some candles, for it was quite dark now, with the wind tugging and tearing at the little structure. The candlelight threw a comforting glow into the tiny room, but flickered and wavered constantly in the draughts.

Raef lifted his brew. "Gotta give thanks to the gods," he said, drinking deeply. Then he stripped completely. It was the first time Gulai had seen any man totally naked. He stood like a god, the candlelight softly gilding and moulding the contours of his body, the dark and pale male strangeness of his sex; she thought she would die, he looked so beautiful. He got under the blankets, snuggled in. "Come," he said, gesturing for her. "You promised."

Gulai turned back to stirring the pot, hardly able to breathe. This man had just saved her life, he loved her, he was asking her to share the pearl of her, the secret hidden in the silky folds of her. He was offering her the world, a doorway into adult life with all its beauty and complexity and stupidity; he was offering her a way to do it differently, not like her father with Veronica, or with that other woman in Sophia's cottage. It would be different with Raef, they would be one, as her father must have been with her mother; they would become something whole and gratifying. She could have this now. They were alone in this rustic hut he had built for this moment, for the moment she would turn and allow him to have his way with her, to enter her. Yet she felt the split, the terrible rift in her: Gail and Gulai, Gulai and Gail, the one who would do anything for this man and the one who whispered: No. No. She recognised the voice now, but it was not her father's voice. It had spoken to her before as a tug of resistance, but now she heard it distinctly: *No*. She recognised it as though it came to her from far away or long ago, like a dream, or a part of herself that she hadn't met yet.

Gulai dished up into two tin mugs, feeling vulnerable, fearful of Raef's responses, out here in the wild. She would stall him, she would appeal to his reason, his honour. She handed him his food. "You haven't taken me to Impossible yet," she said.

Raef took the mug and ate a spoonful. He chewed slowly, a cold anger setting into his face. He swallowed, glanced at Gulai, shook his head. "Sex isn't a ticket somewhere, you know," he said. "Sex is about loving someone." He finished his food, turned over to face the wall, pulled the blankets over his shoulders and went to sleep.

Outside, the storm was not letting up. Gulai sat miserable and shivering in a corner, her back to the wall. Raef began to snore gently. He had given up on her. She was alone, battered by storms, and there was no sign of them passing.

Chapter Thirteen

The doctor didn't believe her. Once she had changed into dry clothes, he marched Gulai straight down to the procedure room at the hospital, gave her a gown and pulled on a pair of latex gloves.

"You shame me in front of the whole island."

Gulai had never seen him like this: turned to ice, cold and hard. She changed, pulling the gown on over her shirt, pulling her jeans and pants off.

"This is statutory rape, I'll have you know. I'll have that bastard's balls." He tore the curtain aside. "Get on the bed."

Tears streamed down Gulai's face. *No!* said her heart. *No!*

Her head said: Never, never say no to your father.

"Hurry up, Gail!" snapped the doctor. "I haven't got all day." He flicked on the angle-poise lamp at the foot of the bed. It shone straight into her eyes. "Lie down!" the doctor commanded. "Stop acting as though I've never seen your or any other girl's vagina before."

Angry, everyone was angry with her. Gulai forced herself

to lie down. She turned her face to the wall.

"Bend your knees! Open your legs! You think what you've got is so special? Then why do you give it to the first horny idiot that comes along!"

Shame, shame washed through Gulai like hot poison. She felt her father's gloved hand on her where not even Raef had touched, she felt his disgusted eyes on her shameful secret, the one so terrible even she had never seen it properly: her womanhood, the thing that made her whole life a problem. She felt herself go numb.

Her father turned from her, peeled the gloves off and threw them into the bin. "Get dressed," he ordered. "Then come to my office."

When Gulai opened his office door, he was sitting behind his desk, smoking, watching the grey curl and vanish. "Sit down," he said, nodding to a chair on the other side of the desk, as though she were a patient to whom he was about to break bad news. Gulai sat on the edge of the seat. She *thought* she was a virgin, but maybe she was mistaken; maybe something had happened while she was asleep, or drunk that one time at the Ball – had she been that drunk? Or maybe . . . could tampons . . . ? She just couldn't remember . . . In any case, her father's face told her she was wrong, wrong, unlovable; she was a whore and not to be trusted.

He was making her wait, tapping his ash into an ashtray, contemplating his fingernails. Gulai couldn't look at him. Her eyes roved over the qualifications framed on the wall, over the bookcases lined with medical books – all evidence of the doctor's intellect, his knowledge about the world and human beings, about how it all worked. All that knowledge, condensed and stored behind his greying temples.

"It doesn't seem you're inclined to listen to me, it seems you prefer your own poor judgement. So I am going to tell you something that might wake you up." He stared at Gulai through the chinks of his shuttered eyes. "Sasha Peters is pregnant." His voice sliced at Gulai through his thin lips. She felt the ground unstable under her. "She was here while you were up to your tricks. Stupid girl thought she had gastroenteritis, vomiting away. Wasn't using anything to protect herself."

Gulai noticed a spider building a web in the corner of the room. Stupid, stupid spider. John Peters would come in and brush the spider's hard work away without a thought. There was a pain in Gulai's belly that made her want to cry for the spider. She wanted to go home and bury her face in her pillow. She was not going to cry in front of her father.

Numb. She wanted to feel nothing.

"Go home and stay there for the next week. Give yourself time to think it over. You're not a stupid girl, even though you act like one. And be grateful it isn't you that's going to be pushing Raef's baby into the world in a few months' time."

"How do you know it's his baby?" Gulai managed to blurt out.

"Everyone knows. Everyone but the people who didn't want to – you and his parents. There'll be hell to pay now. Raef and Sasha, they're first cousins. No wonder this bloody island has so many medical problems, so many funny-looking kids." He put out a cigarette, lit another. "Now I'll have Jerome and Rumer on my neck, trying to persuade me to get rid of it. I won't, you know, never have. I always think, if a woman is stupid enough not to look after herself, she must pay the consequences." He seemed to have forgotten Gulai was in the room; he was talking to himself. "Now why, I ask you, should I be expected to relieve her of that?"

Gulai stood up, made it across the room to the door. She opened it, then turned, her hand still on the handle. "I didn't sleep with him," she said.

The doctor waved his hand in dismissal. "I know," he said.

Outside, the storm was over as suddenly as it had started, the mantle of cloud folding back over the horizon. Up the road was Raef's house, its wet thatch shining in sunlight, with the shed behind – now closed to her. Out across the channel, Impossible Island sailed like a perfect galleon: intact, serene, inaccessible to her.

At least her father hadn't discovered that part. He didn't know the real reason she was out with Raef.

For weeks, Gulai stayed at home, unable to face herself or the world. Every day, she would wake and hope to find everything restored; that Raef was still hers, that Sasha never existed. Pain was her constant companion, except during brief bouts of reading. She paid a visit to the library at Martha Schoones's cottage, took out all her old favourites, and went home and buried her head in the comfort of them. Even that trip took all her courage. She felt the whole island was laughing at her since finding out about Sasha's pregnancy; they all thought she'd done it too, that she was immoral. On the way to Martha's cottage, the sight of Sasha in the distance knifed her; she overheard Frank Bardelli outside the boatshed, laughing about how boys will be boys – falling silent when he turned and saw her.

The doctor was increasingly irritated by her reluctance to go out. It meant he had to do the shopping. One evening he came home from the tavern and announced: "I told those busybodies you're still a virgin. Now tomorrow you go to the shop and stock up, right?"

Next day, Mr Bacon added up the items and put the total onto the doctor's account. He eyed Gulai before passing her the bag of groceries.

"You save yourself for the right man," he counselled. "Pretty thing like you gotta look after yourself."

Gulai put her hand out for the bag, wanting to end this ordeal, but he held onto it; he hadn't finished yet. Drowning in hot shame, she wanted to shriek that *of course* she wanted to save herself. But how? She would lock herself up, throw away the key. She would keep her eyes on the ground in front of her. She would enter a convent; she'd read about such places, where women were married to God, where they were kept safe from all temptation, saved from the ravages of humiliation. What? What must she do?

"Boys can't help themselves," Mr Bacon explained, "so girls have to be extra careful." He shook his head, handed her the bag.

The doctor came home in a foul mood. Gulai got him a drink and put a plate of fish pie in front of him, treading softly to prevent a landmine going off.

"She's gone and tampered, that Sasha Peters," he said.

"Tampered?"

He glanced at her. "That Sasha girl miscarried today. I know who's behind it. Someone interfered, and it wasn't me." He attacked the pie as though it was the cause of his problems.

Gulai was intrigued. Babies died sometimes, didn't they? Mothers too. Yet her father was suggesting something else. Who but Sophia could make someone miscarry? That meant others went to her, that there was a way to get to her.

She thought of Sasha, bleeding, crying; she imagined the scandal that would follow her . . . imagine! She was councillor Peters's daughter and the mayor's niece!

Gulai was glad. Served her right for seducing Raef.

Chapter Fourteen

The December ship brought the boarders back for the summer holidays. Gulai's old schoolmates had changed: there was something worldly about them; they had forgotten who they were. Gulai felt small and shy and stupid as she greeted them – even Phoebe, with her dangling earrings, her forearms ringed with many bangles and her bold new clothing, teetering on heels not designed for daily island life.

"You'll never guess," Phoebe giggled. "The new nurse is on board."

The next load arriving on Frank's barge included Veronica's replacement. A man in a pink shirt clambered awkwardly onto the wharf, knelt his lanky frame down and kissed the earth.

"Oh, Charley!" shrieked Phoebe, escaping her mother's embrace. "There are more interesting things to kiss here!"

Gulai had never before seen a man in a pink shirt, let alone one who kissed the earth. Phoebe's behaviour was equally shocking. The villagers stared at the newcomer as he straightened up unsteadily, with his long pocked face, eyes set a bit too close in his head, curly brown hair and large disarming smile.

"Hell," he exclaimed, "am I glad to be on stable ground!" He hesitated, disconcerted. "Only it's not feeling too stable."

"Welcome," said Mayor Nelson Peters, introducing himself as though he'd rather not.

"Hi, your honour!" said the stranger. "I'm Charley Handley."

"He had a bad trip," explained Hans.

Charley nodded emphatically. "They told me I'd find my sea legs, but I never did. Someone must've hidden them. All I can say, if there's no other way off this place, I'll be staying for good. I'm never getting on a ship again."

Gulai took Charley up to the hospital, with Phoebe following. "I also get seasick," Gulai offered.

"You sure this island is properly anchored?" he asked. "Damn, I wish this rocking would stop."

"Don't worry, this place is the most staid and stable in the world," said Phoebe. Gulai felt the prick of irritation; Phoebe was taking over, even flirting with this older stranger.

"Why did you come here?" Gulai probed.

Charley shook his head. "Long story."

"Lost love, I'll bet," charmed Phoebe inquisitively.

"Your room." Gulai opened the door to the flatlet next to casualty. Charley looked around at the forlorn furnishings, and flopped onto the bed to try it out.

"If you don't like it, I'm sure you can come and stay with us," sang Phoebe, flinging the curtains open.

"You from the city?" asked Gulai, trying to claim the focus. Charley nodded. "It's very quiet here," Gulai warned.

"Quiet's okay. Quiet's what the doctor ordered."

"Are you sick?" asked Gulai, concerned.

"Yep. Lovesick, heartsick, sick and tired. I decided on the

proverbial cure, a long voyage out to a romantic island, and promptly got seasick too."

Gulai laughed. "I hope you don't also get homesick." She liked his gawky, funny manner, his exaggerated gestures, his humour.

"I'm making a fresh start," he explained. "Cutting all the old ties."

"I have too," announced Phoebe, "but I'm off in the other direction. This place is a dump."

The doctor and Sister Lena were busy in the procedure room with Martha Schoones, who had a dog bite gone septic.

"Hallo," beamed Lena, shaking Charley's hand.

The doctor turned his eye to Charley, looking him up and down. "You weren't my first choice," he informed him.

It took only a moment for Charley to recover. "I don't think you'd be mine either," he retorted. A shocked silence descended; no one ever spoke back to the doctor. "But we can probably find a way round that."

Gulai held her breath and glanced at Phoebe, waiting for the explosion. The doctor looked as though he'd been winded, or lost his footing. He swung to Sister Lena. "Give Sister Charley . . ."

"Nurse Charley," Charley corrected him firmly.

The doctor glared at him, then turned back to Lena. "Give him his uniform, then show him his duties. I believe it's time for the medication round."

"I only start work tomorrow," frowned Charley.

"You start work when I tell you!" snapped the doctor. Gulai was horrified. This was going to be a war. Didn't Charley understand? Maybe it was different on the mainland, but here you did what you were told.

"I only work for nothing if I am treated well," said Charley coldly.

The doctor's face went red with rage; he stormed out of the room.

Charley looked at the women, who were shocked into silence, and raised an eyebrow. "Looks like the storms haven't ended," he said. "Is there anything I can help you with, Lena?"

The doctor came home in a foul mood that night and went straight for the bottle. "He's got to go," he grumbled. "He's totally unsuitable."

Where to? thought Gulai, sick to her stomach, for the ship had already sailed. The doctor looked at his supper with distaste. "What kind of a man would want to be a nurse, anyway?"

Gulai looked at her father, crumpled angrily in his chair, a drink in his hand, and saw him as a small, rude man who drank too much. She excused herself and went to her room. She suddenly felt tired, sick and tired of this life; but then, Charley had been sick and tired of *his* life and had changed it, and look where he was now. This was hardly the recuperation he was seeking. She fell asleep wondering about him, imagining him alone in his room with his memories and dreams. What makes a person change their life completely?

Next day, as she was helping Phoebe unpack, her old friend handed her a wrapped present. "It's for Christmas," she said, "but you can open it now, if you want."

Gulai tore the paper open, grateful her friend had remembered her. Inside was a small plastic box, moulded and coloured to take on the appearance of wood, the lid fastened with a catch.

"Open it!" said Phoebe excitedly.

Gulai undid the catch and lifted the lid. At once a tinny tune began to play, activated by the hinge. The interior of the box was covered with a shiny red material, and set into the lid was a mirror. In it, Gulai caught sight of her disappointed face, and snapped the lid closed.

"Don't you like it?" demanded Phoebe, hurt.

"What is it?"

"It's a jewellery box, dumbhead!"

"Oh." Gulai felt slapped, but forced her face to recover. She ran her hands over the dead, pretend surface, wondering what had happened, whether they had ever really known each other. "Thanks."

After that, the two avoided each other. Phoebe hung out with the other students who had returned from the mainland, propped up against the pillars on the veranda outside Mr Bacon's shop, sneaking cigarettes and talking about mainland topics like television and movies. Gulai felt as though her home had been invaded by infidels who no longer valued wild weather and open spaces, the island textures and smells, the shaded palette of silvers and whites and greys where the streaked sea became one with the slashed sky. She was relieved when her contemporaries left on the February ship, leaving her to her solitary wanderings.

The subterranean beast was shifting; Gulai could feel it in her body, in the way things felt different – not better, but different. There was something new in the air, some small wobble in the routine orbit of things.

Soon afterwards, a second newcomer arrived on the island. Gulai was coming out of Mr Bacon's one grey and blustery March morning when Officer Bardelli pulled up in the police van, talking to a male stranger sitting beside her: a teenager, angular, lean, with long hair about an unremarkable face, a nose too large to be called attractive and eyes that landed curiously on her, so full of attention and wonder she found it hard to return the stranger's gaze. Where on earth had he come from? The only time there were strangers on Ergo Island was when the ship came in, and a ship was not due for another two months. Officer Bardelli emerged from the van, still talking – " . . . and this is Mr Bacon's shop," – while the stranger got out of the vehicle and limped, his right leg slightly stiff, towards Gulai. " . . . and this is Gail. Gail, meet Callum. Gail is the doctor's daughter, you know, she's doing correspondence, same as you. You'll have to get together, help each other maybe."

Callum put his hand out to Gulai, shook it in the old way. "Hallo," he said, his voice full of the intonations of the old way of speaking, his eyes looking right into hers. "There's a cloud in you, Gulai," he observed.

"Oh, the doctor doesn't like that," warned Officer Bardelli. "He likes 'Gail', not 'Gulai'. And you'll want to keep on the good side of the doctor, in case your appendix blows. Oh, hallo, Mr Bacon, this is Callum, sent by his mother to come and live amongst us after all these years. Isn't that nice?"

"That so?" smiled Mr Bacon, coming out onto the shop veranda. "Now what made her decide to do that?"

"I've come to find my father," said Callum, looking at Mr Bacon with clear brown eyes. There was an awkward silence as rumour stirred in their memories: the father was the devil, some had said.

Officer Bardelli recovered first. "His mother sent him to live with Elijah – her cousin, you remember? Time for him to be brought up by a man, she said; isn't that right, Callum? Elijah'll make you a good father, although he's not had much practice at it. I'm sure you'll teach him the necessary in no time! I don't like Sophia staying on Impossible by herself, but you know how she is. Nobody can tell her anything."

"You got her onto Impossible," Mr Bacon pointed out. "I'm sure you could get her off if you wanted."

Officer Bardelli shrugged, uncomfortable. Mr Bacon dipped into the shop a moment, and came out with a large bar of chocolate, which he thrust into Callum's hand. "Welcome," he said. "It's about time you joined reality!"

"Thank you," said Callum, turning the bar over in his hands, staring at it. "This is chocolate."

Mr Bacon laughed. "You're right, chocolate! You're what, fourteen years old, and you don't know chocolate? I know all about your habits – I get your mother's orders ready! Lots more pleasures awaiting you, young man. Look at Gail here, delicious as chocolate too!"

Gulai felt her shame revolve slowly in the deep recess of her belly; what was he saying? Contradictory, he was: she had to make herself both delicious and unavailable. He was laughing at her, the whole island was laughing, thinking her easy, an easy target.

"Wait till we get you down to the tavern, Callum!" Mr Bacon chuckled. "We'll put some hair on your chest! You're not the only newcomer in need of initiation."

"Callum's not really a newcomer," Officer Bardelli pointed out a little anxiously.

"Oh yes, he is. Never set foot on the island before – course he is!"

Gulai was anxious too. Initiation of newcomers to the island was a rare occurrence, as rare as newcomers. Jolene Schoones had been the last one, and by all accounts hers had been mild, what with her being a woman; her initiation, organised by the island women, had involved only flour and eggs and cold water. But Andy Brookes, the one man who had immigrated in living memory, had lost his life to alcohol poisoning. For some reason, neither the doctor nor Veronica nor Minister Kohler had been initiated, and perhaps because of this had never been fully integrated into the local community. But Charley and Callum would be seen as fair game. They would not survive it, she felt sure; they were both too sensitive.

Callum's face had gone blank, suddenly turned to a place inside himself. "Can we go to Uncle Elijah now, please?" he asked.

Officer Bardelli put a hand on his shoulder. "Had enough? I'll show you the rest tomorrow."

"Elijah's at the hospital," said Mr Bacon. "He'll teach you to sort what's rubbish from what's not, son!"

Gulai could not take her eyes off Callum. He was like a snail, putting out soft feelers to ascertain the way. She didn't want her brusque father to meet him yet, not the way she was feeling herself: fragile, intrigued; and not after the rough and condescending way Mr Bacon had spoken to him. "I'll find him," she offered, and ran across to the hospital.

Elijah Mobara was coming from the hospital kitchen with a barrow full of refuse for the dump. "He's here already?" he said through his wagging grey beard. He set down his load, and loped along beside Gulai to the shop.

Before long, Officer Bardelli, Elijah, Gulai and Callum were squashed into Elijah's tiny lean-to bedroom tacked onto the back of Mannie and Susanna Mobara's cottage. Elijah, Callum and Gulai were sitting shoulder to shoulder on Elijah's sagging single bed, while Officer Bardelli sat on the only chair. Callum's eyes roved everywhere; there were so many things he had never seen or experienced before. Even Ceylon tea was new to him – he was used to drinking his mother's root and herb teas. He politely asked whether he could leave it.

"The two of you can't stay here," Officer Bardelli pointed out. Besides the bed, a table and a chair, a small gas cooker, and a few clothes hanging on pegs behind the door, the space was stacked and hung with driftwood and woodworking implements.

"We're to live at Sophia's," said Elijah. "I never wanted to live there alone, but now the boy has come . . ." He looked pleased, this old man who had never married, never had his own children, living behind the Mobaras' for as long as Gulai could remember.

"It'll take some work," warned the officer.

"Can I go there now, please?" asked Callum.

So they bundled into the police van, three people quick to respond to this young man's polite yet quietly urgent requests, and drove across to the ghost house. Callum exclaimed at the strangeness of it all – to go to the trouble of making a vehicle when walking would do.

At the cottage they set to, cleaning and clearing. Word had got out, and soon others arrived. Others who, to Gulai's astonishment, knew Callum: Leila Tamara, Martha Schoones, Layla Bardelli and Kali Mobara, then Graça Bagonata, even Yero Tamara; all patients of Sophia's, it turned out, all ready and willing to help. Suddenly the cottage was filled with a weave of something light and happy as people went in and out, fixing and mending, donating a tablecloth here and a picture for the wall there. People often helped each other on the island, that was how things worked, but this felt like a net held up to catch goodness as it fell; the spell on the cottage was broken, and people could breathe and joke and laugh again.

Gulai did not want to go home. There was an aromatic supper of slow-cooking stew in a large pot on Elijah's little gas cooker, for as people arrived at the door with offerings of vegetables and herbs, Callum chopped up portions and added them to the pot, so that there would be enough for all when the work was done. Gulai wanted to stay, to eat with them, to celebrate and give thanks. But her father, her father would not approve.

She said goodbye, refusing repeated invitations to stay, and left the cottage. Tomorrow, she thought. There's always tomorrow. I wonder what will happen then.

Chapter Fifteen

Charley was a kite flyer. When he was off duty and conditions were right, he would spend hours playing with a large red kite, watching it dip and climb, the diamond with a trailing tail dancing the tension between the pull of strings and the tug of the gusting wind. A crowd of island children would gather round him, all looking up into the sky, their mouths open, as if witnessing a miracle.

"Don't see the point of that," grumbled Frank Bardelli. "Pulling a fish in from the sea on the end of a line, now that'll feed a family – but a kite in the sky? Waste of time."

Some villagers called their children away. "You'll need to do something useful, not stand around gawping," Samuel reprimanded his son. "If you're going to play, do something that'll grow you up, like making a dam at the stream."

"You'll all get cricks in your necks," observed the doctor crossly. "Go get some proper exercise."

But the children couldn't help themselves. Charley with his dancing kite was irresistible.

DAWN GARISCH

The doctor wished a large enough gust would carry Charley and his kite off for good. He wanted to be rid of him, his very presence irritated; yet it was hard to find fault with his work. And once the women got over the horror of a male nurse, they started to flirt with him. The doctor had seen it with his very own eyes, how Sasha Peters smiled at him when he injected an anti-inflammatory into her bottom; but that was Sasha, a loose woman, as he well knew. But to see even Cyn Peters come over all peculiar, giggling like a girl when Charley checked her blood pressure, was too much. Charley could be charming but he had no respect, no ambition. He must be an outcast to have come to the island, there had to be something wrong with his past, thought the doctor; and he let slip his suspicion into a number of ears.

So one night in the tavern, when Jojo reminded the menfolk about the tradition of the lighthouse initiation for newcomers, a number fell into agreement. This would put Charley in his place. It would show him up to their women and children for the wimp he was, with his pink shirt and mainland ways. There were those who wanted to deal with the witch's son at the same time.

Nelson felt otherwise, but he was aware that going against consensus could jeopardise his popularity. He was an elected representative of the majority, he reasoned to himself; yet he feared the thought of falling, of broken bodies on rock. The nights were beginning to wake him again, full of ghosts and terror. "We need to be careful," he cautioned. "If we don't welcome newcomers warmly, particularly the youth, they won't stay – and our population figures are down again this year."

"You'd encourage the witch's son to live here?" challenged Jojo. "He'll turn out a troublemaker, just like his mother."

"If he can't take a little fun, he shouldn't have come," remarked Danny.

"He's too young, only just fourteen, and no real match, what with his gammy side," worried Harry.

"Now's the time to get him and break him, before he becomes difficult," Jojo observed, a little smeared from the drink.

"Exactly," agreed Frank. "The only influence he's had so far is the witch. It's our duty to put him right."

Danny shook his head. "And that Charley's not our type, never will be. No initiation'll change that."

Jojo gestured for another round. "He's got secrets, that man. Don't like him."

"I dunno. If he manages the lighthouse race, I reckon he's okay," Arthur said.

"It's not a good idea," Nelson objected again. "We don't want one of our medics injured. It's true he's a bit strange, but we all know he's good at his job."

"You're also good at your job, and look at *your* past!" Jojo smirked at his cousin. The men laughed awkwardly, embarrassed, and looked at the floor or out of the window into the night. What was Jojo on about? In any case, he'd gone too far.

Samuel tried to change the subject. "Great catch you had the other day, Arthur!" But the mayor had heard Jojo; his dart had hit home. It was the spirits talking, the spirits that refused to give Nelson rest at night, licking incessantly at his ear, now tonguing at him through Jojo's mouth.

"Look to the beam in your own eye," Nelson warned.

"Storm approaching." Arthur knocked the barometer glass. "Boats won't make it out tomorrow, looks like."

Jojo and Nelson glared at each other across the counter, across history and complicity, and left it at that.

But as a result, late one stormy night after a heated debate at the tavern, it was decided: the mayor was not to be invited, in case he spoilt the fun. While he lay alone next to his dreaming wife, hoping for the gentle lap of sleep to drift him off, both Charley and Callum were forcibly taken from their slumber. Frank and Jojo came for Callum, marching him down to the tavern despite Elijah's protests. Elijah remonstrated with himself for not seeing it coming. He wrung his hands and followed the men, already deep in their cups, trying to persuade them that Callum was too young, too sensitive, that this was not his way.

"That's the point!" Frank slapped the old man on the back, shouting into the wind. "Sensitivity's gotta be knocked out of him, or he'll turn into a woman like that Charley!"

Charley was brought in by Harry Pelani, Mr Bacon and Raef Peters, bleary-eyed but co-operative, drawn by curiosity. Both Charley and Callum were presented with glasses of dubious brew while the men banged a countdown on the table. Charley's glass was three times the size of Callum's, but he finished first while Callum struggled with his, screwing up his face in disgust. "What is this?" he wanted to know. "This can't be good for you, it tastes too bad!"

"It's the antidote to mother's milk!" proclaimed Frank, downing another tot himself.

"It's the elixir of life on Ergo Island!" announced Samuel Pelani, topping up Danny's glass.

"I don't want any more, thank you," said Callum.

The group of men laughed at him. Frank put his face close to Callum's. "Trouble with you is you don't know hard work. Us men, we've worked months to bring you this brew. You have no idea what went into it, just as you have no idea what goes into being a man. Now don't you be ungrateful."

"Yeah, it's the last time you'll be getting free booze for a while," chuckled Raef. "Drink up and be grateful."

Danny nodded. "Boys your age aren't usually allowed into this sanctum. It's a real privilege!"

"The boy'll be sick," protested Elijah. "He's never had spirits before."

"He's lived with his mother these years," laughed Jojo. "Plenty spirits round there!"

"Come," said Elijah to Callum. "You don't have to do this."

Callum looked round the ring of faces.

"It's not so bad," said Charley, a little blurred already. "'Specially if you throw up after."

Callum pinched his nose and knocked the rest back quickly.

Samuel Pelani, who had brought out bags of clothes, handed Charley a large bra. Charley held it up, astonished. "Put it on," instructed Jojo. "Call it home improvements."

"Well, okay," said Charley, pulling off his jersey. "I haven't worn one of these for a while!"

The men laughed and joked as Charley stripped down to his underpants and put on the women's clothing borrowed from Cyn Peters, who had been tickled at the thought of Charley wearing her underwear, her stockings, her dress and jacket. For Callum, they brought out clothing belonging to Levona Mobara, including a small, flat bra and skirt. He shook his head and crossed his arms protectively over his chest, horrified.

"What's the matter, don't you like women?" Frank smirked. He and Jojo and Harry had a bag of their wives' clothing, and they started changing. "Come on," he cajoled, "it's just a laugh."

"Leave him," said Raef. "It's probably more of an education just to watch."

"Old island tradition," Samuel explained to Callum.

"Just foreplay before the lighthouse," laughed Harry Pelani.

One by one, Frank, Jojo, Harry and Charley staged a strip show, standing on the counter and gyrating to the thudding beat of mainland music, flinging articles of women's clothing into the crowd, men clapping and stamping and yelling: "Take it off!", "More!" and "All the way!" Harry got his ankles tangled in his wife's skirt when he tried to whip it off in one seductive gesture while swaying his hips, and fell off the counter; it was only the following day that he discovered he'd broken his wrist.

Callum watched with his face gone blank. Blank, turned inside himself, unresponsive to the ribald jibes that tried to nudge him into the mood of the event. A sweat broke on his brow, the room was swirling, and before he could find a way to escape, he'd vomited. A roar of approval went up.

"It is rather disgusting, isn't it?" Mr Bacon laughed, referring to Charley's wiggling backside as he removed his blouse with more panache than the other men had managed.

"Never mind," consoled Danny, clapping Callum on the back, "you'll get to hold your drink one of these days."

"Bloody waste of good brew," remarked Samuel, inspecting the carpet unsteadily.

Elijah put an arm round the boy. "Come home now, Callum."

"The best's still coming!" objected Frank, pulling his jersey back on. "You can't let him miss the lighthouse!" He consulted his watch. "Only two hours to go."

"He's in no fit state." Elijah lead Callum outside and all the way home, the earth rising and falling away with every step, the sky unreliable, the world turned inside out. There was an engine throbbing in the chamber of Callum's skull; Elijah made him drink a jug of water before he collapsed into bed. Towards dawn he vomited again, and Elijah, worried, called the doctor for an injection. The doctor looked at Callum lying on his bed as though at an idiot, and told him he'd be better off looking after what brain he had than drowning it in drink, then went out into the rain grumbling about stupid island ways.

So Callum missed the central event, when Frank and Jojo and Harry challenged Charley to race them to the top of the lighthouse as dawn was breaking. The first to extinguish the hurricane lamp would be the winner. Both the winner and the losers would then be required to drink more alcohol. The lighthouse column had six faces made from hewn laval rock fitted together; the chips and cracks allowed minimal purchase for the toes and fingertips of a climber. The only safe ascent was the official one, up the metal rungs set into one face. On the other sides, aspirant climbers were assisted slightly by the gentle slope of the lighthouse walls, which led up to the glass chamber housing the lamp; but the blocks were usually slippery due to wet weather and mosses that grew in the niches of rock. Climbing the lighthouse was a lure and a terror, for the height was enough to kill a man outright if he fell on his head, as Raymond Pelani had done thirty years before. For this reason it was out of bounds for children – but because such decrees render the forbidden object even more desirable, disobedient children regularly had to be plucked off the wall halfway up, crying and terrified, fingers stiff and cramping, legs numb and quaking.

After the long haul of night, as a tepid, insipid light at last spilt over his windowsill, Nelson heard the throng staggering and swaggering down the road, making their way from the tavern to the lighthouse. He heard them, and knew at once what it meant. His foot had slipped; he had lost ground, and with it the ability to influence and direct, the rats now following a different pipe. It was that Jojo, he knew. The two of them were in the same leaky boat, and hated each other for it, for their shared deceit and secrets. He had an urge to rise and slap an immediate ban on the event, to demonstrate who was in charge and make them take notice. But he couldn't. He had scanned the Constitution, looking for a way, but there was none. He would have to be careful, mind his back.

The lighthouse punctured the whitening sky above the revellers, sweeping the water with arcs of light, beckoning all who dared. It didn't take Harry long to realise that his right arm would not take his weight; but, due to the anaesthetising effects of the revelry, he still did not recognise the pain that went with a fracture. He therefore retired early from the race, blaming his boots. So it was between Frank, the reigning champion, Jojo and Charley. Buffeted by the wind, they inched their way up the slopes. Charley, with his long, athletic body and his foresight – retiring outside after the drinking contest to expel the contents of his stomach before they had leached through to his brain – slowly increased his headway over the other two men. When Jojo learnt of this from the crowd's reports and cheers, for the contestants could not see each other, he whipped round to the adjacent face and quickly scrambled up the rungs to the top, out of sight of the other contestants. There was a gasp from the crowd, but no one referred to it afterwards except as an aside to Frank, who naturally understood; better to have a local winner who had received a little help than let the mainland stranger make them all lose face.

The two men were dosed with congratulatory amounts of alcohol, Charley was forgiven his past life as a mainlander and wearer of pink shirts, and everyone fell exhausted and spinning into their beds.

Kali Mobara opened the tavern doors and started cleaning

up the glasses, bottles, vomit and cigarette butts. She gathered up the strewn articles of women's clothing and washed and hung them out to dry while the rain was holding off. The dresses and underwear danced on the line, bright and innocuous, stripped of the role they had played during the night.

Chapter Sixteen

That day, the doctor got Gulai to help Lena in the clinic, as Charley was unrousable. He grumbled incessantly as he checked Felicity Pelani's chest X-ray and Katerina Schoones's blood sugar and haemoglobin results, and removed a grain of soot from Arthur Bardelli's eye. Around eleven, Harry Pelani came in looking pale and drawn, his left wrist all swollen up. This reminded the doctor of his night call, and he sent Gulai round to Elijah's to find out how Callum was doing. Nobody was there.

On her way back, she saw Elijah and Yero Tamara striding up from the harbour towards the police station, their faces set and serious. Callum was gone and so was the police launch, and the wind was busy whipping itself up into a gale. A decision had to be made, and soon.

Frank Bardelli's longboat was commandeered, and a party consisting of Dorado, Elijah and Frank set out. At the last moment, Gulai leapt aboard. Despite a thrill of anxiety that her father would find out, she was determined not to be left behind this time. Besides, she was concerned about Callum – and if he were safe, he would be with the woman she had wanted to meet for years. Frank, who was furious and suffering from a headache, objected to Gulai's presence. This trip, he said, was not for girls. Dorado Bardelli agreed, saying it was too dangerous, she must ask her father first; but then Elijah spoke for her, saying that her presence would be helpful when they found Callum. *When*, he said, not *if*, and no one corrected him. And as time was of the essence, and as people had other things on their minds, they let it slip, and Gulai got her way and accompanied them in their attempt to rescue a boy who did not want to be rescued – assuming he was still above water.

They scanned the sea on the way across the channel. It transpired that Dorado had let the boy steer the launch often enough while she was visiting Impossible, and like most of the islanders he knew the sea and the weather well; also the police launch was a sturdy boat. But the weather was worsening again, although not to the point where visibility was impaired. At the top of each crest, everyone looked for evidence of Callum's safety – all except Gulai, who felt increasingly ill. Why did her body reject the sea so?

Frank saw it first, using Officer Dorado's powerful binoculars: on Impossible Island itself, where they were headed, the police launch was pulled up and secured at the landing beach. He had made it, this young man, he was back with his mother. As Frank's longboat crunched into the black pebble beach, the weather became suddenly wilder; great currents of air pouring round the four of them, to the point of making them lose balance. The men pulled both the boats higher up the beach, a seal lolloping out of their way and seabirds hopping into flight, screaming disapproval at the intrusion. They secured the boats with ropes and rocks and anchors. Frank's headache and mood were getting steadily worse. "How dare he put us all at risk!" he shouted, his face inflamed. "Mummy's little boy!"

The track they took led up the side of a gorge, then zigzagged up and around a headland that overlooked the sea. Four cottages stood in the lee of a cliff cluttered with nests; seabirds flew to their young on the ledges, in and out as though sliding along washing lines. It was a wild place: not hostile, yet not inviting, except for smoke unfurling from a chimney on one of the cottages.

"Damn," exclaimed Frank, looking back to the channel. "There'll be no going back in this weather." He strode up to the door as Sophia opened it. She was taller and more lithe than Gulai expected; no cragged and knuckled Hansel and Gretel witch this!

Frank glared at her. "Where is that boy of yours?" he growled without greeting.

Sophia gestured towards the cliffs behind the dwellings. High up on the rock face, higher than the height of the light-house, a small figure was descending, a bag swinging from his waist. Frank's mouth dropped open. "You let him . . ."

"Eggs for your supper," Sophia said evenly, gesturing them into her cottage. "Welcome to you all. Have a seat where you might find one. Here we do things the old way."

The place was tiny, meant as a shelter for fishermen who couldn't get home, hardly room enough for a crowd; but they squeezed in somehow, finding places to sit on the floor and the bed and the table. There were only two chairs: one for the witch and one for Dorado. Sophia went round the group with a bowl of water and a cloth for each to wash their hands, according to the old custom. Gulai watched with fascination. Without effort, Sophia had stopped Frank in his tracks; this man who reminded her of a large and snarly dog was meekly sitting, stirring the tips of his fingers in water meant for absorbing troubles, for purifying and rectifying. Officer Dorado too accepted the ritual meekly. It was obvious who was in charge here; despite the fact that Sophia had been imprisoned here, she was no prisoner.

"You'll have to stay, one, perhaps two days," Sophia said, looking at the weather through the small window. She was beautiful, thought Gulai, with her wild grey hair tamed into a plait.

"I'm going to have that boy of yours up in front of the council," started Frank.

The wind flung into the shelter as Callum opened the door. He closed it behind him, his eyes sullen, avoiding the assembled company, his hair wild about his head. He undid the bag from his belt and deposited it carefully on the table.

"Thank you, my boy." Sophia's dark, freckled cheeks folded into a smile. Then she addressed the others as she poured root tea: "He owes you all an apology and an amends."

"Officially, it is a crime to steal the police launch," Officer Bardelli pointed out. "And it could have been lost, along with the boy."

"An apology!" fretted Frank. "I should be at work right now, and I'm stuck in this bloody place for goodness knows how long . . ."

"He has promised to make amends."

"How?" The question popped out of Gulai's mouth before she'd thought it.

The witch handed her some tea. "Hallo, Gulai," she smiled. "I was wondering when you'd pay me a visit." She winked at her – a secret wink, for Gulai felt sure no one else had seen it; a quick flicker over an eye. "You've travelled far to get here." Sophia passed a cup to her son. "Gulai wants to know how you will make amends, Callum."

Callum sat at the hearth, poking at the fire as though it were an adversary he had to overcome. He pulled his mouth this way and that, reluctant to speak. Without raising his eyes, he blurted out: "I will go back to Ergo Island and work for Mr Bardelli and Officer Bardelli for as long as it takes to make amends."

Dorado raised her eyebrows at her cousin Frank, who sat back, the wind taken out of his sails. She looked at Callum. "Your offer is accepted, Callum."

Gulai was shocked. How could the witch . . . ? She didn't understand her own son, forcing him back to Ergo! How could she expect Callum to work for Frank, a man who gave her the creeps, and for Officer Dorado, who had been Sophia's jailor for years! This was a terrible betrayal, terrible.

Sophia smiled graciously at her guests. "Now, if you would like to make yourselves comfortable in the cottages, Elijah and I have some business to discuss."

She was dismissing them all like children. Gulai didn't know about this witch, whether she even liked her. But she stood with the others and followed them outside into a gale. Frank mumbled something about mumbo jumbo and went into a cottage, saying he needed to put his head down. Officer Dorado went down to the police launch to radio Yero to let him know they were all safe, only stranded by weather. Callum limped into the third cottage. Gulai stood for a moment in the wind, alone and lonely. The first few drops of rain forced her to a decision. She followed Callum inside. He was sitting cross-legged on a mattress in a corner, unpicking a nest of fishing line. He glanced up briefly as Gulai entered, then ignored her.

"Can I . . . ?"

Callum shrugged, not looking up from his task.

"I could go to the other . . ."

"It's fine," he said irritably.

"I think it's *terrible*, what your mother's making you do," she began. Callum picked furiously at the fishing line. "I mean, do you *want* to go back? I heard they made you very ill last night."

Nothing. It was like talking to the wall. Gulai wanted him to take notice, to notice her.

"Did you ever find out who your father is?" A stiffening; Gulai persevered. "Why can't you ask your mother . . . ?"

Callum stood up and left, banging the door closed behind him. The sound reverberated through Gulai like a shock wave. Why couldn't she just shut up? She didn't talk when she should, and she talked too much when she shouldn't. She wanted to go after him, explain, but that was also probably the wrong thing. She would lie on the bed, still warm from Callum's body, and cry until someone came along and took pity on her. Within a few minutes she was asleep.

In Sophia's cottage, Elijah sat on the edge of the table, his southwester hood in his hands, folding and unfolding it. "I can't, Sophia."

Sophia looked sternly at him. "There's no escaping it. The old ways have power; they cannot die, they can only be forgotten. Our lives are the knots that hold the net of our people together, also knots in the thread that passes wisdom and knowledge from our ancestors' generations down through us to our children's. The threads are unravelling, the nets are breaking. Unless we pay attention, this heritage will dissipate, it will become useless to us! We are guardians of the thread, repairers of the nets." She held her hands out to the hearth. "The ancestors are with you. They will give you the courage you need, as for all of us."

"The boy is too young," protested Elijah. "I was sixteen."

"The times are different now; this needs urgent attention, it cannot wait. And there are others who will help you." She stared at him, willing him. "You have been chosen, Elijah. The bones have spoken, and for good reason."

He shook his head, and clucked his tongue with discomfort. "I am a rubbish collector, not a high priest of the old ways!"

"You're afraid. There's no shame in that. But don't be afraid of the wrong thing. Your fear stems from what people think; the real concern is the ancestors' wrath at being ignored, and the unravelling and waste of things that truly matter." She shifted in her chair, but her eyes never left his face. "We are all called during our lives to a thing that requires humility and faith, a thing that strips us of our certainty and our pride." She smiled, reminiscing. "Look what happened to me!" Her face broke into laughter, laughter poured out of her like a dam overflowing, laughter splashed round the room inviting anyone; look at this, it seemed to say, there is nothing, no terror or pain, that cannot eventually be transformed into laughter.

Elijah was about to protest, but stopped himself, and nodded reluctantly.

Sophia pushed herself out of her chair. "But now I have food to prepare. It's a long time since I had so many guests to dinner!"

Chapter Seventeen

That night, Sophia and Callum served the party a delicious omelette made of petrel eggs, garlic and wild mushrooms. Frank was restless and irritable, going outside every now and then to check the weather. At this time he was usually at the tavern, and every now and then through the lifting mist he could see its lights twinkling in the village across the channel. He got to the point of asking Sophia directly whether she had some brew. She shook her head, but said she had a remedy for those who want to give it up, to help with the craving. This made Frank even more irritable; he excused himself and went to bed.

Officer Dorado and Elijah followed soon after, going to sleep in the other cottages, exhausted after the eventful day. Gulai was about to follow them when Sophia stopped her. "You'll sleep here tonight," she said, indicating a rolled-up bundle near the hearth. Callum glanced at his mother, and by his hurt look, Gulai understood that this had been his bed. Sophia ignored this; she cupped his face in her hands and kissed him warmly. He left without a glance at Gulai.

Gulai helped Sophia roll out the mattress and blankets, rubbed her teeth with salt, then settled down.

Sophia blew out the candles, and they were left in the last glow of firelight. "You comfortable?" she asked.

"Yes," lied Gulai. It was the hardest mattress she had ever slept on.

She lay a while, looking into the dying embers of the fire, imagining Callum doing the same all those years, on this very bed. Perhaps Sophia was right: Callum could not stay here with her forever; he had to go out and face the world with all its madness and injustice. The witch was asleep; she could hear her regular, gentle breathing across the room. For years Gulai had waited for this moment, and now she didn't know what to say to her or how to say it. There was more to this strange woman than met the eye; more, she wanted more of her, to sit at her feet and ask her . . . what? What was worth asking? Where would she live? Whom would she love? What work would she do? What children would she bear? Yet there was a deeper question, a question that could not be asked because it was not made of words, but of feeling; it was made of the tug and yearn and pain she could remember from the earliest days, feelings that underpinned her very life.

She felt safe here, protected against the storms that rocked her, as though an anchor had been released from the vessel of her drifting, restless heart; an anchor that had caught and held fast on unshakeable bedrock. She fell into a heavy sleep.

Something woke her in the night. The room was lighter, lit from outside by moonlight. The wind had died. Gulai turned, her shoulder aching from the mattress, and saw Sophia sitting on the mat at the hearth, stoking up the fire. What time was it? Surely the witch didn't get up this early?

Sophia lifted her eyes to Gulai. "Come," she said. "Sit with me." Gulai got up, pulled on her jacket. She lowered herself onto the mat opposite Sophia. "The storm is spent, you'll be gone first thing." Sophia fed dry grasses into the fire and blew on a cinder, long, slow breaths. The kindling took, flame leapt from the wood. Sophia took a plait of dried herbs, lit the end, then extinguished it. Smoke curled into the room. Then she took a large feather and waved the smoke towards Gulai, dousing her with its pungent aroma. "Let the ancestors be with us," she appealed. She leaned back, regarding Gulai, who sat hugging her knees. "You have come to consult the oracle," she said.

This was a surprise. "Are you an oracle or a witch?" The words were out.

Sophia laughed and pulled a cloth bag out from under her chair. "Neither, and both. You will learn that the whole world is your oracle; you will learn to notice signs that appear in front of you every moment, ready to guide and help and support you; you will also learn to read them correctly. The oracle is always with us if we pay attention. Our lives are constantly reminding us who we are and where we should be heading."

She took a blue cloth from the bag and spread it on the mat in front of her. "As for being a witch . . ." She paused, her eyes wandering away. "There was a time when words had different meanings, a time when being a witch or a virgin meant that a woman belonged to herself, that she was in touch with her own goddess-given power. This had nothing to do with magic tricks or whether a woman had slept with a man or not. Now the words have been corrupted, like many of the old things, and the terms are used to put women down or to raise them impossibly and falsely high. So, cup your hands," Sophia instructed. She opened the bag and shook the contents into the bowl of Gulai's hands, then folded them closed with her own like a careful prayer. "What is it you want to ask?"

Gulai didn't know, all her questions had vanished; there was just that feeling, the feeling with no name, sitting in the pit of her stomach. She shook her head, despairing.

"Never mind," said Sophia. "The oracle knows your innermost question. Blow in here," and she opened a chink between her hands, within which Gulai's were contained. Gulai blew into the cavity, her palms around the objects growing warm and moist. Sophia chanted something Gulai didn't understand, then instructed Gulai to throw the objects onto the cloth. Small bones fell, and a few stones, different shapes and colours, and an old coin, and a piece of blue yarn, a piece of green seaglass, a seed and a tiny shell. Sophia sat a while and studied them, the fall of them, the pattern that made the story. Gulai felt anxious. The sky outside was lightening; soon Frank would be banging on the door. What was it? What had Sophia seen that was keeping her from speaking? Would she tell Gulai, or keep the terrible parts secret?

At last she said, "There is cloud cover over you; you lie under deep water. See, the shell has fallen over the seed. You are hidden, even from yourself. But there are helpers – see how this small knuckle bone lies near, as does the coin. But you are severed from assistance at this time; the yarn has fallen far, and is not connected to anything."

Gulai felt anxious; what was she to do?

Sophia saw the look on her face, and laid a hand on hers. "You have songs in you that long to be sung. Music is the great force that binds the universe; it is the thread with which we call our ancestors to us, the means whereby they sing through us, helping us to discover the secrets of our own hearts. You have a gift. We all have. All we need is the courage to use it."

Gulai felt a stiffening in her, a tightness in her belly. For as long as she could remember, her song had not been welcome in her childhood home. It reminded her father of her mother, and it had annoyed Veronica for the same reason. For most of her life she had kept herself limp and empty, the neck of her tied tight.

Sophia put a large pot of water next to the fire, then put out her hand. "Come," she said. Gulai followed her outside into the growing light and down a path that lead to the top of a cliff. They stood in the play and pluck of the wind, facing the rough-hewn sea far below their feet. Sophia started clapping, her hands releasing a rhythm of beats and off-beats. Gulai stood frozen. What was expected of her? She wanted to please Sophia, to show that she was worthy of her care and attention. Her instruction was to use her gift, but she felt barren. She had nothing of value.

Sophia began stamping in time to the clapped rhythm, her body falling into the sway of an invisible dance. Then Gulai saw it: that Sophia's body was planted into the ground, that she trusted the ground and took the rhythm from it up through her feet, drawing water from a well. She saw that the rhythm watered Sophia's body, and felt with an unbearable ache that her own body was a desert.

Out of Sophia's mouth came a sound Gulai had never heard before: a flying, curling ribbon of bird sound, a shoal of sea sound, the shock of an avalanche. Weaving it together was her body, moving as though no one was watching, her clapping hands sewing the music together into a whole piece: a long dreaming tapestry of song unfolding.

Then it was over. Too soon, for Gulai wanted more, her heart beating with the power and the beauty of it, the magic of it. Slowly, as though coming out of a trance, Sophia turned to her. Gulai felt ashamed; she looked at the ground. "I could never . . ." she began.

Sophia brought a vial of liquid out of her pocket and pressed Gulai to take a sip. Bitter, bitter it washed through her. "What . . ." Gulai wanted to know. Sophia ignored this, and placed one hand in the middle of Gulai's back and the other on her belly below the arch of her lower ribs. Gently she began to massage her diaphragm. Gulai felt the warmth of Sophia's hands stoking the smouldering bitter coal of her, loosening the choked flue of her, coaxing her tiny flame. A sob escaped her lips, an escaped prisoner of sound – and then there was no stopping, for an enormous space suddenly opened up underneath her ribs, a tunnel funnelling up, her throat loosening, untying, sound erupting out of her with such violence that Gulai felt certain she was damaging herself, yet she could not stop; a waste chamber was disgorging its contents, vomiting up a lifetime of swallowed dross. She wailed into the wind, shrieking and sobbing, terrible sounds of lament and terror, until the last trickling whimper trailed away. Spent and shaking, she fell into Sophia's arms. Sophia held and comforted her, murmuring into her ear to calm her, the gentle stroke of Sophia's hand on her back soothing her until at last she was quiet.

She kept her cheek pressed to Sophia's breast till she could hear again: the birds and rustle, the rumble of the shoreline, and a singing in her ears like faraway voices; the lightening day danced red against her eyelids, encouraging her to open them.

Sophia took her by the hand, and led her to the cottage; she sat Gulai in front of the fire and slowly, very slowly, in warm water, she washed and dried her feet.

Chapter Eighteen

Gulai was afraid to go home, she was afraid of her father's hand raised against her. The last she saw of Sophia from the police launch was through Officer Bardelli's binoculars. She was in her blue skirt, high up on the cliff; it looked as though she were dancing. Gulai could not understand why Sophia wished to live alone, and was annoyed she hadn't asked. There were so many questions, now she had left: can I come again? Should I go to the mainland? What should I do about my father? How is my mother? Who is Callum's father?

Callum sat in the bow of the boat, not looking back to Impossible; furled inside himself, he did not respond to Elijah's light and friendly jokes or his large bony hand on his shoulder. Gulai wished she could reassure him, offer him something. She wrapped her jacket around her as the icy wind cut across her neck, and felt in her pocket the bottle of bitter medicine Sophia had given her to make her spirit strong, a remedy against the binding that stopped the life force: medicine that had to be taken each day before the sun came up, for that was when it was most potent and her body most receptive.

Halfway across, Callum became agitated, urging Frank on. Frank shrugged with some irritation; he was going full throttle anyway, back to the call of the tavern.

"What is it?" Gulai wanted to know.

Callum turned wild eyes to her. "The doctor," he said, and wouldn't elaborate.

As the launch entered the harbour on Ergo, Nelson and Jojo came to meet them with the news that Gulai's father was in hospital with what looked like a heart attack. Gulai's body drenched with coldness. First she had killed her mother, now her father's heart had given in because of her duplicity. Gulai ran up to the hospital, past John Peters at reception, who tried to speak to her but she wasn't stopping for anyone, and into the high-care ward. The doctor was lying in a hospital bed. He looked dead, with his eyes closed, his jaw hanging slack and his skin draped grey over his bones.

Gulai realised this was the first time she had seen stubble on her father's chin. He looked terrible, as though a thicket of grey weeds had sprung from his face. Surely, she thought, he can't be dead if he can grow stubble. Then she remembered she'd read that hair and nails keep growing a while after you die. She wanted to fling herself onto him, weeping, but restrained herself because she knew her father hated anyone making what he called "a scene". It was only then that the pulsing of the cardiac monitor penetrated her fright, and she saw the luminous green waves of her father's life rolling across the monitor screen.

Charley was there, adjusting the drip. He gave her hand a squeeze. "I think your father'll be fine," he said.

"But . . ." The doctor looked anything but fine. Something was very, very wrong. Even when Frank had his heart attack, he hadn't been unconscious.

"I had to sedate him," Charley admitted.

Gulai stared at him. She knew nurses were not allowed to prescribe medication, nor dispense anything not written up by a doctor.

Charley sighed with discomfort. "Yesterday afternoon he was in his office with . . . ah . . . Cyn Peters. She came running, saying he'd collapsed. I went straight over with the defibrillator, and gave him two hundred of the best across the chest." He paused, looking pleased with himself.

Gulai knew about the defibrillator; it had only been used once before, on old Rozi Bagonata, but she hadn't recovered. She imagined her father on the floor of his office, being jerked back into his life by a luminous cord of electricity winding and whipping about in his chest.

"Then, well, you know what your father's like," shrugged Charley. "He wanted to carry on as though nothing had happened. Even though he was short of breath, he wanted to get back to work. There was nothing Lena and I could do, he just refused point-blank to accept he'd had a heart attack. So I put a rather large dose of a little something in his tea."

Gulai absorbed this, shocked and grateful. Her father didn't even know she had gone to Impossible Island. She wanted to laugh, to cry. "So he'll live?"

"There are no guarantees, but his ECG is already almost normal. I radioed for help. The specialist was incredibly helpful. Hell, it's been quite a time."

Gulai looked at his haggard face and realised that this man had been up all night saving her father's life, and that he could get struck off the roll for what he had done.

"Thank you," she said, suspecting Charley would probably not receive thanks from her father.

"I was just thinking the other day that it was time for another adventure," said Charley. "I wasn't expecting this!"

"You're not leaving us, are you?" asked Gulai, alarmed.

"No, I really like it here. But I need to . . . dunno, be on my own a while. Think my life through. Maybe stay at Deception Bay for a couple of days, when your father's through this."

Callum was hanging around outside, waiting for news, when Gulai emerged. "How did you know?" she asked.

"What?"

"About my father."

Callum shrugged it off as though he didn't know what she was talking about.

Charley and Lena kept the doctor sedated for two more days. In this time, Gulai took to singing as though her life depended upon it. Something had been released in her, like seed from a tight, dry pod when rains come. She went to the lookout, to the lighthouse or to the harbour wall, and experimented with the instrument of her body: drumming on her chest, her belly, her thighs, dislodging old and dormant music from her muscles and bones out into the air. She sang for her father, that he might live; for her mother, that she might guide her. She sang for her home and the villagers, for Charley and Callum. Every time it was a release; she learned to open her throat, her belly, her sinuses, until her body vibrated with the sound it generated, until she reverberated with life, with the light frequency of stars. She learnt to deepen the place the sound came from, until she felt the slow laval flow of earth, the leap of fire, or the well of water running through her. She sang across the channel to Sophia, she sang across the ocean to the rest of the world, throwing out nets and lines and reels of sound for the man she loved but hadn't yet met, songs of yearning and desire – for desire has a trajectory, always falling beyond the thing you have in your hand; songs for her foremothers and her granddaughters, songs falling like a waterfall from her, like the swoop of seabirds, like a scurry in the undergrowth. She sang as though possessed, and therefore she sang alone or in the dark, always away from others.

From the lookout she could see how the police launch ferried villagers across to Impossible, seeking help during the doctor's incapacity.

People noticed the change in her. Charley said she was blossoming under his very eyes, Mr Bacon gave her a lecture about being demure, Frank pinched her bottom – whereupon she turned blazing towards him, telling him never to do that again, surprising both him and herself – and Raef came again with pleas and promises. She turned him away. He didn't bother her any more; suddenly he looked small and insignificant.

Her father came home to recuperate, and Cyn Peters left Jerome's house and came with him: Cyn, with her straying black hair, looking as though the wind were her father. The doctor looked suddenly old and fallen in on himself, torn between the indignity of illness, rage at loss of power, and a reluctant acknowledgement of Charley's care. Cyn took over the household. She gave the booze and cigarettes away and forced the doctor to have afternoon naps. He protested and sulked, became shaky and belligerent; but Cyn fed him his tablets, and come lunchtime, he had difficulty keeping his eyes open.

A short time before, Gulai would have baulked at the thought of having Cyn move in: a woman older than the doctor, with her false smile and gush, her fussing over her father, her irritating laugh; besides, her father had made her forfeit mainland schooling to look after him. But now she didn't care. It was a relief, actually, to share the responsibility of her father, for she had to admit to herself that he had been a burden. Nowadays her father's moods couldn't touch her; her schoolwork was no longer a boring chore. She still had an ache in her belly occasionally, but now it felt like a tug of life rather than a fearful severance.

She was fifteen years old and wanting to live.

The thing that bothered her was that Callum was so withdrawn around her; or perhaps it wasn't personal, and he was just withdrawn. He was listless, and had lost something of that wonder he'd had when he first arrived on the island. She wanted to know him better, this son of a witch forced out into the world, this young man who had somehow known her father was in trouble and had cared. He spent the mornings doing schoolwork at home and the afternoons working for Frank and Officer Bardelli. He was fourteen now, and his upper lip was darkening. It made Gulai angry to see Callum off-loading the baskets of crayfish for Frank when the boats came in. His making amends was lasting too long; she didn't agree with it in the first place.

Elijah was also concerned about Callum, and was engaged in negotiations with Mayor Nelson Peters for the use of the shelter at Deception Bay. He argued that it should never have been appropriated for the recreational use of a few youngsters. It was sacred ground, meant for initiation. The mayor laughed, said Elijah couldn't be serious – those times were long gone, thank God. The doctor snipped those boys whose parents wanted it soon after the birth: it was less painful, safer, scientific. Elijah looked at the floor, revolving his hat in his hands, and requested that he bring the case to the council. Mayor Peters shrugged with irritation. He could not refuse Elijah, it was his right as a citizen, but the mayor hated wasting time.

Down at the tavern, some of the men laughed to think of old Elijah taking out his knife.

"You'd think he had enough rubbish to sort out on the island without adding bits of skin!" Danny Schoones snorted.

"What if he takes off too much!" chuckled Jojo. "He's not properly trained."

"He is, you know," said Arthur Bardelli. "His father was the elder who performed these duties when Elijah was a boy. His job was to keep the knife sharp."

The men squirmed at the thought of it.

"Well, I'm glad the doctor did me before I was awake enough to realise what was going on," said Frank. "Barbarous idea."

"We should take poor Callum to the doctor to have it done properly. Then Elijah can stop his nonsense." Arthur looked round to gauge the response.

"You don't have to have it done at all," said Raef. The men all looked at him. To his dismay, he blushed.

"Well," pronounced Frank, "they say it's cleaner. And it makes you a better lover."

"It's not just about circumcision," Yero interjected. "It's about becoming a man."

"Hey!" retorted Raef, grabbing Yero's sleeve aggressively. Arthur knitted his eyebrows together under the brim of his woollen cap and pulled him back. Silly boy was drunk already – imagine, looking for a fight with a police officer!

Yero glared at Raef with disdain, and brushed his sleeve. He turned to the others, determined to make his point. "Look at the lighthouse race – that's not safe or painless or scientific. It's about taking on danger, risking your life, proving something to yourself."

"Well, I don't know about all that," said Jojo. "Let Elijah chop it right off! They say the boy's a product of a witch and a devil – we don't want any more offspring from that source, now do we?"

There was uncomfortable laughter. That was the problem with the drink: it let things slip out, things that were better not said.

"So you'll join the chop too, eh, Yero?" jibed Frank, to get the mood going again.

"It's incredible!" Arthur shook his head. "We're living in modern times, we should be showing the world we're no longer savages – and these dolts want to go back to the wild!"

"The only thing that cutting off the end of your dick and painting your face and wearing a blanket in the freeze proves is that you're a bloody idiot!" declared Jojo.

"Takes one to know one," retorted Yero.

That's when Jojo hit him, and after that Yero punched Frank, and then Frank hit Arthur by mistake, and before long the doctor had two people with cuts to be stitched, and two others were sitting in the jail room to cool off under the beady eye of Officer Bardelli. She shook her head. Maybe Yero wasn't cut out for the profession. He was too sensitive, too old-fashioned, too easy to anger.

Next morning, come ten o'clock, Frank and Danny were released from the jail cell with a warning, for Officer Bardelli was due at the mayor's office for a council meeting. Elijah sat down and faced the three council members across the mayor's shiny desk. After Elijah had presented his argument, Mayor Nelson Peters explained that the church had brought a different way to the island and initiation wasn't necessary any more; it wasn't in the Bible, and it was pagan to suggest going back to the old ways.

Elijah shook his head, pinching the brim of the hat between his bony thumbs and forefingers, and tried again. God speaks to us in many ways, he told the three councillors sitting across the table . . . and then could not find the words to carry on. He was uncomfortable approaching the most important people on the island; after all, he was only the rubbish collector, and not good with words and graces. But he suspected the councillors had no real say over what happened at Deception Bay, as it was public land. He did not manage to get support from Jerome Peters either; Jerome pointed out that the boys had worked hard to restore what those interested in the old ways had neglected, and Elijah could not argue with that. Officer Bardelli kept silent during the exchange; it was useless appealing to her. She always went with the men.

The mayor sat pulling his lip after he had escorted Elijah and the two councillors out of his office. God moves in mysterious ways, he thought, *mysterious* ways. He sympathised with Minister Kohler. This community was a wayward one, steeped in superstition and irrationality, distorting biblical teachings and common sense towards their own ends. He knew who was behind this initiative: Sophia. Sophia, who still wanted influence. He had the authority to stop her in her tracks, to fine those who visited her, but he was afraid of the backlash. He suspected that even his own sister-in-law had helped her daughter get rid of her pregnancy with the assistance of that damn woman. He still felt ill at the thought of it, sick to the stomach at the tiny murder of his son's child, his first grandchild.

He would do what he could. The initiation would not go ahead if he could help it.

Part Three

Chapter One

Those in power often do not recognise the dragon forces that underlie life, those forces that cannot be contained by man-made laws and resolutions. The dragon shifted several times that year . . .

Firstly, Mayor Nelson Peters learnt from his wife that he was going to father again – a deeply embarrassing thing, as he and Condolessa were getting on in years, with a son well into his teens. Also, for some time after the dreadful Sasha episode, he had given Raef repeated and emphatic lectures about responsible condom use. Some said, after a few tankards at the tavern, that Condolessa should have kept her niece Sasha's baby rather than have one of her own at her age. You kill a baby, there's bound to be trouble, some said.

Then the doctor had his heart attack. He believed it was entirely due to an obstruction of the arteries of his heart – it did not occur to him that the blockage was due to something much more fundamental than erupted plaque, nor did he register that the excruciating pain in his chest had forced him for one pure moment to experience the full terror of his feelings.

Soon after the doctor had gone back to work, Mayor Nelson Peters, busy composing in his head a decree banning initiation ceremonies, was distracted by something even more disturbing: the ground beneath his feet. He was taking a drive around the perimeter of the village when it suddenly felt as though there were a donkey struggling to free itself from under his chassis. That was his first thought: my God, I've driven over Mannie's donkey, how the hell did that happen?

He stopped, got out and looked under the vehicle; of course there was nothing there but air. At that very moment he felt another heave and shudder, and because he'd forgotten to put the brake on, his four-by-four began to roll slowly backwards down the track. In his fright, the mayor leapt behind the moving vehicle, mistakenly believing his power greater than that of a large vehicle engaged in a tandem act with the dragon gravity; whereupon he was run over in a most ignominious way, losing consciousness and thereby missing out on most of an important piece of island history: the first earthquake in living memory. He ended up in a hospital bed next to Arthur Bardelli, who had dropped an anchor as the earth shifted, resulting in his broken, swollen foot being propped up on pillows and observed regularly for vascular compromise.

The earthquake resulted in little structural damage, except to the mayor's back fender when it came suddenly to rest against a boulder, and to a wall of Jojo's outhouse, which collapsed while he was busy in it. Thus it was that history would remember this as the day the mayor drove over himself, and that Jojo, horribly exposed and the survivor of a near-miss, contracted sudden performance anxiety and thereby constipation; he too ended up at the hospital in need of help.

When the quake struck, the doctor, unable to predict the

severity of the situation, decided to evacuate the building in case it came down. So Layla Bardelli and Katerina Schoones lay in their hospital beds in the driveway, forced to listen to mad Fabio Bagonata proclaiming the end of the world up and down the road, and effectively blocking the way when the police vehicle arrived with the unconscious mayor.

Minister Kohler held an urgent service outside the church to pray to God to forgive any outstanding sins and to deliver the community from terrestrial and moral upheavals. There were those amongst the congregation who, for extra good measure, hurried home afterwards to put out the customary offerings to placate the wrath of the ancient and wakening dragon.

Yet the earthquakes continued intermittently for the next few months, with mild shudderings and settlings, so that when the September ship came in, it brought a vulcanologist, a geologist and a meteorologist to investigate: was it safe to live on Ergo? Was this a warning that the island was going to blow? And what were the consequences for the rest of the world?

What with welcoming and escorting the scientists, the mayor didn't notice that Elijah was preparing Haven Cave as sacred ground for initiation: performing the offerings, saying the prayers, erecting a partial barrier at the opening to protect the initiates from the elements.

Haven Cave had been the refuge of the original shipwreck survivors while they took stock of their situation. When rescue arrived in the form of a ship that happened by three years later, most of them were well settled, having built cottages from the laval rock and thatched them with island grasses. They had water and roots and fish, and some livestock which had also survived the wreck, and in time they imported potato and pumpkin seed, and planted apple trees, and began to flourish in their small island way.

Elijah was pleased with this new location; he realised the ancestors had had a hand in it by making the mayor so stubborn about the original initiation site. This was a good place, a place where the ancestors had come through hardship and learnt to survive – both the white men from Europe who'd thought they knew everything, and the black people, shackled both in their minds and their bodies. They'd somehow had to make their peace, and their offspring had blurred the distinction between master and slave.

Or had they? Elijah felt uncomfortable, thinking about the way the mayor treated him, the way the authorities had treated Sophia and Astrid. Yet through the living the dead could make their amends, and through the dead the living could learn.

Calvin Tamara had approached him, putting forward his two sons as initiates. Yero was keen, but including Gilbert meant they would have to wait for the December ship to arrive. So they waited, and it wasn't long before Mannie Mobara put his son Tomas forward too.

The scientists clambered and roamed, measured and monitored, often with the exclaiming and gesticulating figure of Fabio Bagonata in tow, eager to share with them his own theories about the instability of the world. After a few days, the three researchers resorted to keeping a low profile, sneaking off each morning at random times to avoid Fabio. After two weeks, Dr Turner, the vulcanologist, had had enough. He approached Officer Bardelli, appealing to her for help; so she recruited Fabio to assist her each morning in preparing for Armageddon. As Fabio's schooling was rudimentary, writing out lists took long enough for the researchers to escape.
Other islanders about their daily tasks watched the scientists set off each morning, and shook their heads. Some felt their

very presence was provocation. Measuring the beast would only make her irritable; better to let her alone. But the tremors had subsided, much to the scientists' annoyance, and at the end of their stay all they could conclude was that they were unsure whether Ergo would blow.

"I could've told them that," smirked Arthur at the tavern. "Waste of bloody money, that was."

"Incredible," agreed Danny. "A man could feed his whole family for a year with the money they've spent."

Samuel whisked his hand with exaggerated exasperation. "Or bought us all rounds of brew for a good six-month!"

"Those guys never even got their hands dirty," agreed Frank. "Those university types make pies in the sky, but nothing you can sink your teeth into."

Jojo had been unusually silent. "What's the difference between a woman and a volcano?" he asked.

The men chuckled expectantly. Jojo came up with good ones sometimes.

"Dunno," said Arthur. "Spit it out!"

Jojo sat back smiling and crossed his arms. "Nothing. You never can tell when they're going to blow up, but you gotta find a way to live with them anyway."

Laughter and applause and another round of drinks. No, the scientists could go to hell. They were staying, that was the end of it. Ergo was home, and no smart aleck was going to persuade them otherwise.

Chapter Two

The day the December ship was due, Gulai climbed to the lookout. She went to sing the ship in and to feel the rain on her face, and to give thanks that the islanders were not leaving and that the ground seemed to have stopped shifting uncomfortably under their feet. She sang a high song to the seabirds weaving in and out of the mist, her voice capturing their glide and swoop; she sang low staccato tones learnt from the beetle tapping at her feet.

Her back prickled; she turned mid-song to find Dr Turner standing behind her.

"Please," the vulcanologist said, gesturing for her to continue. "It's lovely."

But Gulai's voice had caught in her throat, snared and subdued.

He waved his hand at the shrouded mountain behind them. "I came to say a last goodbye."

He was trying to be nice to her, Gulai could see that.

Besides, he would be gone that very day. Yet her voice was lost, her full song collapsed.

She looked at him with his goatee and his glasses and his big hat dripping rain from the brim: a mainlander, a mystery.

"Are those local songs? I mean, are they indigenous?"

Well, they weren't from anywhere else. Gulai nodded.

"Lovely, really lovely." He took off his glasses, dried them on his shirt, put them on again, peering through the smear. "Extraordinary place this, really. You plan to stay?"

Gulai shrugged.

He picked up a black stone, examined it and put it in his pocket where it clacked against others. "Strange business, really, that none of us stand on solid ground."

Was he telling her something? "You mean . . . the volcano? I thought . . ."

Dr Turner pointed over the channel. "Look over at Impossible." Gulai could just make out the island, listing in rising mist. "Did you know it once stood where we are now?"

Gulai stared at him, astonished. "Then . . . where was Ergo?"

"Ergo had not yet been formed." He smiled at her incomprehension. "We're talking about millions of years ago. We think these islands were formed by what we call a hot spot in the mantle of the earth, a place where molten magma wells up out of the ocean floor, solidifying and slowly growing until it breaks through the surface of the sea."

"Impossible Island is a volcano?" He was wrong, he must be; Impossible was not the right shape.

"It's extinct now. Long ago, when it was formed over this very spot, it was active. We know it became bigger even than Ergo is now. About three million years ago, it erupted so violently that only the northern aspect remains visible above sea level."

Gulai had always thought that Impossible looked like a galleon leaning into the wind, majestic, elusive; but now she could see: it looked like a broken molar. "You know about plate tectonics?" Gulai shook her head. "The crust of the earth consists of plates that move very slowly. We have found chains of islands where the youngest is an active volcano situated over a hot spot, with a string of increasingly older, extinct volcanoes that have, in a sense, moved on, together with the moving mantle."

Gulai thought of the childhood story she had heard so often, of the dragon lying at the bottom of the ocean, breathing very slow, deep breaths, with two of the scales on her back sticking out of the water. She imagined the beast overhearing them; how she would laugh at this.

"So Ergo will erupt?"

"One day, almost certainly. No one can really say when. Maybe only in five hundred years, long after we're gone."

Gulai looked to the west, out over the expanse of sea, as the sun burnt through the thinning cloud. If the scientist's theory were true, another island would form one day as Ergo moved on.

Out of the haze on the northern horizon emerged the December ship, a flea crawling towards them across the back of the giant ocean. "Look, it's here!"

Dr Turner peered myopically. "Well, I'd better be going then." Out of his wallet he produced a small card. On it was his name with letters behind it, his position at the university and his contact details. "A friend of mine in the music department collects ethnic music. When you come to the mainland, give me a ring, I'll introduce you to him. He'd love to hear you, perhaps even record you."

Gulai thanked him and put the card in her pocket, together with the piece of blue yarn she had taken to carrying around with her. He tipped his hat at her to say goodbye, and strode off down the mountain. Was he the knuckle bone Sophia had pointed out to her? She watched his retreating back, rubbing the card between her finger and thumb.

So the scientists left with the December ship, and life carried on as it always had – except that the structure at Haven Cave was now completed. The students had returned on the ship with their mainland ways and clothes; even their accents were changing. Mayor Peters shook his head. Something had to be done. Like his father before him, he was concerned by how many of the youth left for the mainland once their studies were over, as though there was something better there, something more on offer. He'd been there once, and he knew how the constant roar of traffic ate at your nerves, how neighbours didn't know each other or even greet, how young children were stuck in crèches while their parents worked all day, how television had replaced stories told round the fire, how the elders were neglected and despised. The island should employ a high-school teacher, then there wouldn't be this dreadful tearing apart. Children belonged in their own homes with their own parents, they needed to be part of the local workforce.

So when he heard that Gilbert and Tomas, straight off the ship, had been whisked off by their fathers to Elijah, objecting all the way, he was furious. Forcing them to participate in barbaric rituals was a sure way to chase the youth off. He went over to Elijah's to protest, but the group had already left for Haven Cave. It was getting dark, and Mayor Nelson didn't relish the thought of going across there by himself. That damn Elijah had prepared it as ritual space, ancestral space, and according to the old custom, no one but those involved in the initiation were allowed near during this time. He wanted to talk to Minister Kohler about it, but he was in the hospital, his health poor. He went down to the tavern, where he knew he had support. He was not going to be disobeyed.

There he learnt there was a fifth initiate. "Who?" he wanted to know, anger licking at his throat.

"Guess!" smirked Frank.

Mayor Nelson glanced round the tavern. Raef was there, and Hans and Darius and Harry. He couldn't think of any youngster foolish enough to go and play superstitious nonsense in the wild, when here at the tavern there was a warm fire, good spirits, the camaraderie of men.

They had to tell him. "Charley!" they chorused, enjoying the scandal.

"But he's a mainlander, and a medical man," objected the mayor. "He should know better!" Besides, he had no business in the culture, he was not of it, never would be!

He was so upset, he went around to the doctor's to check.

"Why did you let him go?" the mayor protested.

The doctor glowered. "Nelson, besides anything else, this is December and all the bullshit that goes with it! You think I let him go? I said, forget it! He said, I've been working here a year, I've got leave owing. I was stunned. I had to explain to him that there's no such thing on Ergo – 'leave' is a mainland idea for rich people who work in offices and go to the sea three weeks a year with thousands of others, then go home and say what a lovely time they've had. Then he showed me his contract, and blow me down, there it was, three weeks' leave every year! It has to be changed! I mean, what on earth would you do with three weeks' leave on Ergo Island, I ask you?"

The mayor shrugged, a great wash of impotence coming over him. "Go get your dick cut off, it seems."

Chapter Three

Phoebe came round to catch up. She was taller, her hair cut strangely short like a man's, her breasts beautiful and full like a woman's. She asked about Gulai's life, but she sounded polite, not really listening to Gulai's answer; her attention was pulled to more important things, like her new mainland boyfriend. She wasn't even particularly interested in Callum coming to live on Ergo. Each no longer quite trusted the other because they were no longer the same, and they were afraid to exchange details of their lives in case they were laughed at or misunderstood. So Gulai didn't tell Phoebe about meeting Sophia, or her singing. But she went with her to the Ball dressed as a ghost and pretended to enjoy herself, dancing most of the evening with Darius Mobara – who had suddenly shot up above her, and had lost some of his awkward shyness, and was dressed as a lighthouse with a light flashing on top of his head. He was good company, but her mind kept wandering off to the five men at the cave and the ordeals they were facing. In the face of that, the party felt frivolous and boring.

She said an early good night to Darius and went home.

After three weeks, a few days into the new year, the initiates returned. In accordance with the old custom, Elijah, Calvin Tamara and Mannie Mobara slaughtered a sheep for the homecoming. Few were invited, and no women among them. That evening, Gulai ventured along the track and up the path to the clearing in front of Sophia's old cottage – keeping her distance, keeping to darkness, skirting the edge of the net of firelight. She wanted to see what it was that made a man, what transformation had taken place. At first she couldn't recognise the initiates, for their hair had been shorn off; their bald heads glowed in the firelight. Then all she could see were men eating, drinking out of a communal gourd, laughing and telling stories. It didn't look that different from the tavern – or did it?

Neither Charley nor Callum would talk about what had happened to them. "So, was it worth it?" she wanted to know on meeting Callum outside the shop the next day, her voice tightening.

Callum tilted his head, considering her question. He looked older with his long hair shorn, new growth spiking through his scalp. He took so long in answering that Gulai couldn't wait; out of her mouth came: "I mean, was it worth missing out on all the fun we were having? You've never even been to a Hunt or the Ball, it was such bad timing."

Callum shrugged.

Charley was so busy at the hospital he didn't have time to chat. The doctor was retaliating by insisting that Lena take some time off.

"Why did you do it?" Gulai asked, tailing him as he sterilised instruments.

"It came at the right time," he answered unhelpfully. "It made me face something about myself I've been avoiding for years." But he wouldn't elaborate.

Even Gilbert and Tomas were reticent. "It's not something you can talk about," said Gilbert. He'd hurt his shoulder during his time at Haven Cave, but wouldn't say how, and now wore his arm in a sling.

Gulai was sitting next to Gilbert on the step in front of his cottage, trying to figure out a way to extract information. "But you didn't want to go," she objected.

"I didn't understand."

"Understand what?"

"I said, it's not something you can talk about."

Gulai punched his thigh hard. Gilbert flinched away from her, offended. "What'd you do that for?"

"*It's not something I can talk about*," she mimicked, ashamed and frustrated.

"Why do you want to know anyway?"

Something tried to unfold its wings inside her; she felt the leash that tied her. "Why do you guys get to do the interesting things?" she said. "Why do girls always get left out?"

"Do you?" Gilbert said, genuinely surprised.

"Sure – you get to do the lighthouse race and the Hunt and the fishing competition and the boat races, and now you're the ones going off on a secret camp!"

Gilbert shook his head. "I wouldn't put the other things in the same category," he objected. "Besides, would you really want to do those things, like the lighthouse race and the Hunt?"

"Of course, they're fun and daring and dirty and wild! You get your teeth into something, you feel part of something important, and afterwards you have something to show for it – a broken bone, a huge fish, a prize, a dead heifer, a circumcision! All us girls have got is another pile of dirty dishes!" Her face was heating up.

Gilbert smiled. "You feel strongly about this, don't you? I've never heard you say so much in one go!"

Gulai blazed. "Oh, for God's sake!" And although he tried to call her back, she left, furious.

She would have suffered more, except that she was involved in a project of her own that had begun to consume her. The words of the vulcanologist had unsettled her; they had shifted the earth beneath her feet. Her mood was restless, it dragged her up and down the village in search of – what? She found that since meeting Dr Turner, her singing trailed off mid-improvisation, as though a track she'd been following had ended in a thicket. A strange ringing in her ears was driving her crazy, even waking her at night. She would stand at the Point and sing the tone of the note in her ear, she would dive into water to try to rinse it out of her head, but nothing would stop it. Her father called it tinnitus, and said she would have to learn to live with it; but one morning while walking down to Mr Bacon's, the world fell suddenly silent, and in that moment she heard something she recognised deeply, although it felt like she was hearing it for the first time.

Octavia Pelani was singing to her new granddaughter on her front veranda. An old song, a song plaited into the long thread that linked generations, a song for growing babies into the world. Gulai stood and listened, mesmerised, memorising the pattern of words she had almost forgotten, words linked into a round of meaning, into a net to catch a child as she falls asleep, words and music woven together into a lilting basket cradle.

Gulai ran down to the lighthouse with this new treasure. She sang the lullaby over and over, finding that it grew with singing into something bigger than a basket; it was a ship she could set sail on, it grew wings and could fly. She turned back to the village in search of more.

She began to visit the old people especially, probing them to think back to all the songs that were lying disused and nearly forgotten in the dusty cupboards of their minds. Some she had heard before, others were entirely new to her. The old people laughed with pleasure to share what they remembered; their voices released the old trembling melodies from their memories onto the air as though shaking out old, folded tapestries; they smiled, clapping the rhythm with their knobbly hands. Polly Bagonata even got up onto her thin legs to wobble and weave around her sitting room to the rhythm of the song in her throat. Gulai gathered lullabies and ballads, songs for weddings and funerals, christenings and initiations, childbirth and harvesting, songs of thanks and lament, of desire and mourning, songs about love and losing your way, about survival and redemption, songs that had origins in the time before the island, in the lands of the masters and of the slaves, songs remoulded by weather and hardship and changed circumstances and intermarriage, altered by time and children and shifting memory. She gathered up the seeds of them and planted them again, deep inside herself.

Gulai went to the lookout, she went to the Point, she went to the harbour wall at night, and she sang these songs to the wind and the waves. As she fed the songs, growing them fat, bringing them back to new life, so the songs fed her. Her heart was overflowing; there was a yearning in her, a desire for life in all its shapes and guises.

Soon after the February ship sailed for the mainland, taking Phoebe and the students with it, the storms arrived, much too early for that time of year. The commotion of the skies incited the ocean into its own madness, the frenzy of the elements tearing at stability and structure, unravelling the edges of things, delighting in mayhem like giant boisterous children. The boats were unable to go out, part of Mannie Mobara's roof came off, and young Hannah Tamara was almost blown away as she struggled through the raging weather to her grandmother's cottage across the road; it was only the nets hung up and drying that caught her before she was blown into the harbour. Yet this was the weather Gulai loved to sing in the most; she loved to match her voice to the voice of the storm, entering into the tempest as the tempest entered into her. It was too dangerous to go far from home, so she struggled to the outcrop of rocks at the back of the house, where there was some shelter from the full force of the winds roaring across open reaches of sea all the way from Antarctica. There she sang, opening herself to the torrent of life flowing through her. One night, spent, she went home and dreamt of a shipwreck, of a wooden ship run aground and a sea full of floundering people.

The next morning, the storm had exhausted itself; outside the birds were singing loudly with relief. There was a knock at the door while Gulai was making breakfast. It was young Peter Schoones and Frank Bardelli junior, both excited, breathless from running, fighting with each other for the right to be the bearer of important news. A yacht had run aground at the Point in the early hours; a sailor had by some miracle survived, but he was in mortal danger, would the doctor please come now. Her father grabbed his bag and hurried off to do what he could.

Gulai followed, a stone in her belly. A crowd had gathered in front of the hospital, watching Yero and Charley lifting a stretcher out of the back of the police vehicle. Before she could see who was on it or how badly hurt he was, they had disappeared inside.

Gulai knew this was her fault. She had spent hours singing into the daemon wind, throwing her voice like a net onto the air, willing another life towards hers – her yearning a magnet confusing the compasses of sailors, her desire a jagged rock.

Later, unable to concentrate, she went out again, restless, tormented, wanting to hear how the sailor was doing. Down at the harbour, a crowd was watching Frank's longboat tow the yacht in; it was listing to starboard and trailing a broken mast. As Gulai joined the crowd, Officer Bardelli emerged from the cabin and came ashore in Mannie's dinghy with some information. The sailor's name was Hal Brink, he was seventeen years old, and he'd been trying to break the record for the youngest sailor to circumnavigate the world solo.

The villagers shook their heads, contemplating the tiny yacht. He must be mad, they said. Don't these mainlanders understand the power of the elements? What is this obsession with breaking records – you end up breaking bones instead. They made the sign to ward off evil and said their prayers, for they felt sorry for him, so far from home. It's better to die in your own bed, some said, and others breathed in sharply at this, for the sailor was not yet dead; there could be lots more life left in him, who were they to say?

Gulai went up to the hospital and found her father having a tea break, puffing on a cigarette. "How is he?" she asked.

The doctor shrugged noncommittally. "Punctured lung, head injury. He's come round."

"Will he . . . live?"

The doctor frowned. "Course he'll live. He's been admitted to the best hospital for miles around."

Gulai couldn't help admiring her father, a man who could pull someone back from the land of the dead. "His name's Hal," she said.

"He told me."

"Can I see him?"

"Go cheer him up. Just don't make him laugh, it'll make the poor sod cry." The doctor stubbed his cigarette out. "Stupid bastard," he mumbled.

Hal was in the bed Gulai's father had occupied, his eyes closed. His upper torso was bare in the air-conditioned room, a tube sticking bizarrely out of the side of his chest, a drip winding into an arm. On his temple, under his long blond fringe, rose a bluish swelling. His straggly beard framed a large mouth that pulled in shallow breaths. His hands lay either side of his body on the sheet: strong rough hands with bitten nails. As Gulai watched this broken bronze god who had emerged from the sea – her sea, washed up because of her – he frowned briefly, and swallowed, his larynx bobbing up and down in his throat like a buoy over a wave. She didn't want to disturb him. She wanted to sit and watch over him like a guardian angel.

He opened his eyes and looked straight into hers. "Who're you?" he asked.

"Gulai," she said. "I'm sorry." He would never know why.

Hal winced, then closed his eyes again, shutting her out.

"They brought your yacht into the harbour, it's still afloat."

"It doesn't matter."

How could it not matter?

Charley entered with lunch. Gulai helped to prop Hal up, the bottle connected to the tubing from his chest bubbling every time he coughed. Interest flickered in his face when he saw his lunch of crayfish and chips. Charley pointed out, tact-lessly, that it wasn't often they had a nearly famous person arrive on the island, and that he'd therefore organised an appropriately sumptuous meal. Gulai watched Hal wolf the food down, then sink back, exhausted from the effort of eating.

"It must've been a long time since you ate anything fresh," commented Charley, taking Hal's blood pressure. "I'll bring you spinach tomorrow. I'm growing some." He shone a light into Hal's eyes and filled something in on the chart at the foot of his bed. "Living on this island isn't a hell of a lot different to living on a boat, except it doesn't rock or crash into other things," he rambled on. "But we do have a pending natural disaster which they say could sink us any time. Imagine surviving a shipwreck only to be sunk by a volcano. That would be taking bad luck too far." He closed the curtains. "Siesta time. Visiting hours are over, Gulai." He offered Hal some painkillers. "You want Gulai to come back later? She's really good at making you feel welcome when you first arrive."

Hal shrugged, unconcerned. "Maybe. Tomorrow."

Charley put an arm around Gulai as they walked down the passage. "Fellow's lost his social skills, been alone too long. You could help him discover them again, you know. Imagine volunteering for solitary confinement on the back of a bucking bronco for six months!"

Chapter Four

When Gulai went to visit Hal again, the doctor was checking the chest drain. He shook his head. A couple more days, he said, I'll give it a couple more days. Then what, Gulai wanted to ask; but she knew the doctor wasn't going to reveal all the millions of thoughts and decisions that marched around in his brain.

"You're only seventeen," said the doctor, checking Hal's chart. Hal nodded. "Have you finished school?" the doctor demanded, more an accusation than a question.

Hal shrugged. "Some things are more important," he said, his eyes tracing the perimeter of a stain on the ceiling.

The doctor made a sound somewhere between clearing his throat and disgust. Gulai tensed, wanting to protect the broken sailor; yet she also wanted to shake Hal, to say to him: how could you put everything into this one venture, risk your whole life, so that now it's gone you lie there like a husk, pretending nothing matters?

"You're going to be here a while," the doctor observed, pacing round the end of Hal's bed, preparing to deliver a lecture. "Next ship's in May. Looks like you've been given an extended opportunity to think things over, sort out your priorities."

Hal's face set, but he said nothing.

"Passion is a funny thing, you know, it can lead you by the nose into dead ends, it can lead you over precipices and onto rocks." The doctor caught his reflection in the mirror over the wash basin, and paused to run his fingers through his thinning grey hair, encouraging it to lie quietly over his crown. He glanced at Hal to check that he was listening, then continued: "Youth is wasted on the young, you've heard that before. Look at you, in your prime, wasting your life on a plank in the middle of the ocean, and for what? So you'll go down in some book? So people will remember you?"

Hal's face flushed red. Say something, thought Gulai. This is none of my father's business. How dare he do this with you pinned to the bed, unable to leave.

"You've got courage and tenacity, I'll grant you that," the doctor continued, enjoying himself. "Good qualities, those, in anyone. Put them to good use! Find an occupation that'll get you somewhere, for God's sake. Being shipwrecked on Ergo is not what counts on a CV!"

He harrumphed again, looked at his watch and left the room. Gulai sat awkwardly in the ensuing silence, trying to find the right poultice to soothe her father's lashing.

"He's . . . he's not always like that," she lied. "Don't mind what he says."

Nothing, no response.

"Personally, I think it's wonderful what you've done."

"I don't care what you think." He turned his head away, shutting her out.

Then why are you angry, Gulai wanted to point out angrily; you're a liar, and anyway, I'm not the enemy.

She left, and went looking for Callum to ask him to go over some work with her, to help get the stranger out of her head. But she found only Elijah at home, carving a dolphin out of a piece of driftwood that already held the shape in its grain and weathering. He told Gulai that Callum had gone over to Impossible with Mannie to visit his mother – something she'd wanted to do herself for ages, she'd specifically told Callum, and now she was left out, left behind again. She wanted to scream.

She was too distracted to engage with her school history project, about the early explorers who'd sailed away from home towards the horizon, drawn by adventure and fortune and fame, despite their fear of the dragons said to live beyond the edge of the world. Well, beyond the edge of the world was where Gulai lived, she lived in the place of dragons; she could feel one heaving, breathing in her right now: smouldering, igniting, wanting to set the world alight and take all sailors with her.

She walked all the way to Haven Cave by herself. Haven Cave, now sacred ground. On the path were chicken feet tied to a stick as warning. She continued down the rocky path in the drizzling wind to where the mouth of the cave yawned, and took refuge. She would make up her own initiation, she would defy them all.

The interior had been converted into a room, with part of the mouth boarded up against the elements, dry reeds covering the earth and rock floor, a couple of packing cases to serve as chairs and tables, and a few old mattresses placed where there was level ground. Candles dripped long white stalactites from rocky ledges, and near the entrance was evidence of a fireplace.

Gulai curled up miserably on a mattress, but soon became cold and bored and hungry. She went home to a hot bath, vowing never to go near the sailor again.

Chapter Five

Two days later, the doctor told Sister Lena that the chest drain could come out, and to prepare a tray of instruments. After that, Hal was free to go – although he could go nowhere but the island, for his yacht was lying like a beaten dog in the harbour, listing to one side. He needed to assess the damage and order replacement parts from the mainland, to arrive with the May ship. Then he needed to decide whether he was going to leave with the ship, or wait till Frank and Mannie had completed the repairs, then sail home across the remaining span of sea.

Hal stood with his hands on his hips looking at his home, for the yacht had been his home for one hundred and sixty-two days non-stop; he had almost circumnavigated the globe and made it back home, almost breaking the record. But almost doesn't count.

Almost wasn't nearly good enough.

He went to the police station to radio his parents and his sponsors, and from there he went with the doctor to his house, for the doctor had invited him to stay until the May ship arrived.

"I'm warning you," the doctor said as they went inside, "not to interfere with my daughter." Across the room Gulai raised her head from her assignment. "She's going to be a lawyer, aren't you, Gail?"

This was the first Gulai had heard of her father's plans for her. Hal looked from Gulai to the doctor, only now seeming to register that she was his daughter. She flushed, angry and embarrassed. "I don't know, I thought perhaps I'd . . ." – *be a singer* came to mind; *I thought I'd fill the world with sounds the ear longs to hear, with groundswell sounds that shift and lighten life and make it somehow bearable, sounds to expand a constricted heart into life unfurling, greening, burning . . .*

"You'll sleep here," said the doctor, ushering Hal into his study. Nobody, absolutely nobody had consulted with Gulai about this. She refused to live with a surly boy who ignored her. She felt the beast in her growl, pacing, raging, caged. She got up and left, and found herself knocking at Elijah's door. Callum opened it, his hair starting to spring back into a curly mess.

"Why the hell did you go without me!"

"What?"

"I told you I wanted to go to Impossible!"

"Good morning, Gulai," said Callum slowly, pointedly. "Would you like to come in?"

To Gulai's embarrassment, she felt tears threatening. "Nobody listens to me! Nobody cares how I feel!"

Then somehow she had leaned too far forward, or Callum had stepped towards her; somehow he was holding her against his chest and stroking her hair. It felt so good, Gulai pulled away. "Don't treat me like a baby!"

"I'm not!"

"Yes, you are!" Gulai turned and ran away down the track. She heard Callum chasing after her. She turned, furious, and felt a sharp twisting stab in her ankle. Gasping, she sank to the ground.

"What? What, Gulai?"

So Gulai allowed Callum to hold her while she cried into his shoulder from the pain of it all, the pain of ankles and shipwreck, broken threads and letters never sent, of shame and desire, of lost fathers and lost songs, banishment and the empty reaches of dark sea between islands and people, drowned mayors and fallen girls . . . and all the while her ankle was swelling, till Callum hoisted her onto his back and carried her, weeping, all the way down the track to the hospital, to the admonishing doctor and the X-ray machine, and strapping and crutches.

Now she was stuck, stuck at home with her foot up on pillows and Cyn fussing about all the extra work she had to do, and the stranger sailor wafting in and out like a dislocated, anxious ghost. Get the washed-up waif to wash up the dishes, Cyn, thought Gulai angrily. After six months of living alone, he surely knows how to do that. But she said nothing, and Cyn didn't ask and Hal didn't offer.

Callum came round to do schoolwork. He explained he hadn't been able to find her the day he went over to his mother's, and Mannie had been in a hurry, for Octavia Pelani's granddaughter was in need of remedies and the weather was perfect for the crossing. But Gulai couldn't get rid of her anger, it swelled inside her. When the milk spilt as she was pouring it, she swore and Cyn smacked her shoulder for it, and when she looked again in the mirror, new pimples had broken out, and when her father started up again one evening about her future life as a lawyer, she felt hot tears pricking under her lids. Everything was being done to her, life and people leaning on her with no room for her own breathing and gestures, no thought in her that wasn't planted there by someone else for their own purpose. She felt chained to history and circumstance, and to this speck of land barely poking above the tumbling hungry sea.

She wrote to Phoebe, telling her she was coming to the mainland, that she felt like a prisoner on Alcatraz, like Prometheus chained to a rock, eagles pecking at her liver, like Psyche trying to sort a mountain of seeds, hopeless, hopeless – even when Callum brought a remedy for her ankle from his mother, even when Hal gave her a book to read about sailing. (Was he not interested in anything else?)

"It's good," he offered, sitting carefully across from her, his knee jigging. "And it's a way to leave the house."

He was talking about reading, he was making an effort. Gulai felt a softening in her. "Weren't you lonely? All that time at sea?"

Hal inclined his head, his gaze fidgeting around the room. He didn't belong here, Gulai could see that.

"Don't you have anyone special in your life?" she probed. "Anyone you're looking forward to seeing at home?"

Hal pulled one corner of his mouth into a half-smile, half-grimace. "Sure, but . . ."

"What?"

He cracked his knuckles – one hand then the other. "People aren't . . . reliable. They let you down." He stood abruptly, pulling his woollen cap on, for it was blustery outside. "I'm going fishing," he said, and left, severing her thread as he went.

This from a man who had been let down by the sea, by the wind, by God, thought Gulai. Or maybe that wasn't personal. Perhaps that's easier to come to terms with than when people betray you and love turns sour. She imagined his heart had been broken, that this voyage had been a means of escape. Hal's feelings were caught on rocks, stranded as the full tide of love receded. Gulai's heart went out like a lifeboat, a lifeline; she wanted to call out to him, call him back, explain that he needn't be afraid. She turned to her schoolwork, but it had lost all meaning.

A knock at the door. No one else was at home, so Gulai swung herself across the room on her crutches and opened the door. Callum was outside with a wheelchair. "I've come to take you for a walk," he said, offering her the seat. "It's lovely out." The rain had stopped, so Gulai pulled on her anorak and sank into the chair, leaving her crutches behind.

"You are remarkable, Callum Tamara," she laughed.

He trundled her down the road towards the harbour – Gulai anxious at not being in control of her own propulsion, yet pleased she hadn't been forgotten. It was twilight, the air threaded through with smells unwinding from the fisherfolk as they passed on their way home to their baths. They greeted and smiled to see Callum propelling his charge, Gulai's strapped and elevated foot on the footrest leading the way like the prow of a ship. He pushed her round to the breakwater, where they stopped to watch the last of the fishing boats come in, guided by the long, beckoning arm of the lighthouse and the twinkling village lights, trailing seabirds hungry for the scraps of the day's catch. Seals flopped around on the stony beach below, or poked their brown heads through the slope and fall of the ocean's surface like periscopes, surveying the non-aquatic world. Waves from over the horizon rolled in to prostrate themselves with an exhausted sigh on the shale, and through a breach in the clouds a new moon punctured the dark evening sky with its light. Over to the east, a light blinked on Impossible.

Then Callum leaned over her, awkwardly trying to put his

mouth to hers. She pushed him away, what did he think . . .?

"I . . . I'm sorry," he stammered, turning away.

Gulai's heart raced with bewilderment. She couldn't look at Callum, couldn't walk away. She glanced sideways; Callum was sitting on the low wall next to her wheelchair, his shoulders hunched, his hands gripping the cement blocks either side of him, his eyes fixed on a boat negotiating the entrance to the harbour. What had he done? He was too young for her, too contrary, too . . . naïve, otherworldly, strange. Not good-looking enough. She looked away, not knowing what to say, not wanting to hurt or encourage him.

It should have been Hal sitting next to her.

"We'd better go back," she said, the evening spoilt. How dare he bring her out here and force this on her when she was captive, powerless, marooned! Better pretend it had never happened.

Yet back home, she felt invigorated, blessed with the knowledge that she was desirable, that men could love her. Hal was home with a catch of fish; Callum excused himself and disappeared into the night, looking small and ridiculous pushing the empty wheelchair.

Hal was in the kitchen making supper, slicing strips of fresh raw fish and laying them out on a plate together with a greenish paste, a bowl of soy sauce, and a mound of pink, translucent flakes. "D'you like sushi?" asked Hal awkwardly. Gulai could see he was trying to be sociable.

"I love it," she said, not knowing what sushi was.

A stamping at the front door announced the arrival of the doctor. He took one look at the plate and, to Gulai's surprise, took a piece of the raw fish, immersed it in the soy sauce and the green paste and dropped it into his mouth, followed by a few pink slices. He groaned with delight. "Haven't had sushi for years, not since I've been living in this arse end of the world!" he exclaimed. "Where did you get the wasabi and ginger?"

"I keep it on board," explained Hal. "Best way to eat fish freshly caught."

Gulai cautiously sampled the sushi, following her father's example. It took one moment and her taste buds were wildly awake – followed by a sudden and extreme pain in her sinuses. She gasped, her nasal cavities igniting. "You overdid the wasabi," laughed the doctor, pouring whiskies for himself and Hal. "Cheers!" He raised his glass to the sailor. "Here's to your future running a sushi restaurant, Hal! Gail, get used to it. All the best lawyers on the mainland eat sushi."

Chapter Six

Desire and restraint, those quarrelsome twins, those contrary dragons of character and principle that spat and wrangle – one driving the impulse to proceed, one standing guardian at the gate. One convinces you you will perish if you do not enter, the other stands keeper of that thing just beyond your reach, that thing forbidden – that, once experienced, will alter all else that follows, for better or for worse. Which one to choose today, on which scaly back to saddle your fortune: dragon Yes or dragon No? For they are made equal, yet they approach through different portals: one pouring hot, impulsive resolve into the funnel of your heart, the other stating its case down the spine of your mind: look to the future, hold fast lest all be burned and laid to waste. Which way? Which way? They stand astride the crossroads of every waking moment, forcing a choice, whether we know it or not.

One night Gulai allowed Hal in; she allowed a stranded sailor to bury his feelings inside her so as not to know them – all his disappointment and anger, all his loneliness and self-blame, all his fear and yearning. He was waiting on the sofa for her one night when the doctor and Cyn were out playing poker, with a look on his face of such sorrow and desire that Gulai sat beside him to comfort him. Without a word he kissed her, and when she did not object he took her down the passage to her bedroom, where she allowed him to take off her clothes. She didn't want to hurt him or be a further cause of sorrow and hardship, for had he not suffered enough? Perhaps there was some respite here for them both, some pleasure and restoration. So she did not object, and he laid her down upon the bed and set sail upon her, the salt of his skin on her lips, the wind of his breathing in her hair, the waves of him rolling through her; and her thoughts slid away to Raef and Sasha, and Callum's sad face turning away, and her father, and fear. Then she thought of fresh raw fish arranged on a plate, laid out like an offering, a sacrifice, the moist pink flesh exposed and vulnerable, and she prayed that this time things could be different – that she could find a way to set sail with this man to a place where people lived happily ever after . . . yet all the while feeling how her body was coming apart, splitting in two after the sudden pain of irruption, her lower body sinking like an anchor, heavy and dead, while her upper body filled with the full sail of hope, of going somewhere. Also, she was clenched with worry about protection and contraception; but surely there wasn't a problem – he had been alone for so long, and she was just about to start her period . . . or was she? She couldn't quite remember, and then she also couldn't remember whether that particular time was safe or not; but surely only once didn't matter? Dragon Yes and dragon No arguing again . . . and then it was too late. Hal gave a deep moan and rolled off her and lay looking at the ceiling, his forehead wet with sweat, his hand an anchor on her belly; although who was anchoring whom Gulai did not know. All she knew was that her ears were tuned like radar for the sound of her father returning, her mind occupied with how fast Hal could get under the bed if he needed to.

Hal sighed beside her, and she was glad of the comfort she'd given him, and about the possibility that he might love her. She turned her face to him and saw with a stab of disappointment that he had fallen asleep. She wriggled slowly out from under his hand and limped to the bathroom. Seeing blood on the toilet paper, she was glad that this stranger had been the one to open her, this man who could open the world to her as she would open his heart to trust. While she ran a bath, she went and woke him, gently prising him out of her bed, relishing the moment he kissed her forehead before he fell into a deep sleep again on the bed in her father's study. Above the bed were shelves stacked with books about the mysteries of the body, books which she had dipped into now and then over the years to try to understand her father and herself, none of them describing the way she felt now – rummaged through, alive in a different kind of way, as though Hal's entry had realigned her very centre and all the cells connected to it. She got into the bath and soaked their secretions away, anxiety lurking on the periphery, praying for all to end well, praying, believing in her prayer.

That night realigned everything around her too: she had stepped into a magic circle. Everything looked fresher, greener, more abundantly alive; she felt protected and made whole by the enchantment, yet also strangely ill: feverish, restless, her centre now joined by a thread to Hal's, a thread that constantly pulled at her. The whole universe was run through with invisible threads that bound them mysteriously together. She loved the sound of his footsteps as they entered the house, the sound of him brushing his teeth, the fall of his blond hair to his shoulder, the way he jigged his knee and gave a half-smile when he found it difficult to speak, the way he took the risk of making love to her in her father's house after her father had forbidden it, his toes, all the same length except for the baby one. She couldn't bear it when he went out alone at night to fish, in case he injured himself; nor could she stand his expression on those occasions when he was far away, thinking of things she could not begin to imagine, places he'd been to, people he knew. She wished she could enter him fully, permanently; find out who he was, find him out.

They became increasingly daring, making love in the early morning when Hal could not sleep and came to her bed. They made love silently, slowly, on the carpet or against the wall – for Gulai's bed had a tell-tale squeak that could not be reme-died; dragon No resided there, trying to give them away, trying to spoil everything with his cry: No, No, No; and every time Yes finding a way past to the intimate garden, to the place of enchantment and forgetting, to the caress that both erases and renews like pleasurable drowning, the merged couple gracefully suspended in a boundless and warm sea, carried on currents to a secluded beach where the high tide daily prepares the sand to receive the first paired footprints again.

She was afraid of pregnancy more than disease; when she saw the miracle of her period she took it as a sign: they were blessed, everything would be fine.

The May ship came, with the new mast and some marine ply and fibreglass for the repairs to Hal's yacht – and with it fear of the future, for what was to happen? Gulai was afraid to mention it and Hal said nothing, increasingly turning away towards the task of repairing the yacht, always down at the boatyard with Frank and Mannie. Fear frayed at the edges of her happiness, tightening her heart: she knew very little about this person to whom she had entrusted her self.

One morning he said, "Are you coming with me?"

A moment of blinding happiness flashed through her, then the clamp again: fear of her father, of seizing this thing she wanted more than anything in the world, dragon Yes carrying her in his maw by the scruff of her neck, his breath hot on her shoulders. She was consumed with desire to find a way into the beginning of her life.

She made plans: she would sail away with Hal without telling her father; she would go to the mainland and look up the professor of music and get recorded and become famous. She and Hal would be together for the rest of time, have beautiful children with blond hair and toes all the same length except for the baby one. Or she would ask her father – no, she would beg him or threaten to kill herself, and he would have to agree to send her to school on the mainland, which would mean being a boarder, but she would get special permission to live with Hal and his parents, and they would love her and take her in as their daughter, and she and Hal would get married and live happily ever after. Or her father would say No. No. No. Never – and she would throw herself off the cliff at Ike's Gully, and teach him not to try to make her something she wasn't: a lawyer, and a woman who would never fall in love with sailors. Or her father would say, Not Yet, wait till you go to university. He couldn't stop her then, studying to be a lawyer would require living on the mainland. But that meant not seeing Hal for two whole years, unless he happened to sail past on his travels, and she could not bear that; he was bound to find someone else.

Time was running out. The mast was up and the repairs to the hull were going better than anticipated due to good weather. The following day they were going to launch the yacht.

"I want to go to boarding school," she told the doctor that evening. "I want to go to school on the mainland."

The doctor's eyes narrowed over the piece of pie perched on the end of his fork, which had come to a halt halfway to his mouth. He glanced at Hal. "This has nothing to do with you, has it?"

Hal shrugged. "It's Gulai's life."

The doctor's fork clattered onto his plate. "Gail," he stressed. "Her name is Gail! For God's sake!"

Bad start. Gulai concentrated on keeping her voice even and looking straight and innocently into her father's eyes. "Hal and I get on, but it's not because of him. I miss Phoebe and my other friends. Having Hal around reminds me how lonely I am." She arranged her expression into a lonely and sad face. "If I'm with my friends I'll feel happier and my marks will improve." Not that they'd been bad, but this idea might appeal to the doctor. "They say you have to get very good marks to get into law school, and if I'm in boarding school I'll have no distractions."

The doctor contemplated this, chewing his food slowly, his moustache riding confidently over the wave of his mouth. Gulai waited, forgetting her own food. Was it really going to be that easy?

The doctor swallowed. "Okay," he said. "Next year." He chased the mouthful with a draught of home-brew, his nod a stamp of approval. "I'm moving there myself, so you wouldn't have to board." Cyn looked up sharply. "I've spent long enough in this godforsaken hole. Time for both of us to move on, eh, Gail?" The doctor narrowed his eyes again, and peered at Gulai as into a microscope.

"I . . . I'd like to go earlier," she said.

"May ship's gone, pointless going with the September ship. Year's nearly over."

"Hal's offered me a lift."

The doctor's suspicions were confirmed. He swivelled, setting his sights on Hal. "Never!" he roared.

Cyn leapt up from the table and fled the room crying. They heard the bedroom door slam shut. The doctor glowered. "What the hell's got into her?" he said, flinging his napkin onto the table and standing up, his chair protesting as it jerked backwards. He wagged a finger at them. "I will find out if there's a traitor in this house, mark my words." He pulled on his jacket. Gulai knew where he was going. To the tavern, to the comfort of the bottle. The doctor turned to Hal. "From tomorrow you sleep in your floating hotel, you hear me!" He was gone, also banging the door behind him.

Hal was already on his feet and taking his all-weather gear off the coat rack.

"Where are you going?" asked Gulai, alarmed.

"Fishing," he said.

"Please," Gulai pleaded, "not now!"

But Hal was gone, into the night, out of the same door as her father, tearing a piece of the room away with him. She was left with Cyn, weeping in the bedroom.

She would run away with Hal. The alternative was suddenly horrendous.

Orion ordered a drink and went to sit at a table near the fire. He looked down at his hands, at the way the contractures of his palms were starting to pull his fingers closed into fists, starting with the little ones. Of late, he was unable to open up the little finger on his right hand enough to encompass a glass. He always used his left to raise his whisky to his lips, so as not to draw attention to this fact. The island brew was responsible, he was sure, terrible stuff. Wouldn't touch it again.

It was time to leave, he knew that. He didn't want to die in this hellhole. And Gail – she needed a broader education, and to meet her grandparents. He ordered another double, to douse the old anger smouldering in him. He would make sure they met her soon, so they would see what he was capable of, see the creature of pure beauty he had created in the image of her mother, the woman he'd loved and that his parents had rejected. Yes, he decided, they must meet Gail before she was spoilt by some fool man and turned into whore or housewife. He would open their eyes to what they'd made him suffer – failing, always failing in their eyes; they would see what they had done and apologise.

The dread was leaving him. Miracle stuff, this golden fluid; cost a fortune in this part of the world, all imported, but worth every cent. Soon the room warmed up, and sharp, hard edges blurred into nothing of consequence; soon he was laughing with Samuel Pelani about the time he pulled maggots out of Sally Tamara's ear – mad old woman thought she was getting migraines.

So it was with irritation that he found Charley in uniform at his elbow, saying he'd better come, Kali Mobara had glass in her foot. You know what to do, Orion told him. Call me when there's a real emergency. Terrible job he had, when you couldn't have a break, not one single break in eighteen years. And who did that Charley think he was, with that look on his face – disapproving, how dare he! Orion grabbed the dish-cloth Samuel was using to wipe beer off the counter and rubbed it hard into Charley's face. Suddenly Frank was there, and Mr Bacon, pulling him off Charley on the floor, had he fallen? Stupid git to get in the way.

He shrugged them off and headed for home, sick to death of them all. It was way overdue. He and Gail were leaving.

Chapter Seven

The yacht was ready, riding at anchor in the harbour. Hal was doing the final preparations: stocking up from Mr Bacon's shop, filling the water and petrol tanks, checking the oil and ballast. He and Gulai had hardly spoken to each other since the scene at the dinner table, as the doctor was on the prowl. Gulai felt ill, displaced, filled with both dread and longing. From the harbour wall she watched Hal scrubbing the deck down. Looking at the sea, she knew she would have to stay. It wasn't her father that was going to stop her, it was sea sickness. Like David Peters, who had nearly died at sea as a boy, vomiting his guts out on a fishing expedition, and had never set foot on a boat again; he worked as the island electrician to temper the scorn. She was afraid of the open sea and of dying, and although it would feel like eating razor blades, she could wait till February. But she had to see Hal alone before he left. That evening, when her father set off for the tavern and Cyn was over at Rumer's, she took her chance, pulling on her boots and all-weather gear, for rain had come blustering down. Who knew, maybe the storm would worsen instead of abating, perhaps Hal would be forced to stay longer. Why was he in such a hurry, anyway? He'd been gone so long, surely a few more days or even weeks wouldn't matter.

She opened the front door to find Hal stamping up the path, his face cold in her neck with the weather. Without a word, she drew him inside the house, inside her bedroom, inside her body. Come to me, she offered, find your home in me. Her face was wet, her chest heaving with the sadness of it all, this wrenching apart, this forced separation when it was obvious they belonged together. Hal kissed her eyes, her face, her body, opening her pores to pain and desire, to hope and loss, as they tossed together in the boat of her bed, dragon No in the springs beneath her squealing: Take care! Take care! No good will come of this! So engrossed was she in her journey of heartache and release that she did not hear the front door opening, nor the bedroom door opening; it was only when her father roared that she surfaced – Hal springing off her as the doctor rained blows down on him, Hal's pale, vulnerable body lunging for the bedroom door, the doctor following, bellowing, beating with his fists, beside himself with rage. Gulai cowered in the corner, her blankets pulled up over her naked terror, hearing the clack of the lock as Hal barricaded himself in the bathroom, her father trying to splinter down the door. The fear bundled in her belly tore open; she found herself surprisingly outside herself and looking in, floating above the house like a ghost, the roof off or turned transparent, looking down at these two men either side of the door – fighting over what? Gulai, that's what, they were fighting over her like duellers, like knights astride horses, their lances set to prod each other off and into the mud of shame and disgrace. For a mad moment it felt to Gulai like power. In that second, laughter ripped from her lips like lava. She was unstoppered, laughter welled up unrestrained out of her – bursts of it, sobbing wails of it, she was possessed by an uncontained flaming ghost, running, escaping, falling, filled with a madness that stopped at nothing.

Her father was leaning over her, his livid face swollen. The veins of his temples wound like roots about a boulder, his eyes were set wide and wild with rage. She felt his hands – the hands that had delivered her life – tying off her outburst, closing themselves about her neck, and she smelt the boozy, smoky smell of his breath fanning her face. The noose of his hands tightened, trapping her breath inside her body; she felt her own hands scrabbling and tugging at his, wanting to explain, to take it all back, to ask for just enough breath to tell him she was sorry. Her head was exploding, her chest burning, red spots flaring in front of her eyes, she was set on fire, hanged, drowned, her treason held up to the world by her father's large hands; it was over, everything was disappearing, hazy and blurred, fading and dreamlike . . .

Her father released his grip; blood rushed with a painful burst into her head. The ceiling light flared with sudden brilliance and a great gasp of air flooded her chest, the first breath of a second chance at life, turning at once into a sob, a hoarse and cracked wailing that flailed around the room. Nausea balled in her stomach as she realised what her father had been doing, thank God he had stopped, thank God he . . .

The doctor was face down in her lap, the back of his head a boggy mess of bloody, grey hair. Hal was standing naked behind him, his face white with shock, holding a length of driftwood with two hands carved at either end. The end with the fist was smeared with blood.

Chapter Eight

Officer Bardelli was taking strain. She was good at her job – settling disputes, keeping law and order, being the right-hand person to the mayor. But this was an unusual event. It was the first time in living memory that there'd been a murder on the island. Unless you counted . . . She put that thought firmly aside, as she had many times over the past fifteen years. Both the doctor and Clarence had declared that death a suicide, and she'd accepted that – even though sometimes she would dream of falling, and wake feeling sick to her stomach. This was different: a clear case of one person killing another.

In front of the council that morning, Hal had repeated his story without hesitation or doubt, even when the mayor lost his temper and called him an ungrateful bastard and a liar. Councillor Jerome Peters took the mayor outside for a moment, indicating that Officer Bardelli should return Hal to the cell.

When the meeting resumed, both the mayor and councillor Peters wanted to call in mainland investigators to solve the crime, although it was by no means certain that the authorities would agree to the kind of expense involved: a chartered ship would cost a small fortune. Dorado felt a flicker of anger at their dismissal of her ability to do a thorough investigation, and found herself saying so. Councillor Peters stared at her with some surprise, as though he'd never really seen her before; the mayor responded, with irritation, that she'd never dealt with such a situation before, and therefore could not know what was involved.

Officer Bardelli pointed out that she would look a fool in the eyes of the mainland authorities if at least a preliminary investigation was not completed – and who knew, that might be all that was necessary. Gulai was still sedated at the hospital; when she came round several issues could be clarified.

The mayor retorted bitterly that she'd made a hash job of investigating his father's disappearance. Dorado looked up from taking the minutes, faltering a moment; had she? What else could she have done?

Councillor Peters intervened, pointing out that there were indeed aspects of the case that Officer Bardelli could easily pursue; he suggested they refrain from contacting the mainland until they had more information, or they would all look like fools. In conclusion, Officer Bardelli was given the mandate to come up with as many facts as possible in two days, so that a reasonable decision could be made, and the meeting was adjourned. Before the men left the room, she reminded them that everything that had been said was confidential. It was imperative that Gulai's story, when she came to tell it, was not influenced by what Hal had divulged.

Afterwards, Dorado found her heart racing. Where had she got the courage? She recognised that usually she either did not have an opinion, or did not say the thing that was burning at her lips in case she offended someone or turned out to be wrong. She watched from the sidelines as stories unfolded without her. Now she had spoken out. She was responsible for following this through, for standing up for her point of view.

Terrified, she set off for the hospital to wait for Gulai to wake.

There was crying; somewhere close, the sound rose and fell, stitching Gulai through. She opened her eyes and for a moment thought she was seven years old and a VIP, lying in a hospital bed and bunking school.

She tried to lift her head, surprised to feel that the strings of her neck were painful and wobbly, her head stuffed with heavy gauze. Charley was sitting next to the bed, blowing his nose. She reached out to him and he started.

"Gulai!" His eyes red-rimmed, his smile spilling relief. He stroked her forehead, easing her back onto the pillow.

"What's wrong?" she wanted to know, her voice cracking. "What's happened?" And then it came back like a slap: her father, her father!

She tried to get up, but Charley gently prevented her. "Lie quietly, you need to be still. You're in shock."

From what, she wondered; what had happened? It was a dream, her head was fuzzy with bad dreams. She didn't really want to know. She closed her eyes again and spiralled into deep sleep.

Next time she woke, Liesa was beside the bed. Gulai sat up. "Where is my father?" she croaked. She touched her neck and flinched at her own tenderness.

Liesa stroked the back of her hand.

A strong wind wound incessantly round the building, whining and whistling and banging. Hal. Had he left? How long had she been asleep? "Where is my father?" she asked again, dropping her legs over the side of the bed. Anxiety washed through her; why was Liesa looking at her in that peculiar way? Blood, she remembered the blood. "Is my father okay?" Afraid of what her father would do to her, do to Hal, afraid that Hal had left her. She stared at Liesa. "Why aren't you talking to me?"

"Your father is dead," said Liesa quietly. "Charley had to sedate you."

Dead. Doctors didn't die. There was some mistake.

She had to see Hal, sort this out. But Liesa told her Hal was being held in the jail. Gulai wanted to go to him; she struggled out of bed, groggy and confused. Liesa called out for Charley, and together they persuaded her to wait: Officer Bardelli was coming.

"You don't understand," she insisted. "Hal was just trying to stop my father . . ."

It was coming back in bits and pieces, as though the recent past had splintered and her brain was grappling, groping at pieces of flotsam as they drifted past, trying to retrieve the one piece that would make sense of the whole. "It was a flesh wound, he was just trying to stop . . ." It was too terrible, how could she face her father again after . . .?

Dead. It couldn't be – death was final, and she still had to work something out with her father, he would never allow . . . . dead. Gulai sat on the bed, slowly shaking her aching head. She looked up at Charley with wild eyes: it isn't true, it can't be, I will never forgive myself if it's true, don't you see, if he's dead it means . . .

Officer Bardelli at the door. "Hallo, Gulai," she said, sitting down.

"He didn't do it," pleaded Gulai, weeping. "He didn't! You have to believe me!"

"Slowly now." Officer Bardelli took out her notepad and sat down, looking official. "What happened last night?"

Gulai had seen movies where the accused said, "I won't say anything until I've spoken to my lawyer." Lawyers were people who made sure you weren't found guilty, no matter what you'd done. A lawyer was what her father wanted her to be. There were no lawyers on Ergo Island and no ship to bring one for months. And anyway, she was guilty, guilty, it didn't matter what had happened. He was only punishing her for disobeying him, he'd lost his temper because of the drinking; he wouldn't even remember it now, the drink made him forget. They could all just forget about it and carry on with their lives. He would be more careful about drink, she would become a lawyer, and she would spend her life helping guilty people. And Hal – he'd only been trying to stop the doctor; it was only a flesh wound, he wouldn't hurt a fly. Now he was being charged with what – assault? He'd been trying to help her, that's all, he was only . . . *what*? They surely weren't accusing him of . . . the doctor had saved his life!

"I can't remember," she sobbed.

"You said, when I came in, 'He didn't do it.' Who didn't do what? You do remember something . . ." Officer Bardelli was clipped and professional, pretending they didn't know each other. She saw right through Gulai, saw that she was a criminal.

"He didn't die, my father didn't die!"

"Do you want to see him?" Officer Bardelli leaned forward. Her face broke open; for a moment it fluttered with emotion. "You can see him if you'd like."

*

He was lying on the mortuary table, a replica of her father made out of some synthetic substance, looking strangely peaceful. Gulai stared at him, trying to comprehend. *I am an orphan* were the words that kept surfacing out of the turbulent mess. I am an orphan, I am an orphan. Or Phan. Orph An. Orphan Annie. She was an orphanannie, whatever that was. She shivered, cold as death in a cold room.

Gulai turned away, not wanting to touch him.

He couldn't do it, he was too upset. Death arrives in many guises, but Nelson rarely had to deal with violence. Raymond Pelani's head injury from his fall from the lighthouse; little Celia Mobara, gored by a bull; Will Mobara, washed up on rocks after drowning; Ben Peters when he'd slipped and cracked his head in his own bathroom, drunk. And that damn Tamara girl. Now the doctor's remains, his mother's lover's body, lay defenceless on the stainless-steel table, his grey hair crusted red. Nelson's job was to repair and prepare the corpse, rendering it fit for viewing at the funeral: washing away the spilt blood, sewing up the rent in the fabric of the scalp, plugging the orifices, carefully sewing closed the eyelids and mouth and applying make-up to approximate the look of peaceful sleep. But that was all wrong; what Nelson really wanted to do was to rage, to erupt, to display the doctor just as he was: look! He wanted to stand up high and shout to the whole village, pointing down into the coffin: look at what we have done to this man who gave up his mainland life and came here to help us, who devoted his whole life, twenty-four hours a day, to keeping us well and fit and sane. We have an international reputation as intermarrying idiots, now we will be seen as murderers too! Who would want to come and live in such a place, where the locals bite the hand that feeds them? Oh, he knew it was a mainland sailor who had wielded the murder weapon, and he would pay for that; but there were many factors that added up to murder. Nelson had known for some time that there were those who did not support the doctor the way that they should: sneaking off against the law to consult that woman, the one who'd consistently stood against progress and proper modern medicine.

A murder had happened while the island was in his charge. There was blood on his own hands. He lowered his head into them, turbulent, swirls of night invading the day. Nowhere to go but down.

Chapter Nine

Dorado sat in her office and contemplated the problem. Question: was it self-defence? Or defence of another? Had the boy tried to kill them both, first hitting the doctor over the head and then trying to rape and strangle the girl? Gulai was lucky to be alive. Why wouldn't she say what had happened? Who was she trying to protect – the boy or her father? Could lack of oxygen to the brain or the effects of the sedative cause someone with bruises round her neck and the fine red facial rash of strangulation to deny that anything had happened? The pocket notebook on forensics in the office was not particularly helpful on this point.

She had to act decisively, and quickly. The islanders were in a confusion of grief and disbelief, some baying for the stranger's blood. She had locked him up, partially for his own safety. Yero was at this very moment stationed on the sailor's yacht, searching for further evidence, also to protect the property against reprisals. Dorado believed implicitly in the maxim that the accused is innocent until proven guilty. Hal stuck to his story, insisting he be allowed to contact his parents. He was within his rights.

Without consulting the council, Dorado had radioed Hal's father, her official voice covering over the horror of the news she was delivering. Mr Brink had gone into a rage, saying he would get the best lawyer in the country onto her, she had better not lay a finger on his son, there must be some misunderstanding. She assured Mr Brink that everything was being done to pursue the truth; she would keep him informed. She passed the receiver to Hal and felt stricken to hear him sob when he spoke to his mother.

Now he lay in the cell with his face to the wall. Her emotions could not interfere. She knew very well that psychopaths could be very convincing, and nobody could vouch for the character of this young stranger washed up out of the blue. Imagine, spending six months alone at sea at a time in life when a young man should be having relationships, finishing his education, getting a job. He could have started out unstable, or ended up loony.

If only Clarence were still alive to help her. This was an international situation, not an internal matter. There was no room for mistakes, or the mainland authorities would have her neck. She considered the facts she'd garnered thus far:

1. The murder weapon was a piece of sculpted driftwood.
2. The clearest, most recent fingerprints on the sculpture belonged to Hal.
3. Death was ostensibly caused by a hard blow to the back of the head.
4. There were signs of a struggle in Gulai's bedroom, with blood on the bedclothes where the doctor had fallen.
5. In Hal's statement, he claimed that the doctor had been excessively drunk and had tried to strangle his own daughter.

6. With Charley's help, she had forcibly expelled the doctor's breath from his chest cavity and into a breath-alyser, and he had been way over the limit.
7. Hal's breath had been clean.
8. Gulai asserted that she could not remember anything.
9. There was evidence on Gulai's body of attempted strangulation.
10. There were scratch marks on the doctor's forearms.
11. Dorado had collected samples from underneath Gulai's fingernails.

Dorado got out the microscope and the samples. Following the instructions in the forensic notebook, she prepared the slide, hoping that staining solutions did not become ineffective with age. She put her eye to the eyepiece and turned the knob until a sea of particles came into view. There they were: sheets of cells coming up red with blue nuclei. Skin cells, from underneath Gulai's nails – skin that presumably had been scratched away from the doctor's forearms. In the absence of a doctor, she would have to ask Charley to help her examine both Gulai and Hal's bodies to ascertain whether they too bore any scratches.

Dorado had disliked the doctor ever since he'd seen her for a lump in her breast – and, with drink on his breath, had lingered a bit long over the examination. And because of the time no one could raise him from sleep when Absalom Pelani had a pain in his side, rolling around the bed and crying like a baby. Lena'd had to attend to him by herself till morning, when the doctor had struggled out of his hangover. He'd laughed it off as a kidney stone, saying Absalom would now have better regard for women, the pain of a stone was like labour. Dorado had been worried that the doctor's drinking would lead to a death one day; she'd had no idea it would be his own.

She looked down the microscope at the evidence again, and sighed. It was easy for the mainlanders to criticise, but there were so few resources here: no electron microscopy, no forensic laboratory. With access to such equipment, she could do her job properly, she could find out quickly and without doubt who the skin belonged to.

Dorado's main concern was to avert an international situation; then all she would have to deal with was the local one. Starting with Cyn, banging again on the office door, peering through the pane, her face ravaged with grief and rage. Dorado had locked the door and put a sign up outside, 'Do Not Disturb', just to get a chance to think and work. But here was Cyn again, demanding entry. Dorado let her in.

"This is an outrage! You cannot close the police station during a crisis! You . . ."

"We're not closed, we are trying to do our job, Mrs Peters."

The two women glared at each other, enemies to the last, having fought each other all those years for Clarence's affections.

Cyn was demanding that she get in mainland authorities to deal with the doctor's murder, implying that Dorado was not fit to do her job. Dorado had cause to wonder whether the mayor and councillor Peters had said something to their mother of the council's discussions. It gave her a distinct moment of pleasure to say, "I have forensic evidence that throws light on the case, but it is too sensitive to divulge at present. Now, if you don't mind, I have work to do. I can recommend Sister Lena, should you require grief counselling."

"Grief! You know *nothing* of grief! All those years you broke up our home, and now you harbour a criminal who . . . who's done it again! I am surrounded by evil! Evil!"

This woman was past reasoning, she was a menace. Dorado steered her towards the door.

"Let me go! How dare you lay your hands on me!"

"I have to remind you that obstructing the law is a criminal offence."

"I want to see the murderer! You have no right . . ."

"No one has been accused of murder at this stage. We are awaiting a statement from Gulai."

She wasn't prepared for what happened next. Cyn slapped her through the face. "Gail!" she sobbed. "The stupid whore's name is Gail!"

Chapter Ten

Dorado was furious, the slap still reverberating inside her. The police force on Ergo was understaffed for this kind of situation, there was no doubt about it. If she'd had two jail cells, she would've locked up Cyn Peters as well for contempt of the law, never mind what others might say.

She was down on Hal's yacht, giving Yero a break and mulling over the events of the day: trying to get Cyn out of her head, trying to work out a way to unravel the truth. She felt trapped by the time constraints. Mr Brink's lawyer had been onto her too – as Ergo was a colony of the mainland, he was making arrangements to get Hal off the island for a decent trial. There was a ship in the area that might be prepared to fetch him; negotiations were under way. That was perhaps a way out of this, thought Dorado; but she objected to the inference that she was not good enough. She wanted to prove to everyone, including herself, that she was worthy of her job; that she could resolve more than cattle disputes.

The rigging was snapping in the wind like a taut nerve. The

yacht was tugging at its mooring, eager to depart; it gave little leaps in the chop that made its way into the harbour. Dorado couldn't sit on this wretched vessel while there was work to be done. Both she and Yero needed to be on the case. Mannie was the obvious person to help, he was both respected and impartial; but he had gone off in his longboat early that morning, no one could say where.

She sat in the cockpit, fidgeting inside. In the slanting light of the afternoon sun, her village looked serene, picturesque. What had gone wrong? How was it that these tragic and unnecessary things had happened? Neither the girl nor the stranger had a single scratch mark on their bodies. It would appear that Hal was telling the truth. She needed verification from Gulai, but the girl continued to maintain that she knew nothing. She would give Gulai till the following morning to get over the sedative and the strangling, and then question her again. She had looked up retrograde amnesia in the doctor's books at the hospital, and it was not necessarily permanent.

Dorado looked out to sea, at the endless blue into which Clarence had disappeared all those years ago. She had a fantasy that he had not drowned, but had set off on impulse one day for the mainland in his boat, and had miraculously made it. He was living incognito, as though his island life had never existed. She could understand the impulse to run away to a place where nobody knew you or had any particular expectations of you, where you could make yourself up from scratch.

From the east, a longboat approached the harbour. For a moment Dorado thought it was Clarence returning – Clarence who, despite his best efforts, could not forget her and was coming for her. But it was only Mannie, ferrying someone who'd presumably gone to Sophia for a remedy.

As the boat entered the harbour, Dorado saw that Sophia herself was on board; Sophia, returning to Ergo for the first time in fifteen years.

Already the islanders working at the harbour had stopped to watch, already children were running down the slipway, shouting and pointing. Dorado waved at Mannie to catch his attention; she had to station him on the yacht so that she could leave it. Sophia's homecoming was certain to stir things up still further.

Gulai lay in her hospital bed, unable to erase the image of her father in the mortuary. It should have been her body stretched out on the metal table . . . but then it would be her father in the jail cell.

"Gulai." Sophia was standing over her and offering her a vial. She looked older, tired.

Gulai lifted her head to the bitter liquid and let it burn into her stomach. Sophia took the edge of her scarf and dried the girl's eyes. "I've come home," she said. "You can live with me now."

"But why . . ." Gulai croaked, wanting to ask: why was this happening, why hadn't the oracle warned her, what was to become of her now?

"Rest," Sophia advised. "Your voice is your instrument of will and desire. It will recover." She smiled. "Things don't always turn out as we plan. We must accept that. Look what happened to me!" She settled herself on a chair next to the bed. "When I realised I was pregnant, I tried everything to get rid of it."

"Why . . ."

"Oh, I don't say I never wanted a child; but this child, I knew he was not meant to be. God didn't agree with me, the ancestors wouldn't help me! I had to accept, I couldn't have what I wanted." Sadness softened her features. "I damaged my own child."

"You damaged Callum . . .?" Sophia was talking in riddles. Was she referring to his leg? Gulai's head hurt.

"As a baby he was slow to walk and talk, and he has the limp of mild palsy."

Gulai turned her face away. She wanted to cry for all the pain in the world. This couldn't be true. Everything she relied on was crumbling in her hand. "You didn't cause . . ."

Sophia cut across her. "Some things you just know." Her tone lightened. "But look now what a treasure Callum is. I ask God to forgive me, and I think at last I have forgiven myself."

Gulai looked at this woman she wanted to trust, and tried again: "Why did you try to get rid of . . . the pregnancy?"

Sophia leant back, indicating she had said enough. "When you are ready to hear the truth, you'll receive it. When you are ready to tell the truth, it will fall from your mouth like ripe fruit."

Charley at the door, his face heavy with worry. "Could you help a moment, Sophia?"

She pressed something into Gulai's palm. "The ancestors are with you." Then she got to her feet. "What's the trouble?"

"Clara Mobara is not doing well, it's not clear . . ." The two disappeared down the corridor.

In Gulai's palm was a length of blue twine, rolled and tied into a ball. Gulai lay for a moment, feeling the comfort of it. Sophia had returned. She arched her back and looped and tied the twine round her waist, feeling the circle of it and a bitter taste like truth in her mouth. What was the truth? Her head was full of doubt and confusion, full of other people's voices persuading her this way and that. Truth would come, Sophia had said. She closed her eyes.

She woke after dark, her supper cold on a tray beside her,

the hospital quiet, a shaft of light from the corridor slanting into her room. Her body couldn't stay there a moment longer. If she couldn't ask questions, she was going to find answers, and she couldn't do that by lying there and crying. She got up, found her clothes and shoes in the cupboard and pulled them on. Getting out was easy; John Peters had fallen asleep at reception, his bald, freckled head resting on his arms. Her first inclination was to go home and have it out with her father; every time she had such a thought, a shock bolted through her.

A light was on in her father's bedroom. How dare Cyn – it wasn't her house now. Gulai couldn't bring herself to enter, to cross the threshold into the place that had turned in a moment from home into horror.

It was late; no one was around except those still gossiping at the tavern, their voices twined into the whine of the wind. She headed for the police station. Through the window she saw Officer Bardelli bent over her desk, the door to the jail cell beyond her. She remembered her childhood games with Phoebe: how small the room was, the walls pressing in, with a small scrap of sky imprisoned in a high window, and only a bare globe, hanging exposed and lonely, for light. Poor Hal, Hal of the open sea! What had happened? The stupid, stupid boy had overreacted, he had chained her forever to this terrible story. Gulai stood rooted with shock. She had welcomed this stranger into the centre of her life, her body, and that act had destroyed everything. Now, to save him, she would have to betray her father. Her throat constricted. Her father's voice in her ear: *A disgrace you are. Don't you have any shame?*

Of course she had shame: she was made of shame, shame leaked out of her bones, leaving a slimy trail behind her.

She walked away. Events could unfold without her. Hal

would be let off. He would find a lawyer to help him – he was from the mainland, where anything was possible. Gulai wanted to blend with the landscape, with walls and floors and doors, to become invisible, a ghost like that woman who threw herself off the cliff. She wanted only to watch and to wait, and not have to deal with anyone's reaction to her and her terrible crimes, their eyes striking her like gavels.

Through the window of Sophia's cottage, she could see her lighting a lamp at the table, Elijah watching. Here was a mother and father she could turn to, return to. Sophia had offered her a home.

Sophia turned angrily to Elijah and he shook his head. They were arguing! There was trouble here too. Gulai stood outside, her bones aching with loss and grief, her legs weak with indecision.

Sophia came towards the door, carrying the lamp; Gulai stepped into shadow. The door creaked open and Sophia emerged, adjusting her shawl, Elijah after her.

"It's a mistake," he said. "Leave him." He folded his lanky frame onto the bench outside the door, his bony knees angling out in baggy trousers, and patted the seat beside him. "Come sit with me."

"You forget how young he is," Sophia said, pulling an edge of the shawl into a hood.

"He's initiated. He is a man."

"A man would not behave like this!"

"He'll understand in time, if you don't force this."

Sophia shook off this opinion with an angry toss of her head. "He's closer to the edge than you realise!" she muttered, and headed off down the track.

Elijah stood up and looked after her, hands on his hips. "You'll never meet your son this way," he warned. He turned indoors before Sophia could respond.

Gulai followed Sophia's silhouette, bent into the wind over the glow of the lamp, keeping as close as she dared, hampered by the darkness and the occasional twinge in her sprained ankle. Sophia walked quickly over the rough terrain, agile for her age. She took the track through the fields, then continued through the turnstile, along the path that led to Haven Cave. Gulai stumbled behind her, visibility worsening as black clouds rolled in from the sea, heavy with rain. The sky cracked open with light and for a moment the landscape flashed brilliantly clear, followed by a rumbling avalanche of sound. In front of her, Sophia gave a cry and turned back, too quickly for Gulai to conceal herself. She thought the older woman had hurt herself: Gulai stood still with indecision. Sophia came bearing down, her lamp held out, her features exaggerated by the stark lamplight. She was not at all surprised to see Gulai. "It's not the right time," she said, receding along the path back in the direction of home.

Not the right time for what? For whom? The dragon sky flickered tongues of flame and belly-groaned; large, cold drops struck Gulai's face. She was seized by the thought that Sophia was tricking her – but how? Which way should she go? A violent storm was upon her and she was not properly dressed; the sea was leaping with streaks of white and the path melted into the dark in front of her. It would be quicker to go on to Haven Cave than to turn back for shelter.

I have come too far, she thought. The dragons could have her. Let them skewer her with their tongues of light: inside she was dry as tinder, ready to burn.

She pushed on through the deluge towards Haven Cave.

Chapter Eleven

"Who's there?" Callum's voice from the darkness.

What was she doing here? Gulai couldn't remember. Some foolish impulse, some trick of Sophia's; now she would have to explain herself. She fumbled her way to a rock and sat shivering, wet clothes sticking to her skin, grateful for shelter. Lightning flashed again through the sky, washing the interior of the cave with a quick splash of light. Callum was not apparent; he must be in a pool of shadow.

"Why are you here?" His voice had turned cold and hard as ice.

He had seen her, burnt through by white light – beyond the peacock mask, past the obedient daughter and scholar, through the innocent girl and into her cinder heart; and he hated her. She was glad of darkness, hiding her despair, cloaking her grief-trammelled face. She had come here for the truth, and this was it: Callum had been a good friend and she had lost him too. All the men in her life peeling away.

"Women have no business here." Callum's voice, bitter and tight.

"Then where must women go?" she challenged him angrily. "This cave was shelter to women, too, when the ancestors were shipwrecked. Where must we now take shelter in a storm?"

"If you know a storm is coming, it's best not to go out."

"I live inside a storm. I have nowhere to go."

"Go to my mother!" His laughter slashed out in the darkness. "She owes you."

"She doesn't owe me anything." Gulai feared for his sanity, he sounded so wild and strange. "You're just jealous your mother . . ."

"You have no idea! None!"

"Then it's about . . . Hal, isn't it?"

"Hal's only a pawn."

He was playing games with her, being unbearably cruel. Were all men like this, Jekyll and Hyde? "I don't know what you're talking about." Gulai shivered miserably, violently, her voice hoarse and wobbling with cold.

When Callum spoke again, his voice was softer. "There's a towel. On the mattress to your left."

Lightning helped her find it. She took off her outer clothes and stood shivering in her damp thermal underwear, the towel wrapped around her, shy and ashamed. She couldn't take off all her clothes in case the lightning exposed her further and he looked on her body with disgust.

"There's no need to be shy of me." His voice ratcheted out of him. He was telling her he knew about her, that she was loose and dirty, having been with other boys. "I'm probably your brother."

Her brother? Probably? He must have lost his mind. The only way he could be her brother was if her mother'd had him after she'd died! Or . . .

No. Not possible.

He was weeping – or was he? She thought she heard a sob, but it must have been a trick of the wind. So many tears in the world, the salt sea full of them. She felt for the mattress and lay down and wished for the end of night. Shadows were moving above her: pieces of shadow broke off and flitted across the cave, merging with others. So simple to be a bat, so straightforward. Eat, sleep, make babies, die. No drama, no sudden collapse of your life. No revelations, omissions. She would go to sleep and wake as a bat, warm and dry, with two thousand brothers and lovers and mothers and fathers, all crammed into this communal life. Lose one, find one, it didn't make much difference; it was expected, normal. It was life.

A blanket dropped onto her, and another. Hands tucked them in around her, covered her feet. The smell of him, she hadn't really noticed that before: a warm musk smell. Under the covers, she wriggled out of her damp clothing and drew the blankets closer around her. "What about you?" she asked, her eyes trying to penetrate the darkness, wanting just one lightning flash so she could see any resemblance in his face.

"I'm here for the vigil, not to sleep."

He was doing a vigil for her father. Why? Did he really think . . . ? Her life was brimful of pain and contradiction. The truth. The only truth she could cope with right now was that she was tired and cold. She doubled up the top blanket and tried to get comfortable. The rest could wait till morning.

The whole night she fought the cold in a half-haze of sleep and dreams; the cold was her armour, it shrouded her in ice. She was a ship caught in pack ice, being crushed slowly under persistent pressure; she was in a frozen hell with icicles skewering her back and limbs. All the while, she was aware of a vague presence watching over her: a sun obscured by clouds, a promise of warmth, just out of reach.

When she woke, the storm was over. She felt almost happy, and then her circumstances seared through her. She turned over, wanting to see Callum, to prove to herself that his plain brown face did not contain traces of her handsome father's; but he was gone. Next to the bed was a jacket, and her own clothes spread out on rocks to dry.

Gulai waited, hoping he would return, but when hunger began to gnaw at her she pulled on her cold, damp clothing and the jacket and went outside. A seal regarded her mournfully before lolloping into the water, and a group of penguins slanted their beady eyes at her. She scanned the landscape and made the short walk to Needle Falls, but she was alone. By now they would have discovered her absence at the hospital; there would be an uproar. Gulai didn't care. She had no one to answer to now, no one to worry about or tiptoe around or look after, no one to love. Nothing to do. Nowhere to go. No one to trust. Everyone had their own story, everyone believed their own lies.

She needed to confront Sophia. It was time to determine the truth.

Chapter Twelve

Dorado was woken out of deep sleep by someone banging on the police-station door. If it was that Cyn again, she was going to commit murder. But it was Charley – Charley, turned white and agitated. "Gulai's gone," he said. "Clara Mobara died in the night. We were busy with her, and next thing, Gulai's bed was empty. No one has seen her."

Clara Mobara. She'd been at the co-op only two days before, fit as anything; then came down with a seizure, now dead. A woman of forty, too young to die. And now Dorado's witness run off – where to?

Yero had spent a couple of hours at the tavern, and had reported that feelings were running high. Some said Gulai had persuaded her boyfriend to kill the doctor; some were talking about Satan and witchcraft. Others remembered how Gulai was raised on witch's milk – she might be infected. Some pointed out that the witch had returned as soon as the doctor was dead. Perhaps it was the wrong person in the jail cell; they all knew the influence women have over men, and older women over younger ones.

Dorado berated herself. There should have been a guard at Gulai's bedside; on the mainland, she could have had a witness-protection programme in place.

"The mayor is organising a search party," Charley told her.

Dorado was furious. Nelson hadn't notified her of this, nor had he called a council meeting.

"I fear for her," Charley said, gripping her arm to get her attention.

Dorado locked up the police station. She would fetch Yero, he must come with her. The prisoner would be on his own briefly, but it couldn't be helped. She understood, better than Charley, how important it was that only people who had not lost their heads be chosen for the search party.

Gulai tried to force down some of the breakfast Sophia had put in front of her. She had always dreamed of this, a mother who would care for her; but her hunger had vanished, replaced by a fist clenched under her ribs.

Sophia sat back, cradling her cup in her hands. "So he told you," she said, as though discussing the weather.

Gulai shook her head. "He didn't tell me anything."

Sophia stared, challenging her.

"He told me nonsense. He told me . . ." She couldn't say it, it was too silly.

"Eat your breakfast, then get into the bath. We'll talk one day when you're ready."

Sophia was treating her like a child. The fist tightened. Gulai dragged her fork through the egg, breaking the yolk, the yellow running like lava down the hard white. "He told me he was my brother." She glanced at Sophia's face, trying to see what story lay embedded there.

Sophia's eyes turned inward toward some hidden thing.

"Maybe. Maybe."

Rage exploded in Gulai as she tripped over something left lying years ago like a landmine in the thicket of her feelings. "What do you mean, *maybe*!"

Sophia sat there, inscrutable. How dare she collude with this monstrous lie!

"Why are you doing this, how can you sit there and say *maybe* . . . maybe you had a son with my father? It would mean . . . *how many men were you screwing*?!"

It was out, the terrible words vomited themselves out of her mouth and lay floundering on the table between them. Sophia looked away, as though slapped.

"Tell me!" Gulai couldn't stop herself. "If you won't tell me, at least tell Callum, he has a right to know!"

"Callum knows what happened." Sophia looked down at her hands, cupped in her lap as though they held something fragile. "The day I was sent into exile, I was raped by two men. One of them was your father."

Landmines. Volcanoes. The world turned unsafe, no stable place to take a person's full weight; the very earth polluted, the water contaminated. The egg in front of her broken, congealing, lifeless. Gulai could not believe it; to believe this was to know a world too terrible to live in.

"Who . . . who was the other . . . ?"

"Clarence Peters."

Gulai remembered him vaguely, his short body and sagging face mysteriously lost at sea. The doctor and the mayor, they wouldn't do things like . . . that. Sophia's words entered her ears, carrying with them images she had not asked for, feelings she wanted to run away from. If this was the truth, she didn't want it.

The front door opened: Elijah, bending his frame in under the lintel. His face relaxed. "Thank God!" he said, folding

Gulai to his bony chest; then worry wormed its way back into the lines around his eyes. He turned to Sophia, his hands restless in front of him; he seemed uncertain what to do. "There's a crowd loose," he started. "A crowd who thinks Gulai has run away."

"Run away! Huh!" Sophia's voice was tinged with scorn. "Where to, exactly?"

"Frank said he saw Gulai coming here early this morning, and Rumer told people she's your apprentice."

"She'd be right! Gulai has a calling, although she hasn't heard it yet."

"Sophia, this is serious! Blame is floating on the air, looking for a place to settle. At present it blows towards your cottage. Some also say Clara Mobara died because of you."

"Clara Mobara. I thought she would go. It was her time."

"Will you take none of this seriously?"

Outside, voices were approaching; male voices. They were coming for her, Gulai knew it. They had found out she was responsible for her father's death, for this terrible curse that had befallen the island. She would give herself up; she would confess everything.

Faces at the window, a shout: "She's here! At the witch's!"

Gulai was horrified. She had brought the curse into Sophia's home, she had attracted danger to her very hearth. Everything she touched turned bitter, everywhere she went ignited.

Sophia stood up and went towards the door. "This time we are not going anywhere," she instructed. Before she got there, the door opened and Nelson stooped into the room, Jojo and Frank close behind him.

"It is customary to knock before entering, Mr Mayor." Sophia stood tall and proud, staring him in the eye. "But I'm glad you've come to visit. You have something of mine."

The mayor was caught off guard. "What are you talking about?"

"The figurehead you stole from my house."

"That never belonged to you."

"It is mine. You keep it at your peril."

"The doctor and Clara Mobara are dead and you carry on about a piece of driftwood!" decried Jojo.

Nelson's face had gone red. "Don't you threaten me with your voodoo rubbish, Sophia!" He grabbed her by the arm and for a moment Gulai was afraid he would throw her against the wall. Elijah lunged to help her as Dorado squeezed into the room past Frank's large frame.

Dorado felt like driftwood tossed in a violent sea, jostled by the mood of the men. If only Yero were with her . . . but he'd gone to check on the prisoner, saying he'd catch her up. She had lost control of the situation; she was struggling to keep afloat, shocked by what she saw. "Mr Mayor! Elijah!"

"Stay out of this, Dorado!" But Nelson dropped Sophia's arm, bull-full with rage. "This murderer threatened me! She is a danger to the community, she remains wayward."

"Murderer!?" Elijah objected.

Nelson swung on Sophia, barely restraining himself. "You murdered my father too, a man who often risked his life coming to Impossible to bring you food. I know you killed him, then cut him loose in his boat!"

Sophia pulled up her sleeve to see the red mark blushing on her arm. "Your father was not a fisherman. He misjudged the weather." Her voice was even; she might have been discussing dinner. "He came alone to rape again, not to bring me food. He killed himself with his own greed and lust."

"You bloody liar!" Nelson tried to grab her again, but Officer Bardelli stepped into his path, her face a grimace, unable to disguise her pain.

"Mr Mayor, I'll deal with this. Come, Sophia." She clipped a pair of handcuffs onto her wrists.

A flame flared in Gulai's belly to see the old woman shackled, but her head was frozen, her hands paralysed. She couldn't let this happen, none of this was Sophia's fault; but she couldn't move.

"This village is riveted together with lies, Nelson." Sophia's voice was ice. "Tell us, you were there: how exactly was it that Astrid died?"

"That's enough!" warned the officer, but Sophia was in full sail.

"What do you say, Jojo?" she persisted. "Did the wind push her?"

Elijah put a shaking hand onto his cousin's shoulder. "Go, Sophia," he urged. "Go with the officer, we'll sort this out."

"You too, Gulai," said Officer Bardelli as she guided Sophia to the door.

Meekly, Gulai obeyed.

Chapter Thirteen

The dormant beast was waking, the creature that emerges under any sun that shines too brightly, any light that pretends it has no shadow.

Dorado sat in her bedroom and felt the shifting beast's scaly spine tear open the carefully woven fabric of the lie that shielded her life. For years she had diligently faced away. Now that the monster had stirred, she was afraid it would take her by the neck and kill her.

It flooded back again, after all these years: the pain that had been her life with Clarence, the yearning when he'd been with his wife, the jealous hatred she'd felt for Cyn, the disappointment of changed arrangements, the wasted hours, the deceit, the blame. The long lonely nights, the subjugation of her feelings so as not to upset this important and busy man, the tapering of herself to fit the small crevice of him, the smouldering rage that he was always half-turned away, half-occupied with someone else, something else. Perhaps even that wasn't true. It seemed to Dorado now that perhaps

Clarence was only ever fully occupied with himself; that his passion for her had been a lie – a lie to help them both believe that what they had was real.

She remembered his mood the day they took the exile to Impossible. When he and the doctor had come back to the launch after taking Sophia up to the cottage, he'd lashed out at her for no apparent reason. Then, that night, she remembered the violent way he'd taken her: like punishment, a forced entry, her very centre recoiling from his assault; yet all the while she'd pushed down her recoil to keep herself available, arguing with herself that he needed this release: he was stressed, under pressure, without this he would blow. She lay beneath him like a burnt field while he ploughed and ploughed, plundering her. She'd been afraid of his power over her: that he would leave her.

Truth was, she'd never really had him. Neither, she saw now, had Cyn. Yet the two of them had been set up as adversaries, fighting over – what? A man who was capable of the thing Sophia had named? He was, after all, capable of cheating on his wife, of lies to them both, of manipulating both women into silence and collusion. And he had not acted to prevent Astrid's wrongful death. But then neither had she.

Neither had she.

It was intolerable, that thought, the thought she had carefully papered over. During the years Sophia had lived on Impossible, Dorado had come to love and admire her. She knew from experience that Sophia could be trusted to tell the truth to your face if it needed to be told, even if it was painful; and to tell the truth about herself, even if it meant looking human and stupid and vulnerable, even if it meant that there were those who would not like her.

Dorado had asked Yero to take Sophia and Gulai to the station to ensure their safety while she came home to compose herself. She couldn't be seen crying. She went into the bathroom to wash her face, forced her eyes to the mirror and took a long, slow look at herself. Nowadays, she avoided mirrors and photographs; she'd always hated the way she looked, and had increasing difficulty with the creeping age that had taken hold of her features. Now, if she was going to face herself, she'd better start by staring at the truth in the mirror. It might tell her something she needed to know.

Her dark hair was streaked about with grey; disobedient hair, she'd always thought; the wrong kind of hair for a stormy island life, where the wind seized the thickness of it every time she set foot out of doors, unless she trapped it in a scarf. Her brow was creased, her eyes too small, the soft flesh beneath them starting to sag, her nose set slightly skew, her teeth uneven, her neck loosening into lines. This was the face she had considered lucky to be loved by Clarence when she was younger; primarily, she now saw, because she did not love it herself. Yet as she gazed upon the features that were somehow attached to the person she was, she noticed a light in her eyes that was truly beautiful, and that the streaks of grey on her wild, wavy hair were like white ribbons of surf adorning the sea at the foot of the cliffs. She saw that her eyes had served her well, and that the bones of her face showed strength of character, and she was grateful for both her beauty and her ugliness, the full spread of life in her features. She put her fingers to her cheekbones, and felt how they structured the soft tissue, how they provided secure foundation. She knew in that moment that she was responsible for something she had not wanted to acknowledge till now: that she had broken a law, an unwritten law that says we should not do things behind people's backs that will hurt them, nor lie to their faces about what we have done and thereby hurt them further.

She knew what she had to do. But first she was needed at the station.

Gulai sat in front of Officer Bardelli and Officer Tamara and told them everything. Her heart was breaking, and she let it; it was the only way to allow the words to spill out. Words like: *I disobeyed my father in his own house, I was sleeping with Hal and I wanted to, my father put his hands around my neck and started to strangle me, I was afraid I was going to die, my father was drunk.* The yarn around her middle dug into her, for she had tied it tightly to give her courage as the details of that night unravelled from her lips. Each time she said, "It was my fault," Officer Bardelli stopped her and said quietly, "Just tell the story as it happened. Who is responsible for what will emerge, and no one needs to be protected." Dorado offered her tea, she gave her tissues, she gave her a break when it all got too much. But the officer's own eyes were red, as though she had been crying. Gulai had never seen her like this.

All the while, Gulai was aware of one man in the cell next door, another somewhere out in the wild, and yet another in the cold mortuary room, ready for the earth; all the while she was aware of Sophia resting on the officer's bed in the police station tearoom, purple blossoming on her arm, a stillness come over her like deep water. And outside: the islanders, restless, stormy, wanting blood for blood. "Hal was trying to stop my father," she said, as Yero wrote her terrible words down. "If he hadn't done something, I probably would have died." She looked up through her horror, expecting to be struck down. "That's everything."

Dorado nodded. "Thank you, Gulai."

Gulai nodded in turn.

"Are you prepared to swear it is the truth and sign it?" Yero put the statement in front of her, four pieces of paper full of words fallen from her mouth and pinned there forever by Yero's beautiful writing. Was this the truth? Signing this would change her ideas about herself and her father forever. She picked up the pen and signed: Gulai Tamara Prosper. She needed her mother's name as well from now on, an island name.

A name that would remind her where she came from.

Chapter Fourteen

Dorado typed the last full stop and leaned back, her shoulders aching from the effort of typing the most difficult document she had ever authored. She urgently needed to call a council meeting, Dorado knew that; but there was another, even more pressing issue. So while young Hector Pelani went to summon the mayor and councillor Peters to the police station, she pulled on her coat and went over to the doctor's house.

Cyn stood at the front door of the doctor's house, not inviting her in. Behind her were boxes; she was packing her things. She looked at Dorado with tired, inflamed eyes.

"I'm sorry," said Dorado. "For those terrible years. For the lies. And for hurting you."

Cyn stiffened. "I don't know how you can forgive yourself."

Dorado felt something leap up in her like a dog, growling. How dare Cyn stand in judgement, as though her own behaviour was faultless? What about the time she'd thrown a brick through Dorado's bedroom window? And that slap in the face? What about the way she'd tried to undermine the community's trust in Dorado's capabilities? But now, as Dorado looked at the woman in front of her, she saw that her eyes were two wells of pain.

Cyn turned away, indicating that Dorado should go. "Words mean nothing," she said.

She was asking for amends. That was fair enough. Dorado remembered Callum, carrying crayfish, scraping down and painting the police launch. "What, Cyn? What can I do to heal this?"

Cyn stared back at her coldly. "It doesn't matter any more," she said. "My life is over." Cyn closed the door. She wasn't going to make it easy; why couldn't things be easy?

Dorado turned and left, taking a piece of pain with her. She went down to relieve Yero at the police station, then waited for the other two council members to arrive. She knew she was on trial here. She would not go down without a fight. The island Constitution allowed for action to be taken when two out of three councillors were in agreement. But could she win one of the brothers over?

As the mayor and councillor Peters entered, she sat down behind her desk – the seat of authority, the place the mayor usually sat when they had council meetings. She gestured to the surprised Nelson to take a seat next to Jerome. She handed the two men copies of both Gulai's statement and her own report, watching the mayor's face as he read them. This was the man she'd known as a boy, the man she'd been envious of when Clarence spent time playing cricket with his son. She owed him amends too, but this could not interfere with the matter at hand, and she was still furious about the way he'd behaved that morning. She watched him pulling at his lip in an unattractive gesture not unlike his father's, and wondered for a moment what she had seen in Clarence all those years.

She reached behind her to pull a large volume out of the bookcase: *Murray's Criminal Justice, 2nd ed.* "Based on the evidence, I am satisfied that Hal is guilty only of involuntary manslaughter," she said, banging it down onto the desk. She turned to the relevant text, pointing out paragraphs for the two men to read. Her report had concluded: "Clearly the incident was not premeditated, nor was there use of undue force, in that a blow to the head with a wooden sculpture does not necessarily cause death. We must conclude that the accused was merely trying to prevent the deceased from murdering his daughter; therefore, according to precedent, the prisoner is free to go." She had worried for ages over the wording of the report. It was in the language, she'd decided, this question of authority; in language and posture, in where you sit and how you speak. Yet the legalese jarred in her: there was something in it that disconnected the heart. Something else needed to be appreciated. "Hal did what any of us would do, I hope, if faced with the same situation."

Jerome closed the manual and looked at her guardedly.

Nelson stood, objecting. "Orion wasn't capable of murder! It's inconceivable! He was a medical man, he invested in life – he didn't even want old Rozi to die, and we all knew it was her time. He wouldn't do abortions, and you, Jerome, know it! Officer, how can you so easily accept the story of two youngsters?" He paced. "Next thing, you'll want to release that woman without a proper investigation!"

Jerome contemplated the report lying on the table. "Orion could put a drink away, too much for his own good, and when he did he could get into a temper. But I can't believe he tried to kill his own daughter." He put on his hat. "We'd better radio the mainland in the morning and get some help. This problem's not going to go away."

Dorado looked at the faces of the two men, desperate,

trying to find a chink. "What's your theory then? I have a good argument, on what basis do you discard the evidence?"

The mayor laughed a hot, tight laugh, then lunged his face close to Dorado's. "You're no detective or lawyer, you're a third-rate officer in a backwater village. You see devils where there are none, and angels where there are devils!"

The office door opened, and Yero ushered Sister Lena in, her face ploughed with fear. "Sophia's needed," she appealed to Dorado; then she glanced apprehensively at the mayor. "Your wife's waters have broken, sir, the baby is coming too early, and she's bleeding." The third child, a latecomer, and the mother too old for it.

Everyone was looking at Dorado, even the mayor, his face torn open.

"Go with Sophia," Dorado instructed Yero. "And if anyone tries to stop you, anyone at all, lock them up."

Yero stared from her to the mayor. Nelson was red in the face, his mouth grasping randomly at words. "You can't . . . that woman . . . she isn't fit . . . I will not allow it! Why is it no one listens to me!"

"She has delivered many on this island," Dorado pointed out firmly. "And she was apprenticed to Aunt Kora, who helped deliver me. Be sensible, Nelson; you have no choice."

Sophia emerged from the tearoom with Yero. Already she was rolling up her sleeves, asking Lena questions: for how long had Condolessa's contractions been painful, was she otherwise well, was she on any medication, what colour were the waters, what had happened with her other pregnancies, had the doctor documented any problems during this pregnancy? The mayor stared with horror as she walked out with Lena and Yero into the evening.

Some islanders stopped and watched as Sophia strode up the road to the hospital, casting their minds back to a time before Doctor Prosper came and this was a common sight; casting back in their consciences, trying to remember what had happened, what had happened? This woman who had helped them in the middle of the night, who had helped them even in the year when the potato crop failed and they could not pay her, this woman who had known their hearts, who had been part of their hearts, what had happened?

There were others at the tavern and round their tables at home who were busy with the news of the mayor's accusation, and the fact that Clara Mobara had died after Sophia had tended to her, and that if the doctor were still alive Clara would probably still be alive too and not lying next to him in the mortuary. Still others shook their heads and made the sign to ward off evil, saying that perhaps it was better if Sophia stayed away from the birthing room; but they stopped before they reached any conclusions about what was true and what wasn't, who was right and who was wrong, what was superstitious and what was from God. A baby was being born, that was what mattered. A new citizen of the island was arriving in the world to take the place of the departed. It was essential to support those assisting; to put differences aside and to pray.

Chapter Fifteen

Mayor Nelson Peters sat in the tavern that evening, nursing a drink while the dragons of life and death fought over his wife and child at the hospital. His ragged thoughts turned from Sophia and her dreadful accusation, to a red-haired woman falling, and he knew: this was her revenge. If only he'd not been so fit in those days, nor followed so closely, he would not have seen; if only he had not seen. But he had, and since then there'd been a memory fastened in his head that no drink or drug could loosen, that no argument could prise out. But still . . . it was surely possible that he'd witnessed incorrectly? That his eyes had cheated him? It was so slight, the difference between wresting loose from a man's grip, stumbling, then falling through one's own misjudgement and loss of balance; and fighting to wrench loose from a slight but murderous thrust . . . What had he seen? Not enough, he'd argued again and again with himself, not enough to go to . . . whom? Dorado? To say what? That Jojo had thrown Astrid off the cliff onto the rocks? Jojo appeared to live comfortably enough with what had happened, with a little help from the drink, so why couldn't he? Yet here, here was death again, calling. He was complicit, death's accomplice. God forbid that he must lay his cold wife out tonight, and no room left in the mortuary.

Outside in the night wind, he thought he could hear the cadence of mad laughter; the sweat ran from his armpits despite the cold.

There are moments in life that unfold like miracles: places where the paths of conflict intersect at unexpected oases, where the relentless contest of dragons for dominance is transmuted into a harmless and playful wrestling; and sometimes, if the conditions are right, it mellows still further into the sensuous embrace of lovemaking. The birth of the child that night opened other passages, freed other spirits, released stories from their eddies to flow again unimpeded.

When Sister Lena arrived to tell Nelson that his wife was well and his son safe in the world – another son, another boy to hunt with and hand his business down to – he swallowed the rest of his tankard to wash away the tears brewing under his lids. Then he accompanied Lena to the hospital to marvel at the sight of a brand-new child, formed perfect in his own image, suckling at his dear wife's living breast. A bag of dark red blood hung above the bed, with a tube of red winding down and into his wife's arm.

"Sophia was wonderful," Condolessa explained weakly, her face almost as pale as the pillowcase. "We're the same blood group."

Shocked, the mayor was, looking at his wife – now part Sophia. He took himself for an unaccustomed walk up to the lookout point, panting his way through thoughts of life and death, fathers and the meaning of blood.

He stood a while, looking down at his small, impossible

kingdom, weeping and giving himself a good talking-to. Blood, he realised, was also courage, and he needed some of that to do what he knew he needed to do. Moved beyond his own comprehension, he went down to the police station and told a surprised Dorado that he agreed to the release of the sailor, and that he wanted to meet with her about an important matter at her convenience; thereafter, he went on to the mortuary to prepare both the doctor's and Clara's bodies for burial.

It was midnight by the time Dorado turned the key in the lock and handed Hal his stamped passport. He followed Dorado out of two days in a cramped cell into a calm night flooded by a full moon's light, his rucksack slung over his back.

Hal's eyes found his yacht. "It's . . . as I left it? Provisions and all?"

Dorado nodded. She wanted to take this boy's hands in hers, to rub his wrists where she'd snapped the handcuffs on. Instead she took his hand and shook it. "I hope . . . you won't think too badly of us," she said.

Hal shrugged, impatient to be gone. "Radio my parents, please," he said. "Tell them I'm on my way." He headed off down the road. Then he hesitated. "Where's Gulai?" he asked.

Gulai was sleeping at Liesa's home. Liesa had taken her into her own bed and comforted her there, sending her husband to sleep with their children.

When the knock came at the front door, Gulai was lying awake, her thoughts circling, turbulent, replaying how things might have been, should have been, could have been. On opening the door, she saw at once with a tearing that it was over between them. Hal stood in front of her, shuffling his feet, a stranger. Who was this man? He had saved her life, he had changed her story. She saw he was a small, scared boy who had found himself out of his depth twice in the past two months, and wondered about her own capacity to love – for the magic had slipped away, ephemeral, unknowable. Hal was looking past her, looking for something that had nothing to do with her. He was restless to get back onto the sea again, shifting his weight from one foot to the other, rocking as though he were already riding the ocean's broad back. Gulai was not the horizon his eyes were searching for. He kissed her cheek, said he was sorry. Then he walked off down the moonlit road towards the harbour, towards home. Gulai followed to where she could watch him row out in the soft light to the yacht. *Goodbye* was stuck in her throat, choked up in a painful knot. She hadn't been able to say the word, or *will I ever see you again or what's your address or please write or have a good life.*

She watched as Hal motored his yacht out of the harbour and then hoisted the mainsail. She could just make out his dark outline, busy on the deck, occupied with the details of his life – forgetting already, leaving this tragedy behind him, leaving her with her life unravelled, wrecked, floundering. If only he would look back, to acknowledge what had happened between them, so she'd know she meant something more than a harbour he'd briefly visited on his travels. The sails caught the wind and the yacht leaned into her journey with grace and ease, the wet, white hull luminous in the moonlight. Hal was merging with the darkness of the night and the sea, the yacht becoming smaller. As she looked, she thought she saw him turn. She felt certain he turned to take one last look at her.

She felt sure he turned and waved goodbye.

Chapter Sixteen

The doctor's funeral was held the next morning, with Clara's planned for the following day. On their way to the church, some noticed the landscape had changed somehow, though they could not recall what was missing. It was Harry Pelani who spotted it first: the stranger's yacht had sailed. He hurried to the station to report the news, only to find a large notice informing the community that Hal Brink had been released from custody, having been conclusively cleared of all charges against him through due process of law. The notice was signed by two of the three council members. The reaction to this news, which Officer Bardelli had been afraid might cause a riot, was tempered by what evolved at the funeral.

Minister Kohler wheezed and panted his way through a sermon fit for a king. The manner of the doctor's demise was not alluded to; he was held up as a man of integrity and honour, a man who had given up his illustrious mainland life to serve their small and insignificant community. The women who had loved him and the men who had drank with him felt sad and happy at the same time, for there is nothing that holds secrets better than death, and the doctor was the repository of many in both his personal and professional capacities.

The doctor was an example, said the minister, of sacrifice

and service, of fortitude and knowledge, of humility and kindness. This oratory might well have let loose a vengeful spirit in the congregation, but for the distraction of a latecomer. Halfway through the service, Callum limped into the church and headed down the aisle, his hair unkempt, his eyes wild, his face half-covered by a straggly beard.

Whose face? wondered Gulai. Whose genes were embedded in the matrix of his being?

He went straight to the front pew on the left, reserved for family only, and sat himself next to Gulai. A murmur rippled through the congregation, but this was not the time for speculation: Minister Kohler beckoned for them all to come forward and to file past the coffin, paying their last respects. Callum took a position directly behind Gulai, then assisted the bearers to take the coffin outside.

The mayor had had his father's gravestone repositioned outside the community hall, bequeathing his father's gravesite to the doctor so that he would not have to lie in the new cemetery beyond the potato fields. Gulai watched as the coffin was lowered into the stony earth, aware of the eyes upon her and Callum, aware that the islanders were standing in judgement of her, one way or another. She knew she was supposed to cry, but she could not feel her heart. She was glad of Liesa's arm around her shoulders; the weight of it anchored her to this moment.

Frank indicated to Gulai that the time had come for the family's part in the ritual. She stepped forward and took the spade from him. "Dust unto dust," Minister Kohler reassured his congregation from under his umbrella, as Gulai dug the blade into the mound of damp soil and threw it with a splattering thump onto the lid of the coffin. She straightened, and then, with a ceremonial deliberateness, handed Callum the spade. The crowd was suddenly silent as he too delivered a clod of earth. Later, at the wake, there would be time enough for tongues to wag, for people to turn their attention from what they thought they knew to what they did not.

Callum gave the spade to Frank, then turned, pushing his way through the crowd. He was leaving again, disappearing into himself, cutting Gulai off after this display of family ties. Gulai found herself following him, not caring what people thought.

By the time she was out of the church grounds, Callum was climbing up the path to Deception Bay, striding quickly along despite his limp, his body blurring into the fine mist swirling down from the peak. She hurried after him, afraid for him and of the mist that was swallowing her too, afraid she would lose both him and her way.

That morning, she had helped to lay out the tables in the community hall for the wake, and by now the islanders would be trickling down from the church to feast and drink to the memory of her father. She was expected there, but she didn't care. The important thing was to find Callum. She needed to tell him something that had not yet fashioned itself into words, that niggled her like toothache.

It was hopeless; he was too far ahead, caught in nets of vapour. Vague shapes appeared suddenly like ghosts in front of her, then turned into bushes and rocks as they arrived at her side. This was the path that headed over the cliffs at Ike's Gully. What was he thinking? Was he planning to hide out in the shelter at Deception Bay? Didn't he know that someone had fallen from those cliffs, long ago? "Callum!" she called, stumbling, feeling like a ghost herself. Her voice stopped dead, muffled by the blanket of mist. She had to slow down; she was afraid of coming upon the sudden drop. "Callum!"

To her left, she heard the roar and suck of incessant waves gnawing at shoreline; the salt breath of the sea exhaled into her face, the salivating monster waiting below to swallow anyone who did not respect her, anyone who thought themselves greater than her. Gulai knew she had ventured too far. She was about to turn back when she almost fell over a dark shape in the path: Callum, sitting, she could see, with his legs dangling over the edge of . . . what? The mists swirled and lifted a moment; she could make out a cairn to her right that marked the correct path. They had strayed towards the cliff. Callum was sitting on a high edge of the island, at the extreme edge of his life. Gulai felt the sudden catch of the world turning, like water swirling down a plughole; her legs buckled towards the pull of the void, she felt the drop leap up and take her by the ankle. She sank trembling to her knees and grabbed Callum's shoulder, trying to pull him away, fearful he would fall and take her with him.

Callum turned dead eyes to her, his wet fringe sticking to his brow. "Go home," he said.

"You're at the cliff edge!"

He looked dispassionately down into the haze below his feet.

Gulai stared at him, shocked. He was here with intent. "Why . . .?"

He sat with hunched shoulders, fixed on the eddying void. His voice was so soft she could hardly hear it. "I failed," he said.

He wasn't the one who'd failed. "What do you mean . . .?" Any moment, he could push himself forward and slide down into the mist. She was shaking with cold and grief. "You're my only family," she heard herself say.

He sat, unmoved. Would nothing move him? "I'm sorry," she sobbed, "I'm so sorry . . ."

"This has nothing to do with you." Callum wiped the drizzle from his face – or was it tears?

"I took you for granted, I didn't understand . . ." He turned his face away, silent. Gulai tried again, snatching at any thought or word to save them. "Your mother . . . told me . . ."

"My mother!" Callum's voice cracked with anger. "My mother killed those two men."

"She didn't, Callum! I was there when my father died!"

"You know nothing, nothing about this . . ."

He was unhinged – how could he believe such superstitious rubbish? Besides, Sophia would never *murder* . . . a vision of Hal displaced the fog, standing in front of her, naked, pale, shaken, a piece of stolen driftwood in his hands, one end red with blood.

"My mother worked a curse on the mayor, I saw her do it! I came here to tell your father, so he could make amends. You've been brought up in mainland ways, Gulai, you are ignorant of our culture. You make amends, or the ancestors can be called upon . . ."

The wooden fist of the ancestors, coming down on her father's head. The revenge of the spirit world as Sophia's curse worked its way through, the helplessness of a boy who wanted his father to say he was sorry. To acknowledge that his brutal act had created a life. Could it be true?

"I . . . didn't have the courage."

Gulai's legs were numb from kneeling; she shifted carefully so as to sit, acutely aware of the drop. Her arms found a hold around Callum; she wept into his shoulder. They were both in danger, but the earth still held beneath her, the earth made of dead things, the earth that gives life to the living. Gulai kissed Callum's neck, tasting the salt of his skin. If only the right words would fall from her mouth. "He didn't want to be saved," she sobbed as the words arrived – meant for Callum, meant for her own ear.

Callum stiffened. She felt despair in his heaving shoulders;

and then she felt how he half-turned to her, his desire for life
stirring. He pulled back and looked into her face, his eyes two
stabs of pain. Then his body shifted, and the ground under her
slid towards the cliff edge. A shaft of horror plunged through
her. Callum was taking her with him, he was going to pull her
into oblivion. In that moment Gulai knew she wanted to live,
more than anything she wanted another chance. "No!" she
yelled, trying to escape from the deadly embrace, her free
hand scrabbling to find a root, a crevice, anything to give her
fingers purchase; then she felt how Callum's arm tightened
around her and lifted her up, pulling her away from the edge.

Chapter Seventeen

On the doorstep stood Sophia, holding a black and mewling kitten. "Good morning, Gulai. Can I come in?" she asked. "I can do a clearing, if you'd like."

Gulai hesitated. This had been her father's house. There was so much to cleanse, to expurgate – but was Sophia not part of it? Yet she greeted her and pulled the door open to let her in.

"And this is for you, if you'll have her." The kitten struggled in Gulai's arms, wanting to explore. She put it down and watched as the woman worked her way through the house, sprinkling water and burning herbs, calling on the ancestors to clear the space and help Gulai reclaim her life. Was restoration as easy as that? An anger sat uneasily in her belly. Her father whispered at her shoulder to throw the woman out. Caught, she was still caught in the old dance, despite the change of circumstance: here before her was the woman she'd waited years to meet, and now her father was the exile. He was an ancestor, but because of his crime he wandered restlessly as a spirit or animal, an outcast, unworthy of mediation between humans and God. Gulai was rent, the house of her body home to torment. Clear me, she prayed.

She was aware, too, that the track of her life branched each moment, a different life heading off at every bifurcation, her decisions or lack of them leaving every other possibility behind. So many options. She stood at the helm of a ship, her hand on the wheel, terrified of making the wrong move, wishing for someone to relieve her of the responsibility. Should she take the ancestors or Jesus as the mediators of her life? Or something else? Should she apprentice herself to Sophia? That was what the old woman wanted, but did Gulai? What would she be in service of, and for what purpose, if she chose that life?

She had spent nights awake and restless, turbulent with thoughts that argued between forgiveness and revenge, tied to a wheel turning first towards anger, then towards compassion. Choices everywhere, attitudes that inform the way one lives.

Since the day on the cliff, she and Callum had been careful not to touch each other. There was dry tinder between them, and Gulai was afraid to let it ignite and burn, not knowing whether she should or could and what that might lead to; yet she was quietly moved to discover that love has a plain face. She had decided to invite Callum and Elijah to live with her, as she did not want to live alone.

Should she finish her schooling on the island or go to the mainland? Her father had left her a trust, so money was not an immediate problem. Should she track down that university professor and sing for his research, or should she take up Samuel Pelani's suggestion and start a cabaret at the tavern for visitors from the cruise ships? Should she become a doctor or lawyer or restaurant owner? Should she travel the world, looking for other choices to complicate her life? Was there only one true path, or did all paths lead to the top of the mountain?

The kitten mewed, stuck and hanging from the top of a curtain; Gulai unhooked it gently from the fabric and gave it milk in a saucer to drink. She would keep it, she thought, to help her make a home.

The evening before Gulai's sixteenth birthday, the subterranean beast roused and stretched, waking from a hundred-thousand-year-long slumber, forcing change on those who had forgotten the power that underlies life. Gulai was going over a history assignment with Callum, astonished by how political geographies change depending upon who is in power, when her kitten began to behave strangely, restlessly, running about and mewling; then the kitten disappeared under the sofa and stayed there, refusing to come out. A while later, there was a sound like the earth clearing its throat. One moment, Gulai was sitting in front of the fire in conversation with Callum, and the next the earth grumbled and heaved, shrugging half her house to the ground, the thatch roof tearing open, black rain tapping onto her face, patting dark splotches into the carpet. Elijah was caught under a falling rafter, injuring his chest, but managed to extricate himself without too much difficulty, but Gulai, Callum and the kitten were miraculously unhurt. The house had split in half, her bedroom squashed to the ground, the kitchen displaying itself unashamedly to the world. From the sofa, Gulai had a view of the volcano peak glowing its warning: red-rimmed and overflowing, the white snow cap gone, spattering flares into the night sky.

Only one person died that night. Due to the lie of the land, the river of spilt lava and mud split in two on its way down the slope, one branch falling hissing into the sea at Ike's Gulley, the other at Needle Falls, sparing the settlement and even the fields. The islanders watched in awe and horror from the hospital – the structure singled out as the safest temporary shelter, as it was made from modern brick and mortar, with an asbestos roof that would not burn should a flaming spear descend in that direction. Through windowpanes streaked black with ash rain, they watched how the forked tongue of molten, radiant rock slid down on either side of them, the temperature rising until they stripped down to one layer of clothing, even though it was midwinter. Officer Bardelli had sounded the alarm on the radio, and a ship had altered its course and was on its way to rescue them. The islanders knew that at any moment the mountain could blow; every moment could be their last. They clutched the few treasures they had snatched from their homes before congregating at the hospital to prepare for evacuation, and prayed as they had never prayed before. Sophia, Charley and Lena had their hands full dealing with injuries sustained in the earthquake, yet all gave an ongoing litany of thanks for the miracle that none had yet died, hoping that Jesus, the gods and the ancestors were listening.

It was only hours later – after the ship had arrived in the bay and Frank and Jojo and Mannie had ferried the terrified islanders across, after they had embarked through a night drizzling black-stained rain and lit by the eerie glow of the earth turning itself inside out, the dragons of destruction and creation battling it out beneath their very island, indifferent to the havoc wreaked upon individual lives – only then did the effort of sustaining and encouraging his flock in the midst of distress take its toll on Minister Kohler, who knelt down on the deck and succumbed to a heart attack.

So it happened that plans and choices were swept away by the earth's impulsive shifting of contours. Sophia never recovered her birdwoman from Nelson; rather the sea reclaimed her, charred by the tide of lava that eventually washed through half the village, taking Nelson Peters's house with it. Raef's concern about how to break the news to his father that he wanted to leave the island to work on oil rigs was also washed into the sea. Dorado never got to make amends directly to Cyn Peters, nor did Nelson Peters ever get to meet with Dorado to report his complicity, and Minister Kohler was buried at sea after years of worry about whether he should retire to the mainland. Mad Fabio Bagonata's prediction of the fire and brimstone end of the world came true, proving God's righteous vengeance on a sinful community, although he was puzzled by his inclusion in the punishment. The doctor's estranged family's attempts to have his remains relocated to the family graveyard on the mainland were thwarted, as a mud slide flattened the church, burying the graves under four feet of rubble and hard mud. Rumer Peters's cow, which she had been trying to pluck up the courage to kill for the pot, watched unconcerned as the ship sailed away, and lived out the rest of her life happily feral, eating potato and pumpkin plants, as did the other island animals that survived the eruption. David Peters's resolution never to set foot on a ship again was overridden by fate, and he spent two days vomiting and on a drip in the ship's sickbay, green to his gills; and Charley had to review his idea of escaping the mainland and the heartache that resided there.

Gulai stood at the bow of the ship early the following morning, feeling a little seasick herself, her eyes on the whitening horizon, trying to see ahead. What was to come?

It was her birthday. She looked out over the expanse of sea to where the sun surfaced through the spilt red and orange of its own light, as it had for millions of years. In the sky, an albatross wheeled and lifted, holding its long wings in an open embrace, its black eyes watching, following. Somewhere behind lay her old life, which now existed only in her memory; somewhere ahead was a new beginning, where she could find out more about who she was. Genetically they would be able to find out who Callum was, which father he carried in him. Whatever the case, the two of them were connected by the filaments and catches of their past; that was something to hold onto.

In between the old and the new was the ocean, its surface shredded by the cold winter wind, its depths a mystery. Somewhere inside she felt her desire and fear at play with each other, that electric, heightened feeling that was both a tiny flame of hearth warmth and a forest fire in the making. She wanted to learn how it was that the one turned into the other, how to ride this power, how not to go under.

Looking across the blue reaches, Gulai thought of Hal and his solitary journey, and wondered what guided him. She knew there were stars and satellites to help him, but what inner guide could save him, or anyone else, from floundering and disaster? Gulai wedged her feet into the ship's welded metal angles and cradled her hips against the rail. Leaning forward into the void, over the skimming blue surface of the sea far below, she rode high and inspired and terrified over the bow of the ship. She was a figurehead with slightly furled wings, who could learn how to fly. Her eagle eyes promised clarity of vision and an overview of life. Her mouth hardened both to defend the truth and to eat it; in her hand she held a snake for protection.

Somewhere inside she began to recognise herself. Somewhere inside stirred the dragon, flicking through its dreaming mouth a silver lick of flame.

Acknowledgements

Although the loose idea for the novel came on the one hand from *The Tempest*, and on the other from stories I heard about Tristan da Cunha, an island I have not yet visited, the story is in no way based on any actual people or events. Some details of weather and life on a remote South Atlantic island I gleaned from the book *Tristan da Cunha and the Roaring Forties* by Allan Crawford (Oxford, 1966). Wonderful books that have also informed my thinking about the characters in *The Tempest* are Marina Warner's *Indigo* (Vintage, 1993) and Helen Luke's *Old Age* (Parabola, 1992).

I would like to thank the following people for their help, witting or otherwise, with the evolution and pinning-down of this story:

To Shakespeare, who explored the extraordinary themes of life; to my son Luke, for performing fabulously in two school productions of *The Tempest*, as Ferdinand in 2000 and as Prospero in 2002; to Jonathan, my second-born, who arrived in this world in a tunnel of sound; to the late Kobus Booysie, who told me strange stories of a remote island in the Southern

Atlantic; to my parents, Pat and Stanley Garisch, and my publisher, Nèlleke de Jager, for believing in me; to Colleen Crawford Cousins, Frederik de Jager and Mallory Attwell for making me go deeper; to Henrietta Rose-Innes, Veronica Cecil and Kate Highman for their generous feedback and editing skills; to Roget, who edited the best book of all; to the Board of Trustees at Lavigny in Switzerland for awarding me a writer's residency, which enabled me to devote three whole weeks to deleting tracts that didn't work; to Colin Miller at Pro Helvetica, who assisted me with airfare to get to Switzerland; to Gus Ferguson and Robert Berold, who have encouraged me over the years; and to my insistent daimon, who is really at the bottom of it all.

Dawn Garisch has published three youth novels and poetry, has had a short play and a short film produced, and has written for the newspaper and for television. She is a practising medical doctor.

She has two grown sons and lives in Cape Town.